Deep Black

Samuel Best

ISBN: 9781712683941

DEDICATION

For Toccara

CONTENTS

PROLOGUE

Rain pounded the helicopter as it flew low over the Gulf of Mexico.

The sleek craft was like a tiny dragonfly beneath a dark, endless sky. Lightning streaked the blanket of clouds above. Below, gray water churned, slashed with white.

Noah Bell sat in the passenger cabin, staring into the dense storm that smothered the Gulf two-hundred miles off the west coast of Florida. Despite the steady drone of the helicopter and the fact that he'd been awake for nearly twenty-four hours, Noah couldn't sleep.

His gaze drifted down to the tumultuous waters.

"I can't see anything in this mess," growled the cabin's only other occupant.

Noah leaned back in his seat and regarded the aging billionaire opposite him.

John Harris strained against his safety harness to look out through a rain-smeared window, further wrinkling his tailored gray suit. At sixty years old, he had only recently succumbed to the slight paunch he'd fought to keep at bay for most of his adult life. His tan face contrasted his stark white hair, which was so immaculately tended that it looked good even at his most disheveled. Noah remembered hearing a story about Harris and his thousand-dollar haircuts.

"It's out there, John," said Noah easily. "Trust me."

He plucked at a loose thread on his jeans and tugged down the plain T-shirt under his blazer. His wardrobe favored the casual ever since he lost control of the most infamous private space company in history.

"I'm not here because I trust you, Junior," Harris said, using a family nickname he knew Noah despised. "The only reason I'm here is because your old man went and bought the farm before I could repay a debt." He settled back in his seat, cursing while he tried in vain to loosen his harness.

"I'm glad you're here, John," said Noah, forcing a smile. "I wouldn't want to do this alone."

Harris snorted and gave up on the harness. "Like you had a choice. I know your well is dry, kid. It's a crime, what they did to you. It really is. Taking your company like that." He jabbed a beefy finger in Noah's direction. "But you tried to keep the government out of the biggest discovery in history. It's no wonder they're holding such a grudge."

Noah fell silent and looked at his own reflection in the window. Almost twelve months had passed since the first Titan mission, yet in his mind he looked many years older. Strands of white had appeared in his short, dark hair. Shadowed lines creased the corners of his eyes when he smiled, and he was far too pale. Yet whenever he looked in a mirror, his eyes held a boyish exuberance that belied his tired features.

Harris sighed. "I'd just as soon get this nonsense over with so I can go home," he grumbled. "Told Charlotte I'd catch the red-eye from Tampa tonight."

"Are you so sure I'm wasting your time?" asked Noah.

Harris stared at him a moment. A slow, condescending smile spread across his face. "Junior, I know enough not to bet on promises, no matter who's offering. It's bad business. If your father had called me, I would have wired him the money no questions asked. But *you* called, and, well..." Harris shrugged as if that explained the rest.

The pilot spoke over the intercom. "Almost there, gentlemen. The platform's bucking quite a bit, so hold tight when we touch down. The anomaly should be coming up soon."

"Anomaly?" said Harris. He frowned and leaned forward to look out the window. "You didn't mention any anomaly."

Noah suppressed the urge to smile as Harris scanned the ocean below, his curiosity temporarily outweighing his doubt.

"I believe the word I used was 'disturbance'," said Noah.

"I don't care what you call it," Harris said. "If I think for one second that..." His voice trailed off and his jaw went slack as he looked at the crashing waves below. "Sweet mother," he whispered. "What is that?"

Noah leaned forward and looked down at the ocean. It was an unbroken plateau of gray and white, except for a large area of water near a half-finished floating research facility. The ocean floor was a mile below.

Next to the floating research facility, the surface dipped down unnaturally to form a deep bowl more than three-hundred feet in diameter, as if a giant, invisible sphere was pushing gently down on the surface. Waves thrashed around the edge of the bowl, but the water inside was perfectly calm.

Harris plopped back against his seat, staring at Noah. A moment later, he slowly closed his gaping mouth, regained his composure, and said, "How much do you need?"

"Quite a lot, actually," Noah replied.

Harris adjusted his collar and cleared his throat. "Right." He nodded. "Well. Yes. I'll want someone who knows what they're doing running things down there," he said. "I won't back anything with just your name on it. No offense."

Noah grinned. "Don't worry, John. I know the perfect person for the job."

PART I

1

Jeff Dolan shielded his eyes and squinted up at the towering 61-meter Neptune III rocket as it waited on launch pad LC-44 at Cape Canaveral Air Force Station. Beneath his dark blue coveralls, his undershirt clung to his sweaty back in the humid Florida air. Blazing sunlight pummeled the tarmac under his shoes with enough July heat to fry an egg.

The rocket's fuselage glinted as its smooth black exterior vaulted up to its dart-like nose fairing.

Jeff never tired of the sight. Whenever he stepped out of the cool, single-story launch prep facility, he felt like he was seeing the *Catalyst* for the first time.

Old memories danced in his head, as vivid as if he'd lived them yesterday. He remembered climbing into the crew section of a different Neptune III almost a year ago—*Explorer I.* He remembered the raw power of four nine-engine Hydra cores igniting at the base of the rocket, pinning him and his three crewmates to their seats as they hurtled into space.

He remembered Titan.

Jeff shook his head, trying to clear away the thought of that distant, icy moon. He preferred to focus on the newer Neptune III, the one still firmly pinned to Earth's surface. It held no mysteries for him to unlock, and it presented no dangers beyond the mapped potential hazards of such a wondrous machine. He knew every nut and bolt inside it, every strip of wire, and every length of pipe. No more mysteries, just the way he liked it. There were already enough unknowns thrust on him in the wake of the first mission—unknowns he now realized he'd be forced to struggle with for the rest of his life.

Behind him, the door to the Deep Black launch prep facility opened and Manuel Lopez stepped out, sunlight bouncing off his bright orange Constellation spacesuit.

"Afternoon, Commander," Jeff said, squinting.

"Jeffrey!" Manny said, as if he were surprised to see him. "Nervous?"

"Not a chance. You?"

Manny laughed. “Never!” He clapped Jeff on the shoulder and gave it a shake as he turned to look at the rocket. “Beautiful, am I right?”

The door behind him opened again and three more astronauts wearing matching orange Constellation spacesuits walked outside. Their gold sun visors were pulled down, hiding their faces. Out of the pool of twenty or so potential astronauts, only a handful had been invited to complete the final stages of training. Jeff and the other ground workers weren’t allowed in the training facility. The only member of the crew he ever spoke with was their commander.

“Ah, here they come,” Manny said. He rested his hand apologetically on Jeff’s shoulder. “They want us up there early, I’m afraid.”

He turned to lead the other three astronauts across the tarmac, toward the rocket.

“Good luck up there,” Jeff called after them. Manny looked back and waved.

Jeff didn’t wait to watch them ride the elevator up the gantry. He ducked back into the launch prep facility and paused as the door closed behind him, shutting out the heavy Florida heat. He wiped sweat from his brow and stared at his glistening palm as he recalled the events directly following the first mission.

He remembered waking up on the beach after returning from Titan, still wearing his spacesuit, with no explanation as to how he got there. The rest of his crew had been flying home, months away…yet he beat them back to Earth.

Jeff wiped his palm against his grease-smeared coveralls and headed for the locker room to shower. On the way, another member of the ground crew stopped him and said he had a phone call.

Besides the astronaut prep area and the locker rooms, the facility was a grid of unused conference rooms and offices. Jeff found one with a working phone and pushed the blinking *Hold* button.

"Jeff Dolan?" asked a deep voice on the other end of the line.

"Mr. Kemp," Jeff said, surprised. Richard Kemp was the head of Deep Black's Human Resources department—a man Jeff hadn't spoken to since he was hired by the rapidly-growing private aerospace startup months ago.

Kemp cleared his throat. "First of all, I want to thank you for your hard work on the Catalyst," he said. "The ship wouldn't be half the marvel it is without your direct influence."

Jeff nodded slowly, sensing what was coming. "I appreciate that."

"We were lucky you were available to help get us into shape before our return to Titan."

We, us, our. The meaning behind the words didn't extend to include Jeff, he noticed.

"When the crew arrives safe and sound at their destination," Kemp continued, "I want you to take great pride in knowing it was your dedication and determination that got them there."

"That's very kind of you to say."

"Unfortunately, it falls on me to inform you that Deep Black is terminating your contract and that your expertise is no longer required."

Jeff stared at the blank wall on the other side of the office.

"You'll have two weeks to wrap things up, of course," Kemp offered, a bit more gently.

"That won't be necessary," Jeff said vacantly. "I wanted to transition to a monitoring station in Mission Control."

"Hm," Kemp said. "Yes. I see. Regrettably, Mr. Dolan, those positions are filled. I hope you understand."

Jeff hung up. He understood just fine.

Deep Black had wanted to glean as much knowledge from him about his previous mission to Titan, and about the company that had sent him there.

Noah Bell's Diamond Aerospace was defunct, its assets seized by the government in the messiest and most public takeover in recent history. Those in charge of the takeover had been especially eager to get their hands on the plans for the *Explorer I* spacecraft that carried Jeff and his crew to Titan.

Granted, Deep Black's yearning for Jeff's knowledge was rooted in the desire to make their own mission as bulletproof as possible, and he couldn't fault them for that.

As such, he only told them what they needed to know—everything that would make their ship safer for the journey. Jeff had spent much of his time with

Deep Black retrofitting the hybrid thermal antimatter engines for greater stability. The rest of his hours were devoted to safeguarding the air circulation system from the same near-catastrophe that had befallen his own crew on *Explorer I*. Even a small portion of his technical knowledge was a great boon to any company who wanted to toss another ship Titan's way—until they were ready to launch, it seemed.

Jeff skipped the shower. He emptied the meager contents of his locker into a duffel bag and left the building. After tossing the duffel into the rusted bed of his beat-up blue pickup truck, he took a last look back at the *Catalyst*.

At the top of the tall gantry, two ground technicians worked to move the circular hatch into place, sealing the crew inside.

The truck's door creaked loudly as Jeff opened it. As he prepared to sit, he noticed a black town car approaching the launch prep facility from the direction of the security gates. Heat shimmered up from the road, blurring its edges.

"You gotta be kidding me," Jeff said.

Kemp had the nerve to send security to escort him off the property. He sighed and slammed his door shut, waiting in the heat with his arms crossed.

He grew more uncertain as the car approached. There were no markings of any kind, no decals identifying the car as a security escort. A yellow government license plate reflected sunlight as the car turned and pulled up next to his truck.

Jeff slowly uncrossed his arms as one of the mirrored back windows rolled down, spilling out cool air.

A sour-faced man in his early fifties sat in the back seat. He wore a tailored suit with a narrow black tie, and he studied Jeff with cold, blue eyes.

"Hello, Mr. Dolan," he said gravely. "Rough day at work?"

Jeff wiped sweat from his upper lip and looked around the parking lot, half-expecting someone to jog up and tell him there had been some kind of misunderstanding.

"What's this about?" he finally asked, eyeing the car's dark interior. Someone else was in there, as well.

"We heard about your recent termination," the man said, adjusting his tie. Jeff looked at him skeptically. "News travels fast," the man explained, "if you know where to listen."

"News travels," Jeff repeated warily. "Who are you?"

"Your second chance, if you want it." The man in the car stared at him for a moment, as if he were deciding something, then said, "How would you like to go back to Titan?"

2

Kate Bishop hated packing.

Throwing together a bag for a long weekend was enough to put her over the edge, but having to box up all of her belongings for the big move to Texas was the absolute worst. She spent a long time staring at all the empty boxes set up on her floor in a neat row before she finally chucked something into one of them. It was a little plastic astronaut figurine Jeff had picked up in a souvenir shop when he first started training for his mission to Titan.

She should have tossed it in the garbage, like she had done with almost every other reminder of their relationship, but it wasn't just a gift from him anymore. After her time in the command building at Diamond Aerospace, watching the events of the Titan mission unfold with a heavy weight in her gut, the plastic astronaut became a totem. Holding it in her hand brought back memories of the fear, elation, pain, and joy she had experienced when *Explorer I* found the alien torus orbiting Titan.

It also brought back the good memories of Jeff before he drifted away.

The front door opened and Juan stepped inside, running a wide hand across his sweaty forehead. Her ex-coworker from the first Titan mission looked for a dry spot on his shirt to wipe his palm but couldn't find one, so he smeared it on his jeans instead.

Behind him outside, the moving truck Kate had rented for the long drive from Cocoa Beach to Houston was backed into the small parking lot, its bed half-filled with her belongings.

"You waited for the hottest day of the year on purpose," said Juan.

"Just to torture you," Kate replied.

She looked around the living room. Everything but the rattan love seat and reading chair had been cleared out.

Juan eyed the furniture warily.

"Don't worry," Kate said, smiling. "The wicker stays. I'm not sure it's allowed in Texas, anyway."

She went into the kitchen and brought back two

ice-cold beers. Juan slapped his pudgy midsection in preparation and accepted his with a grateful sigh. He plopped down into the reading chair, which protested with a squeak.

Kate sat on the love seat and took a long drink. She pulled her knees up to her chest and swept back her shoulder-length brown hair.

As her body slowly relaxed, the silence bloomed with thoughts of her time working as Ground Teams Manager for Diamond Aerospace, and of the time before that, when she worked in a cubicle at Boeing. Besides playing a very small role in the rare spacecraft systems projects, most of her shifts at Boeing had been spent double-checking timeline spreadsheets.

The job that awaited her in Houston was not so different. It was the kind of job she had been fighting to leave behind ever since Noah Bell offered her a position at Diamond Aerospace.

Needless to say, she was not in any hurry to get there.

"I'm going to miss your free beer," Juan said, ending the deep silence.

She gave him a weak smile.

"You could have stayed here," he continued. "I got a gig with a telecom last month. I drive around and fix antennas. Most of the time it's just a loose cable." He plucked at his jeans. "You get your own van and everything."

"I thought about staying," Kate said. "My old boss gave me a sympathy call after he heard about the whole mess." She took a swig of beer. "Offered me my old job. I said no at first. But night after night in this place," she said, gesturing at the room, "day after day thinking about working out at the Cape again..."

She shrugged.

"It wasn't all bad," Juan said. "We had a lot of fun, too."

"That we did. It's just getting harder and harder to remember those parts."

He frowned at her. "You gonna be okay?"

The phone in the kitchen rang before she could answer his question.

"I thought I unplugged that stupid thing," she mumbled. She drank the rest of her beer in several long gulps and took her time getting to the phone. A few minutes later, she wandered back into the living room, half-dazed.

"You're not going to believe who that was," she said, leaning against the wall and crossing her arms.

Juan lowered his beer and wiped his mouth. "Must have been bad news. You're white as a sheet."

Kate shook her head numbly. "No, no. Nothing like that..."

"Then who was it?" he asked.

She rubbed her arms, feeling the goose bumps that erupted as soon as she hung up the phone.

"It was Noah Bell."

"Uh oh," said Juan. "Did someone die?"

"No. He...he offered me a job."

3

Jeff rode silently as the black town car drove through the last security checkpoint and left Cape Canaveral Air Force Station behind. The car had passed through all of the security gates without being stopped, the stone-faced guards barely watching as it passed, if they looked at all.

Other than the driver and the stern, middle-aged man who did all of the talking, there was only one other person in the car, sitting across from Jeff. He was in his early thirties, tall and spindly, with thin glasses on a pinched face. His thick, shiny auburn hair was cut short and combed to the side, and his expensive suit hinted that he made more money in a year than Jeff ever had in a decade. He sat with his knees together, atop which he clutched a worn leather briefcase.

The older man spoke up. “I’m Colonel Brighton. Retired.” He gestured to the younger man, who adjusted his glasses and blinked. “This is Will Chapman.”

They both stared at him.

“What do you do now that you’re retired, Colonel?” Jeff asked.

“Way too much. Will, if you wouldn’t mind,” he said to the younger man.

Will snapped open his briefcase and produced a single sheet of paper. He handed it to Brighton, who gave it to Jeff.

“This is a non-disclosure agreement,” said the retired colonel. “You’ll sign it before we arrive.”

Will fished around inside his briefcase and pulled out a pen. Jeff took it slowly as he read the document.

“And if I don’t sign?”

“It’s a long walk back to your truck,” said Brighton.

Jeff smiled thinly and he scrawled his name on the bottom line. *What else could I possibly lose today?* he wondered. He returned the paper to Will, who nodded as he glanced at the signature and tucked it away in his briefcase.

"Where are we headed?" Jeff asked. Neither of them offered up a response. "I signed the document." More silence. "Is it a surprise?"

Brighton answered him with a question. "Do you believe the Catalyst and its crew will reach Titan?"

"I don't see why they wouldn't," said Jeff. "Solid engine, solid crew. Deep Black has refined a lot of the harsh edges we endured on Explorer."

Brighton grunted. "With your help."

"Wasted knowledge helps no one."

"Depends on who you're helping."

The car turned off the main road and onto a narrower lane that led away from the Air Force base. To the left, glass-and-steel warehouses sprawled over acres of land—a collection of buildings known to those who worked in them as the Rocketyards, or the Yards for short. As they drove past, Jeff looked through one of the open sliding warehouse doors and into the cavernous space within. A giant of a rocket lay supported on its side, half-finished. Workers crawled over its surface like ants.

The town car turned right, onto a single-lane paved road leading away from the Yards. A few minutes later, they came to a small guard shack and a yellow barricade arm blocking the road. This time, the car stopped. The driver rolled down his window and showed a badge to a frowning guard with an automatic rifle strapped to his back. He nodded, then buzzed the car through.

Two signs flanked the road ahead, each with blue text on a white background. Jeff knew what they said before he was close enough to read them.

"Diamond Aerospace," he muttered with disbelief as the car drove past the signs.

Noah Bell's company.

"Surprise," said Brighton.

4

Saltwater from the Gulf of Mexico sprayed over the low concrete barrier and pelted Kate's shoulder as she turned away.

She hadn't seen rain the entire helicopter ride across the state, from Cocoa Beach to St. Petersburg. Fifteen minutes after landing, the sky clouded over gray and wind lashed the tops of frothing waves as if to make up for the rain's absence.

The helicopter pilot had told her to wait near the concrete landing pad by the water where he'd set down, then took off east, back the way they'd come. A dark sedan with severely tinted windows waited nearby, idling. Kate had tapped on the window and looked questioningly at the driver, but he didn't acknowledge her.

Now she stood at the water's edge, turning away from the waves with her lonely black duffel bag in hand, waiting for the next part of the mystery to unfold.

She surprised herself with how quickly she'd agreed to meet Noah Bell in person. After the Titan incident, she never expected to see or hear from him again. Immediately following the government takeover of Diamond Aerospace, he'd disappeared from the public eye, presumably too embarrassed to show his face. The media painted him as a recluse, the next Howard Hughes, lost to myth and conjecture.

Apparently, that was not an accurate assumption.

In the few minutes she had spoken with him on the phone, it was obvious that he had been very busy indeed...and whatever he had in mind was certain to be a lot more enticing than retreating back to her old job in Texas.

She looked across the churning waters of the stormy Gulf. It took her a moment to pick out the black speck just above the horizon, slowly growing larger.

Her pilot hadn't said anything about getting into a second helicopter. Of course, he hadn't said anything. Kate tried talking to him over the intercom during the flight, but he had either switched off her microphone or he was ignoring her questions.

Even Bell was reticent. The most she had been able to glean from their brief conversation was that he meant to offer her a job similar to the Ground Teams Manager position she held at Diamond Aerospace during the Titan mission.

It had been enough to prompt her to send a polite email to her old boss in Houston and let him know she would be delayed. If it didn't work out with Bell after a few days, she could always buy another plane ticket.

The approaching helicopter swung wide around the landing pad before touching down. Kate backed away slowly, clutching her bag to her chest and shielding her eyes as the rotor blades blasted stinging water from the ground.

The side door opened and a short, older man with stark white hair and a deep tan hopped out. He buttoned the coat of his tailored suit as he strolled casually away from the helicopter, oblivious to the wind. Kate couldn't help but stare at his brilliant white teeth as he smiled and shook her hand.

"You're in for quite a treat, Ms. Bishop!" he shouted over the propeller noise.

"I don't suppose you want to spoil it for me," she shouted back.

The rotor whine nearly drowned out his laughter. "Bell would never forgive me if I did! Trust me, it's worth the wait."

He winked at her and gestured toward the helicopter. Without knowing what else to say, she ducked as she hurried under the rotor blades and climbed into the passenger cabin.

"Go ahead and slide that closed, would ya?" said a friendly male voice over the intercom.

It took Kate a moment to realize it was the pilot, and another to realize he meant the door. She dropped her duffel on the empty seat next to her and grunted as she pulled it shut, clipping off the high-pitched whine from the spinning rotor.

Outside, the man she spoke to on the landing pad got into the back seat of the dark sedan with heavily-tinted windows. As the car pulled away, Kate noticed the license plate: "BIGMONEY 3".

She pegged him for an investor. Bell would certainly need people like him if he was planning to start another company. But what kind of company? One of the more contentious stipulations of the government takeover of Diamond Aerospace forbade him to launch any space-bound vehicles from Earth as a private enterprise.

As the helicopter lifted off and flew over open water, Kate wondered—and not for the first time—what exactly she'd gotten herself into.

5

The driver let them out in front of a large box of a building, its façade an enormous mirrored checkerboard of reflective windows. The air inside the building was refreshingly cool. Brighton told Jeff to wait in a small lobby staffed by a lone woman who never looked up from her computer to acknowledge them. Then he was gone through a plain door, one of several leading from the lobby, Will Chapman hot on his heels.

Jeff stuck his hands in his pockets and looked around. There were no magazines; there was no television. He glanced out the tinted windows at the long road which led back to the Yards. He thought of the roads beyond, which led back to the base, and to *Catalyst* on its pad, ready to launch.

He had signed on with Deep Black to be near a ship again—*any* ship. It had only taken Jeff a month back on Earth after his mission to Titan to get that familiar aching in his bones, the longing to work on engines once more.

Engines to the stars, he thought. It was difficult not to wax romantic when he dreamed of traveling to other worlds.

Kate had suggested there was a different reason he was so eager to get near another spaceship: he wanted to go back to Titan.

"Why would I?" he had asked as they sat close together on the back porch of her beachfront condo, watching the sun dip below the horizon. "I survived, I'm back home, and I have you." He gave her a squeeze.

"You also have something else," Kate had said. "Something you brought back with you. A question neither of us can answer."

How did I get home? Jeff thought.

By rights, he should have died on Titan after setting the rest of his crew on their journey back to Earth. He should have died there alongside Tag Riley, the mission commander.

Riley had been swallowed up and spit out by the alien torus they'd found orbiting Saturn's largest moon. The black ring had turned him inside-out within his spacesuit as he was pulled through its center. Jeff had been swallowed by a different torus, but instead of dying, he emerged from yet another obsidian hoop in the atmosphere of Titan. Then he was pulled into another, and emerged yet again, closer to the surface.

He broke through the dense fog of Titan's hazy, orange atmosphere as he fell, and saw an expanse of ice and lakes of liquid hydrocarbons. Alien structures rose from the ice: arches, walls, and bridges, all constructed by the tori. Wherever a torus hovered, the arms of a new structure reached out from the black hole in its center to take root on the icy surface of Titan. Human figures clad in bright orange Constellation spacesuits with black face shields hovered amongst the structures, tweaking and pulling and bending them into shape.

They were building a city, Jeff thought.

But not a living city. It was a city of machines built by machines. Jeff had stayed up countless nights thinking about its purpose. Simple habitation seemed unlikely given the frigid, remote location. Yet he had to admit his own arrogance at assuming alien biology wouldn't tolerate the extreme conditions on Titan. Whatever built the tori could be as different from humans as humans were from rock crystal. Perhaps, for a non-Earth culture, Titan was a holiday getaway destination—the alien equivalent of Hawaii.

None of these thoughts had gone through Jeff's mind when he fell toward Titan's surface. All of his thoughts were dedicated to Kate and to the rapidly-approaching impact.

He was, however, able to notice a very specific detail on the way down.

One of the figures hovering about the nascent alien city had the name RILEY stitched on its suit.

Immediately afterward, Jeff slammed into a deep lake of liquid methane and woke up on a beach in Florida, the gentle waves rocking him inside his spacesuit.

That was where Kate found him.

There had been no small amount of personal implosion after that...a lot of stumbling around in the proverbial dark, shouting for answers he soon realized he would never find on Earth. Jeff knew now that he had been too stupid to take Kate's hand when she offered to help him. He thought he could walk the path alone.

He was wrong.

They had spoken on the phone several times since they separated, growing farther apart with each conversation. In hindsight, the gap had only been widening from his side, directly *because* of him.

The last time he tried to call her, she didn't pick up.

Standing in the lobby of the government building, Jeff had the sudden urge to call her again—to apologize and do whatever he could to get a fresh start.

The woman behind the front desk put a finger gently to her ear and listened intently.

"Mr. Dolan?" she said without looking up. "You may go in."

6

Kate sat alone in the passenger cabin of the helicopter as it flew low over the Gulf, heading southwest.

The slow-rolling waves were mesmerizing. She leaned forward and bonked her forehead on the window.

"Some view, right?" said the pilot, startling her as she rubbed her forehead. She looked up at the ceiling, trying to find a headset she could wear. "It's alright," the pilot assured her, sounding amused. "You can just talk."

"Some view," Kate agreed as the pilot banked steadily to the south.

"It only gets better."

"I imagine you're not allowed to tell me where we're going."

"Let's check the map," the pilot said. "Ah, here it is. Another couple of miles, south by southwest."

"Very funny. Any other details?"

"Promise you won't tell anyone I told you?"

"Cross my heart."

"Well…okay," he said, his voice tinny over the intercom speakers. "I'll give you a hint. It's really wet."

Kate sighed, but couldn't help but smile. She leaned back and looked out the window toward the horizon, seeing nothing but gray water beneath a gray sky.

"Smack in the middle of nowhere," she mumbled.

"Oh, I wouldn't call it nowhere," said the pilot. "At least not for long. See for yourself. Straight ahead now."

He banked to the left, turning so she could look southward. The Gulf was an unbroken line across the entire horizon…except in one spot. Kate squinted, trying to make out the details of a disturbance in the water.

"Is that a…?" she asked. "What *is* that?"

"This might help a bit," said the pilot.

The craft dipped and flew just over the water as they approached the disturbance. Kate's breath caught in her throat when she realized the surface dipped down to form a deep bowl.

"But what's keeping the water from rushing in?" she asked quickly. "How is it maintaining its shape?"

The pilot laughed. "They don't pay me enough to know those answers, Ms. Bishop. Don't worry, Mr. Bell is waiting for you at the research station."

"What station?" she asked absentmindedly, her eyes still fixed on the disturbance.

The pilot took them a hundred feet above its rim, where raging stormwater suddenly calmed and sloped downward to form a smooth, empty hollow in the ocean's surface.

She got her answer a moment later. The helicopter dropped even lower, came around, and gently touched down. Kate had been too busy staring at the disturbance in the water to see any kind of surface structure. Outside the helicopter was a landing pad and a series of low, flat buildings arranged in a grid on a wide, floating platform.

"Enjoy your stay, Ms. Bishop," said the pilot. "It's been nice talking with you."

The rotor quieted as a man wearing a black turtleneck came running up to the helicopter to open the passenger cabin door.

Kate was shocked to realize it was Noah Bell. Since last she saw him, his youthful face had been infiltrated by several weary lines that showed at the corners of his eyes as he smiled. The first hint of gray was hesitantly creeping into the dark hair at his temples, yet his hazel eyes still sparkled with ambition.

"Ms. Bishop!" he shouted. "So nice of you to come!"

He gestured for her to follow him across the landing pad. Grabbing her duffel, she hopped out of the helicopter, managed a hasty thank-you-wave back at the pilot, and hurried after Noah. He paused next to the nearest structure, a nondescript black building with a low roof, and smiled at her.

"What's the matter?" she asked after a few moments.

"It's just...it's good to see you again," he said. "I underestimated how meaningful it would be to have a familiar face around. I feel like I've been on my own for so long."

Kate waited, but he didn't seem like he was going to say anything else. He just stood there, grinning at her.

"Well, where are we?!" she finally asked. Her impatience was only half-feigned.

"Oh, right! Your first time here. Sorry."

He turned around and swiped the cuff of his sleeve across the wall of the black building. A green light glowed in the surface. Noah pushed gently against the wall and a door swung inward. Kate admired the craftsmanship as they walked inside.

"Impresses potential investors to no end," Noah explained. "It's kind of the point."

"I can imagine."

They were inside a small wet room with metal grates in the tile floor and a low, dark wooden bench in the middle.

"Ninety percent of asking for money is wrapped up in your first impression," Noah continued. "Did you know that?"

"You may have mentioned it," said Kate. "A couple dozen times."

"Forgive me," he said, smiling. "I'm very excited." He gestured around the room. "I jokingly refer to this as the airlock. When we're fully up and running, we'll have lockers for the staff and equipment bins for outdoor maintenance."

"Investors don't really care much about that," said Kate.

"Exactly," Noah agreed. "Not in the beginning. Or ever, if you've hooked one that will stay out of your business."

"I met one of them on the mainland," said Kate.

"That would be John Harris, yes. I hope he was pleasant."

"Pleasant enough," Kate admitted.

"Good. Well, I don't want to keep you waiting any longer. This way, please."

He led her through a door opposite the entrance and into a long, black-tiled hallway that gradually descended. The floor undulated with snakes of soft light, mimicking sunlight shining through the ocean's surface as seen from underwater.

"I understand you've told your boss in Houston that you might be delayed a few days," Noah said as they walked.

"How could you *possibly* know that?"

"I may have run out of money, but I'm not completely out of resources. Not yet, anyway."

She looked past him, toward the end of the hallway, where it opened onto a small viewing area. The wall there was noticeably different: a diffused dark green that covered the entirety of it from edge to edge.

"It's a lot easier to see on a sunny day," Noah said cryptically.

They stopped inches away from the wall, and he crossed his arms. Kate saw that it wasn't really a wall...it was a window. They were below the surface. The deep waters of the Gulf stretched away before her, transitioning to an impenetrable darkness farther out. In the distance, at the very edge of her vision, something shimmered.

"Look straight ahead," Noah said, pointing. "It might take a moment."

The shimmer spread as her eyes adjusted to the darkness. It formed an angled wall in the water, sloping gently downward. It was one side of the bowl she had seen from the helicopter.

"How is this possible?" she asked.

"There's something else in the water," Noah answered.

"Something...else?"

"Something *deeper*."

He pointed below the bowl...far below. Kate's gaze drifted lower, but she saw only shadowy, sun-starved depths.

"What's down there?" she whispered.

A slow smile spread across Noah's face. He held the cuff of his sleeve to his mouth and said, "Lights, please, Tom."

Kate looked at him, confused, and he nodded out toward the water.

A halogen lamp flicked on in the darkness below. At such a great distance, it appeared as a tiny flashlight beam. Another flicked on next to it, then another. The lights formed a vast circle, all facing inward. At the edge of their beams, inside the ring of light, another shape became visible. Its black surface absorbed the light, seeming to make the surrounding waters even darker.

Yet she couldn't deny what she was seeing: a giant obsidian ring floating parallel with the surface, untethered.

Kate's mouth moved as she tried to speak, but she couldn't force out any sound. The size of the object was staggering. The one Jeff's crew encountered in orbit around Titan was nowhere near as large.

Yet this wasn't Titan.

It was Earth, and Kate was most definitely looking at the unmistakable shape of an alien torus.

7

Jeff went through the door.

A long hallway ended at a grand meeting room. The space was clearly meant to accommodate dozens of people at a time, but now it was empty except for a solitary conference table. Colonel Brighton sat with two other men in suits and one woman wearing jeans and a T-shirt. Will Chapman stood behind Brighton, holding his briefcase with one hand and smoothing down his tie with the other.

"Elizabeth?" Jeff said as he stared at the woman, his voice pitching up in disbelief.

Elizabeth McCall was one of the astronauts aboard the International Space Station when Jeff and the crew of *Explorer I* set out for Titan.

"Hello, Jeff," she said with a mild Texas accent, smiling broadly. The freckles on her cheeks stood out against her fair skin. Fiery red hair cascaded over her shoulders in shining ringlets. "How's Gabriel?"

Jeff took a seat in the empty chair across from the quartet.

"Happy as a clam, last I heard. He married a schoolteacher and settled down in Colombia."

Elizabeth shook her head fondly as she smiled. She and Gabriel had got on quite well during *Explorer I*'s brief visit to the ISS.

"Mr. Dolan," one of the suited men cut in. "I'm sorry to rush your reunion, but we have a lot of information to get through."

Jeff turned toward him. Aging, like the other man who sat beside him, though with drooping jowls where the other man had sunken cheeks white with stubble.

"I'd love to hear it," said Jeff. He glanced at Brighton, who sat silently, watching him.

"I'm Director Welling," said the jowly one. He gestured to the thin man next to him. "This is Clay, our lead engineer. You've met Ms. McCall."

Clay wore his white hair in a short, flat-topped military style that made his narrow head look like the eraser-end of a pencil. He frowned at Jeff as Elizabeth smiled warmly.

Welling cleared his throat, drawing Jeff's attention back to him.

"In the interest of time, I'll get right to it," he said, his jowls quivering with each word. "We're prepping a mission to Titan."

"Military?" Jeff asked.

"Military oversight," Welling corrected. "Scientific in nature. We'd like you on board."

Jeff blinked. "Just like that?"

Brighton eyed him coolly, and said, "Your expertise would be an asset." His persistently-scowling face ran contrary to his compliment.

Jeff studied the others on the panel. The lead engineer, Clay, clenched his teeth in frustration, but held his tongue. Apparently, they were not all of the same mind to invite him along.

"The Catalyst is launching today," said Jeff. "Deep Black will get there months ahead of you, or more." He thought about it a moment longer. "Unless you already have a ship."

Director Welling cleared his throat again. "When we, ah, *acquired* Diamond Aerospace from Noah Bell, he was nearly finished with a new spacecraft."

"Explorer Two," said Elizabeth. "He intended the crew to continue work on Space Station Freedom in orbit around Titan."

"The station we never started," Jeff said quietly, remembering *Explorer I*'s cargo hold full of unused construction materials.

Clay unclenched his jaw long enough to say, "She launches in six days."

Welling pulled an 8x10 photo out of a folder and slid it across the table. Jeff turned the blurry image toward him and tried to make sense of the shapes. He thought a blue smudge on the side of a gray building could have been the Diamond Aerospace logo.

"It's the mining facility on Mars," said Director Welling. He jabbed a pudgy finger at a dark spot in one corner. "Look here."

Jeff tilted his head, then rotated the picture. In the shadows, beyond what he assumed was the hulking mass of an excavator, was the distinctive circular shape of a torus—the same alien artifact he had encountered near Titan.

"It's eating the ore," Welling explained.

"Eating it?" Jeff said numbly. His mouth was suddenly dry, and his blossoming eagerness to leave the dependable comfort of *terra firma* wilted.

"Sucking it right into that black hole of a mouth. And it's not coming out the other side. We tried pushing it away with one of the excavators, but it sucked that up, too, and spit it out piece by broken piece. We had to shut down operations. That cursed thing is still chomping at our facility like it's an all-you-can-eat buffet."

"Where's that ore going, Mr. Dolan?" asked Brighton.

Jeff pushed the photo away and leaned back in his chair. "It has to be Titan."

The others at the table exchanged wary glances, and Welling nodded. "We thought as much. We've been peppering the surface of Titan with surveillance drones for months. Most don't survive long enough to send back images, but the ones that do tell a very clear story. Whatever's on that moon is building something big."

"It's siphoning construction material," Jeff said, finally understanding.

"We believe so."

"For what?"

"That's what we aim to find out," Colonel Brighton said. "We're not going to Titan to stake a claim, as Noah Bell wished to do. This isn't manifest destiny, Mr. Dolan. This is exploration, this is communication, this is—"

"Enemy surveillance," said Jeff. "You want to make sure they're not hostile."

"That's part of it, yes."

"Why did you go to work for Deep Black after you got back from Titan?" asked Welling.

"I could only sit on my hands for so long," Jeff replied. "Rent doesn't pay itself."

"You were hoping for a spot on the crew."

Jeff was about to deny it, but instead he said, "Maybe at first. But as I followed the preparations, I realized I was more content down here."

"Content," Welling snorted. "Don't lie to yourself. When has 'content' ever been enough for someone who's seen what you've seen?"

"You have Bell's mission files," Jeff said, "his blueprints, even his ship. I still don't know what happened to me on Titan. I don't have answers for myself, let alone anyone else, and I have to live with that."

"You've been there," Welling said. "No one else on the crew has gone that far. You might even find some answers if you go back."

"Why are you asking me at the last minute? What's changed?"

"One of the crew failed his training," answered Welling. "You're to be his replacement."

"Failed."

"That's right."

Jeff looked at Elizabeth. "You're going?" he asked.

She nodded.

"In that case, you're in good hands. Best of luck," said Jeff, pushing back from the table. He looked at Elizabeth. "I'll give your regards to Gabriel next time we speak."

He stood and was pulling the door open to leave when Brighton said, "Show him the rest."

Jeff hesitated, then released the doorknob and turned back.

Will Chapman opened his briefcase and handed an x-ray scan to Brighton, who set it on the table. It showed a man's head in profile—the ghostly lines of his nose, lips, chin, and brow, and the glowing outline of his skull. The brain was shaped by a whisper-thin line that followed the inside of the skull. Inside the skull, near the back of the brain, was a perfect dark sphere the size of a golf ball.

"What is that?" Jeff asked.

"That's your brain, Mr. Dolan," Brighton answered. "You've got something inside, something you brought back with you from Titan. Lodged in there pretty good, too."

Jeff studied the x-ray. It must have been taken in the days after he washed up on the east coast of Florida. The doctors had crawled over him like he was a newly discovered species, poking and prodding...but no one had ever mentioned a foreign object lodged in his brain. They gave him the all-clear; said he was even healthier than when he'd left, in fact. He squinted at the x-ray. Perhaps it wasn't even him. Yet his profile was unmistakable...

"What is it?" he whispered, his shaking hand drifting up to the back of his skull.

Brighton laced his fingers over his stomach and leaned back. “We were hoping you’d find out on Titan.”

8

"How did you find it?" Kate asked.

Noah sighed tiredly and leaned against the window. "Persistence, luck, and every last penny," he answered. "I hired a dozen research vessels to run search patterns out here for weeks."

Kate stared at the torus far below. It remained as motionless as a rock—except this particular enormous rock hovered in the water and sucked in light from the halogen lamps, giving nothing back but darkness.

"The size of it..." she said, shaking her head as she trailed off.

"Three-hundred feet in diameter, give or take," Noah told her. "The one orbiting Titan was just under a hundred."

"But why did you start searching *here?*"

"I didn't. Jeff Dolan washed up on the east coast of Florida. That's where I started. Then I worked my way around to this side of the state, and here we are."

He paused and closed his eyes, swaying gently in place. Kate waited awkwardly, thinking he had fallen asleep standing up. She was about to nudge him when he spasmed once and coughed into his hand.

"I'm sorry," he said. "You'll have to excuse me. I've been under the weather lately. That and a lack of sleep is a bad combination." He took a deep breath and steadied himself. "I was happy to learn Jeff is alive, by the way. He never should have been left behind on Titan."

Kate felt the same, yet it had been Jeff's decision to remain there while the surviving crew members set off on their return voyage. Because of the fail-safe protocols hard-coded into *Explorer I*'s operational systems, manually sealing the ship's damaged airlock door from the outside had been the only way to unlock the engine start-up sequence.

"What does Jeff have to do with this?" Kate asked.

"I can't think of a way he returned to Earth before his ship other than by hitching a ride with a torus. Can you?"

Kate remembered the day she found him, rocking gently in the surf near her beachfront condo, still wearing his spacesuit.

"Why would the torus dump him all the way on the east coast and then move to the Gulf?" she asked.

"Scientifically, I have no idea," he admitted. "But if you're asking hypothetically...maybe the torus put Jeff back where it thought he belonged."

"I see," said Kate. "But you were still just stabbing in the dark."

"With a needle," Noah agreed, "trying to hit a mosquito. Then one of the research ships got lucky. I still had a few favors left, and I cashed them in by borrowing a few weather satellites to scan the surface. Back then, the bowl in the surface was only a few feet across. But I knew what to look for under the water."

"I thought we couldn't detect them with scans."

He smiled a bit sheepishly. "Actually, I'm rather proud of the solution. How does one detect the undetectable?"

He paused, obviously waiting for a prompt.

"Okay, how?" said Kate.

"Sonar bounces a signal back from whatever it hits. I just had to look for the spot where it didn't bounce back."

Kate smiled as she figured it out. "Because the torus sucks in every signal we throw at it."

"Precisely."

"That *is* clever," she admitted. "Wait a minute. You said the bowl used to be smaller. Does that mean it's still growing?"

"Its diameter hasn't changed in two months." He looked into the deep waters of the Gulf. "I thought I was finished with Titan, but now..."

"But now one of those things is here. On our planet."

"It seems we're not finished after all. That artifact is here for a reason, Kate. We can work together to find out why."

She took a deep breath and let it out slowly. "Guess I need to let my old boss in Houston know I won't be taking the job." She held out her hand and Noah shook it eagerly, his face beaming.

"Welcome aboard," he said.

Kate laughed, surprised to find herself relieved. Her words came tumbling out in a rush.

"I have so many other questions. How is it creating the surface bowl? Have you sent anyone down there?"

Noah held up his hand patiently before she could launch her interrogation.

"Plenty of time for that soon enough," he said. "Let me show you around first."

"You mean there's more?" she said jokingly.

"The rest of the team, for starters. I've been out hunting investors, so they've pretty much been running the place without me. You're the final addition to my all-star roster."

"Because you saved the best for last?"

"Because up until a few days ago, I didn't know if I would have the money to keep this facility afloat. Pardon the pun." He smiled. "Want to see where you'll be working?"

"Abso-*lutely*."

They walked the length of the window until they came to a black-tiled wall.

"I'll show you a trick," said Noah. He pointed to one of the tiles. "Notice anything different about this one?"

Kate studied it for a moment. “It’s matte instead of polished.”

“Exactly.”

He held the cuff of his sleeve up to the dull tile. A green light pulsed slowly beneath the surface. With an easy push, a hidden door swung open.

“Be honest,” said Kate as they stepped through the doorway. “You didn’t have these installed *just* to impress investors, did you?”

“Well…not exactly, no. When you’re dealing with a mysterious alien artifact, regular doors just seem so mundane.”

Noah led her through a warm room humming with racks of mainframe equipment.

“The facility is a little over two-hundred feet from top to bottom,” Noah explained. “It starts out wider at the top and tapers down to the drydock room at the bottom.”

“How on Earth have you kept this place a secret?” she asked. “Besides not telling prospective employees anything about it, I mean.”

They left the mainframe room and entered a long hallway. This one had none of the flair of the first. Presumably by this point, any investor wouldn’t need to be won over by polished tiles and a glowing floor.

"It hasn't been easy," said Noah. "You'll remember that scans from Explorer One wouldn't penetrate the torus near Titan. It was invisible to the on-board computers."

"I remember," she replied as they walked down the hallway.

"The big one in the water is utilizing the same obfuscating technology. Or the construction material absorbs our signals instead of bouncing them back. Or any of a hundred other possibilities." He was speaking faster now, growing more excited as he explained everything to her. "The point is that unless you're looking right at the torus, it's undetectable. That's why I had to find dead spots in the sonar."

Noah paused politely to wait for any questions. Kate raised her eyebrows and gestured impatiently for him to continue.

He smiled. "To answer your question, whatever scan-blocking or signal-absorbing field the torus is emitting creates a bubble around itself. With the smaller torus near Titan, that bubble wasn't very large. But with *this* one," he said, jabbing his thumb back toward the observation room, "the bubble is much bigger. *Massive*, actually. I built this research facility inside of it."

"But you saw the surface disturbance with a weather satellite."

"I was looking for it. I'm counting on the sheer size of the ocean to keep the disturbance hidden as long as possible."

"There are no heat signatures from the torus, either?"

"Nothing," he said, shaking his head. "No outbound signals of any kind."

"Noah," she said hesitantly, "you can't expect to keep it a secret forever. Considering what the government did to you after Titan, I can imagine they wouldn't be too happy about being left in the dark on this. By your own admission, they let you off easy."

His smile was resigned. "Believe me, I haven't forgotten. They took everything from me, Kate. Everything I built. Diamond Aerospace, the mining outpost on Mars. My money." He took a moment to regain his composure, then nodded. "This time will be different, though. Trust me on that."

"I have another question," she said as they neared the end of the hallway.

"Don't hold back now."

"I don't have to wear one of those turtlenecks to open doors, do I?"

Noah burst out laughing and shook his head. "No, of course not. The access chip can be sewn into any garment. Though I *would* suggest a jacket of some kind. It gets a little chilly at the bottom."

Noah waved his cuff over a matte tile in the wall and an elevator door slid open.

He gestured for her to go first. "After you, Ms. Bishop."

9

"Look right here, Mr. Dolan," said the young medical technician. "No, not the little black circle. That's the camera. This glowing light, down here."

Jeff gave the tech an icy look, which went unnoticed, then reluctantly dragged his gaze to the little blue light in front of him. His head was secured in something like a mad optician's phoropter, with blunted platinum screws turned in far enough to rest against his jaw, temples, and the back of his skull. He had been sitting at an awkward angle on an uncomfortable stool for almost twenty minutes while the tech swapped out various equipment on the rack in front of him.

This one's to test your depth perception, Mr. Dolan. This one's to measure cornea response, Mr. Dolan. This one will make you blind for a few seconds, Mr. Dolan.

That one was the worst. Jeff had cursed at the tech through his clenched jaw, but the kid was an expert at ignoring him.

"That's the last of it, Mr. Dolan," said the tech as he wheeled away the rack of equipment.

When the kid finally loosened the screws holding Jeff's head hostage, he opened his mouth wide and cracked his neck, then stretched his back as he stood.

"What's the prognosis?" he asked.

The tech picked up a tablet and scribbled notes with his stylus.

"Everything's normal for a man your age," he said without looking up.

Jeff's eyes narrowed. "I'm forty-one."

The tech smiled thinly. "And you have perfect eyesight for a forty-one-year-old. Which is to say you're ready for the next round of testing."

"There's more? When are you going to get that ball out of my head?"

"If you'll just step through that door, Mr. Dolan, one of my colleagues will get you all set up..."

* * *

Half an hour later, Jeff was floating inside a coffin-like transparent glass tube, suspended in viscous pink fluid. Electrode discs clung to his shirtless torso like remora, sending the occasional electric pulse into his muscles, making him twitch. A different tech, a young girl seemingly fresh out of med school with the same indifferent demeanor as the optician, had fitted him with a mask and breathing apparatus for his stint in the cylinder of goop. She told him to sit on the lip of the tank, then she unceremoniously pushed him into the thick liquid.

Through the goop and the thick plexi tube, her distorted form wandered around the small lab, swiping at her tablet and reading data from one of a dozen pieces of equipment monitoring Jeff's vitals.

When it was over and he was dripping pink jelly onto a grated floor, waiting for a hose-off, he said, "And what was all that about?"

"Just testing how your body reacts to zero gravity, Mr. Dolan," she replied.

"I've already *been* to space. My body handles it just fine."

She gave him a thin smile identical to her

colleague's. "It's safer for everyone if we don't simply take an applicant's word about their previous experience." She reached over and turned a handle. Icy cold water sprayed down from a nozzle in the ceiling and spattered against Jeff's head. "Just be happy you're on the accelerated testing course," she continued loudly. "The real astronauts have been doing this for months."

He sputtered water from his mouth and swiped it from his eyes. "Oh, I'm *very* grateful. What's next in this house of horrors?"

* * *

Jeff climbed down from the treadmill after forty minutes of continuous jogging, dripping sweat and breathing hard. He sat on a nearby bench and a technician appeared at his shoulder, holding out a bottle of water and a towel. He made good use of them both.

"That wasn't so bad, was it?" asked the tech.

Jeff looked up at her as he mopped his neck. At least this one seemed to have a glimmer of personality.

"Depends on what you do for fun," Jeff answered. "I don't usually run in place wearing a wetsuit just for kicks."

He plucked at the skin-tight neoprene suit he had squeezed into at the tech's insistence. Thin wires ran out from the elbows, chest, waist, and thighs, and disappeared into a boxy machine on a cart, from which the technician took her readings.

The tech smiled. "Most people don't."

Jeff grunted. "One of your friends said I should be grateful I'm on the accelerated course."

"That's true," she agreed. "Otherwise you'd be exercising every day."

"Heaven forbid," he said as the tech began detaching wires from his suit. "How many more of these tests do I have?"

"Just one."

"Yeah?" he asked her, unable to believe it.

"Promise. You might actually like it."

"And why's that?"

She smiled again. "All you have to do is sleep."

* * *

Whether purposeful or not, Jeff had latched on to the idea that he was deliberately being isolated from the rest of the crew. All of his questions regarding his shipmates were evaded—sometimes clumsily, but other times with such deftness that he was convinced the ground crew had undergone training in the fine art of changing the subject.

Jeff had asked to speak with the commander so he could get a better grasp on his responsibilities during the voyage. He had been told, politely at first, and then rather pointedly, not to worry about it.

Like a rat in a maze, he had walked from hallway to lab room to hallway to lab room. Yet, unlike the rat, Jeff never got his piece of cheese.

The last laboratory was a wide, sterile room with a lone gurney in the middle. Next to it stood an intravenous cart and a middle-aged technician with a receding hairline and wireframe glasses. He waited patiently as Jeff walked over to him.

"Mr. Dolan," he said. "Congratulations on the passing of your tests thus far."

"Uh huh," Jeff replied, studying the gurney. The only thing giving him pause was the thick syringe filled with milky pink fluid next to one of the arm straps. "Are you going to cut the, um, the *object* out of my head?"

"Oh my, no," he answered quickly. "It's stuck in there for good, I'm afraid. Buried too deep. If we yanked it out, we'd pull your life out with it."

Jeff swallowed and found he couldn't speak.

"Oh dear," the tech said quietly. "They hadn't told you yet." He *tsk*ed and shook his head.

Jeff cleared his throat, and said, "To be honest, I'm surprised they didn't cut it out as soon as they found it."

"They can afford to be patient. After all, you are an organ donor, are you not? Besides, I imagine it is all very exciting, this opportunity. Yes? Only a very lucky few will ever see what you're going to see. The rest of us must be content with the grainy video feeds."

Jeff stirred as if waking from a trance, then looked at the tech's name tag.

"Doctor Strauss," he read. "I take it you're not going with us."

Strauss frowned sharply and adjusted his glasses. "Most unfortunately, no. Not for my lack of trying, if that is how you say it. Alas."

"Any idea when I'll meet someone else who *is* going?"

"It saddens me I cannot say, Mr. Dolan." He gestured to the gurney. "Won't you please?"

After a moment of deliberation, Jeff stretched out on the lightly padded metal rack and immediately regretted his decision. Strauss swabbed the crook of his arm with a small alcohol pad.

"What are you testing?" Jeff asked.

"Sensitivity to a very unique sedative. I need you to relax, Mr. Dolan. Can you do that?"

"Sedative? What for?"

Strauss raised his eyebrows dramatically and leaned in closer. "It's top secret." He grinned as he inspected the gleaming syringe. "You are wondering why you signed all that paperwork without reading it thoroughly." Before Jeff could rise, Strauss stuck the needle into his arm and quickly injected the milky pink fluid. "Nobody ever reads the paperwork," the doctor sighed.

A wave of nausea rolled up from Jeff's belly. His head clonked back onto the gurney and he mumbled something unintelligible as his vision swirled.

"Don't worry, Mr. Dolan," Strauss said from very

far away. "After this test, it's Titan or bust. I know which one I would choose..."

His voice trailed off as Jeff's consciousness slipped into a deep, dark cavern.

And then, nothing.

10

As the elevator descended, Noah told Kate about his quest for funding to get the research facility up and running. The last of his own property to be sold off was his New York penthouse, and the profits from that had paid for the first layer of heat insulation on the operations level, where they were headed now.

Kate chuckled, and Noah looked at her, curious.

"It's nothing," she said. "This is surreal. I think I just expected you to end up somewhere...*different*... after the Titan mission."

"Oh?" he asked, arching an eyebrow. "Like where? Prison?"

She shrugged. "Maybe a beach in Thailand, drowning your sorrows in cheap beer. Anywhere else but *here*, really."

"I'm hurt you think of me as a walking cliché."

"Oh, come on, Noah. You took a pretty heavy hit. I'm not the only one who thought I'd never hear from you again. No one would blame you if you laid low for a while."

He smiled, somewhat sadly. "Not really my style."

Kate gestured at the facility as a whole. "Obviously."

The elevator stopped. The first thing to greet her as the door opened was a shower of sparks from the hallway ceiling. A bundle of exposed cables hung from a gaping hole.

"As you can see," said Noah as they avoided the sparks, "we're not *quite* finished yet. Another round of funding should land within the next couple of weeks. Crew quarters and the cafeteria are a little primitive at the moment, but at least the coffee's good."

"That's what you said about the coffee at Diamond Aerospace, too."

She followed him down a dark hallway. A fluorescent lamp in the ceiling tried and failed to click on, emitting a steady electric buzz.

"This is the operations level," said Noah. "The only thing deeper is the drydock room."

"Did you get one of those little submarines?" Kate asked, holding her thumb and forefinger an inch apart.

"We will get *two* submersibles—one remote and one that can hold three passengers. The drydock room is also for the divers."

Kate stopped in the hallway. "Divers?" she repeated. "You're not thinking about sending people *out* there, right?"

"After the remote sub checks it out, yes."

Kate's eyebrows went up slowly. "Noah, one of those things killed Commander Riley."

"I haven't forgotten," he said gently. "No one is required to dive. Only those who want to go."

"Yourself included?"

He hesitated a moment. "I can't think of any greater adventure. But don't worry. The dives will happen mostly during construction. After that, we'll go everywhere in the passenger sub."

They walked on. The dark hallway ended at a simple door with a missing handle. Noah pushed it open and gestured for Kate to go ahead.

"The operations room," he said.

She walked past him and into a large room with three wide, blank screens on the opposite wall. In the middle of the room were several computer workstations arranged in an arc to face the massive screens.

Noah came in and stood next to Kate as she admired the setup.

"It looks like the bridge of a movie starship," she said.

"It was inspired by some of my favorite science fiction shows as a kid," Noah admitted. "With a little artistic license, of course."

"Of course."

Thin strips of recessed lights ran up the walls, softly illuminating the room. Harsher squares of light from the desktop monitors splashed in bright colors over the shiny black floor. The architecture-magazine sterility of the room deepened the chill creeping into Kate's skin.

"Where are the others?" she asked.

"Tom's in the mainframe room, Dominic is visiting family, and you and I are right here."

She glanced sideways at him. "That's it? You only have two other people running the place?"

"They can handle it, and so can you. I wanted to get you in here first to get a feel for the place. Tried to spare you having to hit the ground running."

Kate looked around the room again. "It's a lot smaller than the control room at Canaveral. Shouldn't be too overwhelming."

"I'm glad to hear it." He tilted his head toward the ceiling and said, "Main view."

The three large viewscreens flicked on, showing a panoramic live image of the large torus outside the facility. Light from the powerful halogen lamps vanished into the black exterior of the object.

"Oh," Kate said quietly. "Well now, that's impressive."

"It was rotating when I first found it," said Noah. "Floating in the same spot and spinning in place."

"Spinning?"

He nodded. "And the surface bowl was growing."

"Now it's stationary," Kate said. "What changed?"

"That's one of the many things I hope to find out. I was watching it rotate, and I looked away for just a moment. When I looked back, it had stopped. It's been immobile for a month now."

She studied the video feed, following the edge of the torus until darkness swallowed its far side.

"You think Jeff traveled through that thing? From Titan?"

"I think that's just one of their many tricks."

"A very profitable one."

"Beyond compare," he agreed. "But I'm not here for that."

She looked at him doubtfully.

"The *investors* are," he clarified, "but I'm not."

"Then why are *you* here?"

Noah joined her in admiring the torus. Light from the screens painted their faces a soft blue.

"I can think of no greater questions than the ones that artifact poses. For humanity, for the *future* of humanity...and for myself."

Kate smiled knowingly. "And you want to be the first to find those answers."

"*We*," Noah corrected. "*We* want to be first. Our team. Who knows how long the torus will be here? It could disappear tomorrow. If we don't find the answers, no one else will. No one else *can*."

"What questions?"

"Where do they come from? Not Titan. They were visiting, like us. Are they sentient? Who's controlling them?"

"I can think of a more important question," Kate said.

"Which is?"

She hesitated a moment, then said, "What do they want with us?"

Noah's watch beeped. He glanced at it and sighed.

"I'm sorry, but I have to leave you alone for a while."

"Is everything alright?"

He waved her concern away. "Fine, fine. Just some business that won't wait. The gears are always turning."

He smiled wanly. Kate couldn't help but notice how pale his skin looked in the harsh lighting.

"I'm sure I'll manage," she said, moving closer to a workstation while trying not to seem *too* eager.

Noah left quickly. Kate sat in one of the workstation chairs and looked up at the object on the viewscreens.

"Hello again," she muttered.

The torus floated in darkness, still and silent.

11

The tide pulled warm saltwater around Jeff's ankles, back into the Atlantic. Golden late afternoon sunlight shimmered over the surface.

He stood in the exact spot he washed ashore after the Titan mission: Cocoa Beach, Florida, not more than a hundred feet from Kate's old condo.

He looked behind him. Thick weeds choked the small backyard garden. It was easy to imagine her standing casually in the doorway, holding a cup of tea and smiling at him. Jeff offered a ghost of a smile in return, but the only true recipient was a vibrant orange *For Sale* sign staked into the ground near the back door.

The tide rolled out once more, bubbling over his feet and pulling his attention back to the Atlantic.

He recalled snippets of his brief fall to Titan. Mostly, he remembered the vast white expanse that opened beneath him when he emerged from the lowest layer of the atmosphere.

There had been hints of immense machines in the orange clouds above him; monolithic behemoths tumbling in the fog. And below...below was the surface of Titan, stretching to every horizon, pristine in its raw form except for the area directly beneath. There the surface was marred by an artificial presence: aliens on that alien moon.

As Jeff fell toward the surface, he glimpsed a wide field of burgeoning structures wrought from the same material as the ring-shaped tori that floated over the icy ground, constructing their silent city.

And moving between the tori and the buildings, floating above the surface as if repelled from it by intense magnetism, were humanoid figures wearing spacesuits just like Jeff's, though one generation older: the Constellation Mark III.

As he rapidly plummeted toward a large pool of liquid methane on the surface, Jeff didn't have much time to ponder the minutiae. He saw spacesuits, tori, black arches emerging from the ice and burrowing back in thirty meters away, a cryovolcano bigger than Mt. Everest spewing ice from its glistening caldera—and the methane lake as he slammed into it, pulling him down faster than he'd been falling, toward the open mouth of a torus as it rushed up to meet him, his suit sizzling as methane ate through the fabric like acid, smoke pouring into his helmet as the polycarbonate face shield melted like butter—

Jeff gasped and stepped back, his foot sucking out of the sand and splashing back down into the surf. He breathed hard and listened to the gentle rush of water as it washed over the sand, over the sand, over the sand...

His heart slowed, and tension left his shoulders.

No, he hadn't been able to ponder what he witnessed as he fell. In the quiet hours following his return to Earth, however, all he had was time. Breaking up with Kate had certainly helped to free up his schedule.

He had tried to call her, to tell her he was going back to Titan. Her landlord said she hadn't left a forwarding address and none of their mutual acquaintances who answered his calls knew where she might be. Not answering his calls was something he could understand, but for no one in Kate's social circle to have any idea where she'd run off to was quite another.

Perhaps that was his own fault. Maybe she didn't want to leave him any breadcrumbs to follow.

By his own admission, Jeff had changed after he got back. It didn't take Kate pointing it out to realize that his focus was inverted. He spent more time sitting on that beach, staring out at nothing than he did interacting with other people, especially her. A singular notion had crept into his mind and was so overpowering that it smothered his every waking thought, making it impossible for him to move on with his life: that the Jeff Dolan who left for Titan wasn't the same one who returned.

When Kate found him on the beach, his spacesuit was undamaged. It looked brand new, she said. And his helmet—the helmet that was a millisecond from disintegrating when Jeff blacked out on Titan—was as pristine as if it had never been worn.

New clothes could be overlooked. Any alien race sophisticated enough to wield the kind of technology employed by the tori could certainly manufacture a new spacesuit for him.

It was the scars that bothered him.

On the outbound trip to Titan, Jeff sustained a severe injury to his chest when an oxygen compressor exploded. A mangled scar bloomed from his sternum like a gruesome octopus, extending over his ribs and tracing several lines down his stomach.

Yet upon his return to Earth, there was no trace of an injury. All his other scars had vanished, as well. Little white nicks on his hands; a jagged circle on his forearm from a rusty nail; a zig-zag line on his shin from a compound fracture when he was sixteen...all of them gone.

And now, the doctors were telling him he'd brought something back: a small sphere tucked neatly against the base of his skull, emitting no electrical signals of any kind (*detectable* signals, one of them clarified during his most recent round of tests), releasing no chemicals, affecting none of his mental processes, absorbing nothing from Jeff so far as they could tell.

It was simply...inside.

He looked down at his feet and wiggled his toes, making small depressions in the wet sand.

His one small and distant hope was that all of his questions would be answered on his second voyage to Titan. If he found those answers, Kate would look into his eyes the next time she saw him and know that he was back...*truly* back.

Explorer II launched in six days. Jeff needed only to endure a few more rounds of poking, prodding, running, and sleep-testing to be declared fit to join the crew—a crew he'd yet to meet, besides Elizabeth McCall. He had been repeatedly assured it was the same story for the rest of the crew. The reasons they were kept apart changed every time he asked the question. Security, isolation testing, and emotional independence were the ones he heard the most.

Jeff thought he and the crew of *Explorer I* did just fine living and working together in a confined space for months on end. They endured their fair share of isolated psychological profiling before the mission, but they also trained as a unit.

Yet that was a private endeavor funded by Noah Bell's Diamond Aerospace. *Explorer II* would fly with government oversight. If Jeff's years as a government contractor had taught him anything, it was the need for such organizations to do it their way.

If getting to Titan meant shutting up and strapping in, that's what he would do. The only other option was to stand on the beach and stare at a body of water that held no answers.

Jeff shook his head. He knew it was better to be up there, in the black, with the pinpoint light of Titan in the distance. Whether or not that tiny light held hope or oblivion he would discover in due time.

PART II

5 MONTHS LATER

12

Explorer II was very similar to its predecessor.

Besides a few minor alterations, it looked the same on the outside: nine meters of bulbous command module at the nose, followed by thirty meters of wider crew module (including the centrifuge). A sixteen-meter storage hold behind that steadily tapered to meet the last section of the 140-meter-long spacecraft: the Thermal Antimatter Propulsion System, which could boost the ship to speeds in excess of seven-thousand kilometers a second.

Eighty-five meters of engine.

It was enough to cut the journey to Titan down to just over five months.

When the government took control of Diamond Aerospace from Noah Bell, the majority of the propulsion systems on *Explorer II* had already been constructed. Also ready for installation were the guidance and life support computers, the oxygen filtration system, and most of the upholstery and furniture, including bunks for the crew.

Production stopped during the takeover, but not because of a bureaucratic snafu or a clerical error. It stopped because the government had a new technology they wanted to incorporate in the design of *Explorer II*—a technology that needed a good deal of space inside the always-turning centrifuge. The artificial gravity generated by the centrifuge fought bone degeneration in the crew, so the technology had to be placed within the spinning ring. This meant the removal of less vital equipment, such as the eating tables and privacy shower.

As the need for these luxuries shrank considerably without a waking crew on the months-long voyage to Titan, it was thought they would hardly be missed.

Yet when Jeff Dolan spilled from his stasis chamber after five months of sleep and hit the floor like a boneless fish, the first thing he wished for was a hot shower. He shivered as cold, pink goop dripped off his body and splatted onto the hard floor.

Since he was now awake, that meant *Explorer II* had begun its slowing process two days from Titan.

He rolled onto his back, groaning in pain. Thick fluid squished under his skin-tight body suit. Since he couldn't have a shower, the next thing he wished for was a towel.

What he got instead was a blurry view of someone's feet as they stepped in front of his face. He squinted up at the bright ceiling, trying to identify the fuzzy shape looming over him.

"Clean yourself up," said the fuzzy shape in a deep baritone. "Drink some lemonade. There's a briefing in ten minutes."

Jeff tried to say *Lemonade?* but all that came out of his mouth when he opened it was a stream of thin liquid that tasted like strawberries. When he finally managed to pull himself up onto his unsteady feet, the fuzzy shape was gone, and Jeff was alone in the stasis section of *Explorer II*.

Six coffin-like sleep chambers had been evenly spaced near the forward part of the spinning centrifuge, just behind the narrow crew bunks. Jeff leaned against one for support as he wiped his eyes, hoping to clear some of the blur.

His sleep chamber contained a mass of pinkish gel that formed to the interior. It was flat on the surface except for a pulpy line down the middle where he had emerged.

The hazy details of launch day slowly came into focus.

Explorer II had made a pit-stop at the International Space Station, just as *Explorer I* had done on its first and only mission. The command module that carried all six astronauts to space inside the modified Neptune III rocket mated with the rest of the ship, which had been constructed ahead of time near the ISS after the individual parts were sent up on previous launches.

Even as he joined the other astronauts in the crew module during launch preparation, Jeff still didn't meet half of them.

Two pilots sat at the front of the cockpit. Jeff had been sandwiched between Elizabeth McCall and, of all people, Will Chapman. Another man sat next to Will, but didn't respond to any questions. For whatever reason, Jeff, Will, and Elizabeth seemed to be on a different comm channel.

He was just getting around to asking Will what he was doing on the rocket when the nine-engine Hydra cores fired, crushing everyone back into their seats and filling the cabin with a tremendous roar.

In the split second before the engines ignited, the look on Will's pale face within his helmet was one of abject terror. He had been unwilling to offer any meaningful answers after that.

In the stasis section of the ship, Jeff straightened up and plucked at the white neoprene bodysuit he'd been forced to squeeze into before *Explorer II* left the space station. It was still slick from the gel compound they had pushed him down into when they stuffed him into the stasis chamber and flipped the night-night switch.

To give himself more time to gain his composure and balance, he re-counted all of the chambers in that ring of the centrifuge.

Six.

Six crew members for this mission. There had only been four of them on *Explorer I*, and that was cramped enough. Yet he did have to admit that sleeping through most of the journey in the stasis chambers would probably extend everyone's tolerance of each other moving forward.

Speaking of others, he thought.

His wet feet peeled off the floor with each step as he padded into the nearby crew section. It was separated from the ring of stasis chambers by a cushioned wall cut with several open doorways and a one-meter hole in its center, aligned with the centrifuge's axis of spin.

Jeff walked quickly around the centrifuge, hunting for an empty bunk. He finally found one and gave a loud, shivering sigh of relief when he saw the folded blue towel on his pillow.

"It's the little things," he said through chattering teeth.

Someone groaned a few bunks over. Jeff wiped his face and rubbed his hair with the towel as he walked in the direction of the sound.

Elizabeth McCall sat on the edge of her bunk with her eyes closed and her head cradled in her hands. She wore a black tracksuit. A piece of string held back her curly red hair in a loose ponytail.

"Where can a guy get some clothes around here?" Jeff managed to say between shivers.

Elizabeth opened one eye slightly to look at him, offering a weak smile.

"Clothes locker," she whispered. Then she pointed above her head.

Jeff looked up at the floor of the crew compartment on the opposite side of the centrifuge. Next to one of the bunks was a short plastic storage bin with a sliding lid.

"Someone told me to drink lemonade," he said, as if it made all the sense in the world.

Elizabeth nodded, then immediately seemed to regret it. "Kitchen," she whispered. "S'post to help."

"Can I bring you a cup?"

"Had three."

"Well, there's a ringing endorsement," said Jeff.

Another weak smile. She turned away and curled up on her bunk.

After searching through the clothes locker and finding a dark blue tracksuit that (mostly) fit and a pair of white sneakers, Jeff climbed the ladder at the forward section of the centrifuge that led to the command module. Gravity slipped away slowly as he climbed until he was floating freely while gripping the top rung. He pulled himself forward using handholds in the wall of the cylindrical passageway, floating past the airlock at a T-junction as he drifted toward the nose of *Explorer II.*

He popped up through the hatch in the floor of the command module, just behind the pilot seats. A bench holding four more cushioned seats was bolted to the back wall of the compartment to allow for the additional four crew members. Besides that, Jeff thought it was identical to the module in the first *Explorer.*

A man with short salt-and-pepper hair sat in the left pilot seat, facing away from Jeff, holding a thin tablet and scribbling notes into a small dialogue box with an illuminated stylus.

Jeff steadied himself behind the two pilot seats and peered out through the narrow slit of a window, into the darkness of space. Tiny pinpoints of white light pierced the veil, glimmering madly without a gauze of atmosphere to dull them. In the center of the window, Titan glowed bright, a slightly lopsided sphere of muted ochre the size of a quarter.

"We're still two days out?" Jeff asked, hoping to kick-start a conversation.

"Mmm," said the man, noncommittally.

"I was told there would be a mission briefing," Jeff continued. After another moment of silence, he added, "And lemonade." No reply. "I'd sure like to know what I'm supposed to be doing up here."

The man in the pilot seat chuckled. "So would I. If you see one of the commanders, try asking them."

Jeff's next breath froze in his throat, caught there in a vise. He knew that voice—had flown with the owner of that voice from Earth to Titan. The last time he heard it, the owner was screaming for help as a torus turned him inside-out.

It was the voice of a ghost.

The pilot seat spun around.

"Good to see you again, Dolan," said Tag Riley. "You look terrible."

13

Kate waited behind a thinning veneer of patience as billionaire John Harris tried to pull his wetsuit up over his paunch for the third time. He was pleasant enough wearing a three-piece suit, but apparently his grumpy alter ego despised skin-tight outfits that accentuated his rounded midsection.

The drydock room at the bottom of the research facility was empty except for the two of them. The only sound besides John's heavy breathing was a gentle splashing from the moon pool. The five-meter-wide pool was in the middle of the floor, glowing soft green from diffused lighting below its surface. It sat atop a seven-meter water tunnel that led down to the bottom of the facility and into open water.

Nautilus, the larger of the two submersibles, and the only one that could carry passengers, bobbed gently in the moon pool, its vertical hatch rising from the surface. The remote sub *Pequod* hung suspended from the crane arm off to one side. It looked like a cross between an escape pod and an oversized robotic lobster.

"I still don't believe this is the only size you have," John growled as he fumbled with the zipper of his wetsuit. Grasping it tightly, he sucked in his gut, held his breath, and yanked it up to his neck, overcoming the main obstacle.

"The sub is like a little spaceship, Mr. Harris," Kate said. "If the hull is breached, we need to have our own air supply."

"But they don't usually wear dive suits in submersibles, right? I've seen the documentaries. Some of them are in T-shirts, for God's sake."

"This isn't the usual situation, Mr. Harris."

"And what about the pressure? We'll have air, but wouldn't we implode at that depth?"

"We're only a hundred feet down," Kate assured him. "The transition would be extremely uncomfortable, but the suits we're using were designed to withstand the pressure. You're in good hands, Mr. Harris."

Kate thought it was best not to mention that if the sub's hull integrity failed, they should be more worried about getting out of the compromised metal shell before it sank to the depths than whether or not they could still breathe.

Harris sighed and relaxed his stomach, then grunted happily when he noticed the slimming effect the wetsuit had on his figure.

"Call me John," he said.

"Alright, John. Are you ready for the rest of it?"

His shoulders drooped. "There's more?"

Kate nodded to her left. Against the curved wall, three gray, brand new dive suits hung from the wall.

"They look like spacesuits!" John said with genuine glee.

"Noah says appearance is ninety percent of your first impression."

"He got that part right. Look at those beauties. We get to wear them?"

Kate smiled, unable to avoid catching a little of his enthusiasm. "Standard issue for anyone riding in Nautilus."

"But where's the rest of the suit?" he asked. "The mask and the breathing apparatus?"

"In the sub," Kate replied. "Easier to get in and out that way."

Kate slipped into her dive suit and was ready to go in less than thirty seconds. After a few minutes of grunts and curses while Harris got into his suit, he bowed his head in deference and gestured at the open hatch.

"Lead on, Ms. Bishop."

"Call me Kate."

A small platform extended a foot over the water. Kate stepped onto it, then to the lip of the hatch. Supporting herself with her hands, she dropped down into the sub's airlock, landing easily. From there, she climbed down into a cramped compartment with barely enough room to turn around.

"Best to use the handholds!" she shouted up the hatch.

Tom Willis sat in the pilot seat. He grinned at Kate as she squeezed into the bucket seat next to him.

Noah hired Tom back when the facility was still in the blueprint phase, months before Kate joined the team. Tom had refined the computer systems before they were installed, then switched projects to help design the two submersibles, which turned out to be his real passion.

Kate thought he looked even more like a rebel computer programmer from decades past than usual. He wore thick glasses instead of contacts. His long hair trailed from a red baseball cap with a string of binary stitched on the front. Kate wasn't surprised to see him in the faded death metal band T-shirt he wore six days of every week. Flat-soled skater shoes under torn blue jeans completed his ensemble. If it weren't for the streaks of gray in his hair and in his face stubble, she might think he was ten years younger.

"Having fun yet?" he asked.

"I just love these press tours," Kate said quietly with a fake smile as she inserted her comm earbud. "Almost makes me wish I was staying behind, filling out all those forms Noah keeps giving to me."

"Yeah, NDAs can be a real pain. I just close my eyes and scribble my signature everywhere."

"It's another thick binder of paperwork," Kate said, holding up her fingers inches apart to demonstrate. "Never seen so much red tape. And I thought it was bad when I signed up." She sighed and flipped a comm switch amidst a myriad of other controls in front of her. "Comms check, comms check, one two three."

"I got you," Tom said, adjusting his own earbud.

John plopped down to the floor behind them, albeit less gracefully than Kate had managed.

"The hatch is still open," he said as he looked around the sub. "Hot dog, this is really something."

"Your money well spent," Kate said. "We can close the hatch from down here."

Tom reached over his head to a bank of controls and slid aside a protective plastic cover. He pushed the glowing red button underneath. There was an audible *whumph* from above as the hatch swung shut, sealing them in.

John maneuvered himself into the only other seat, directly behind the other two. Protruding equipment forced him to sit slightly hunched forward. Kate turned around and gave John an earbud, then she lifted a rectangular metal panel off the floor. In the space beneath were three polished, full-face helmets. She handed one to John and another to Tom, then donned her own.

"You can feel the slider by your chin," she said, pointing to the bottom of her own helmet.

John pawed at it clumsily, his helmet bonking against the equipment behind his seat.

"Here, let me," said Kate.

John leaned forward dutifully. Kate rotated the metal slider under his chin until she felt the soft click that indicated a good seal.

"Detaching now," Tom said.

He grasped a lever attached to the side of his seat and jerked it upward. With a brief expulsion of ballast, the sub descended. Silver bubbles roiled up past the wide window.

"What about the breathing tanks?" John said, alarmed.

"Did you notice the flat metal circles on the backs of our suits?" Kate asked.

"Yes..."

"Lean back in your chair."

He did, slowly, then he laughed as the metal circles clicked into grooves in the chair.

"I read about these," he said.

Kate leaned back against her own chair until the six metal rings on her suit clicked into place. "See the big orange button by your left hand?" she asked.

"I see it," John said.

"If there's a hull breach, that little guy pops up. Smack it back down, and your oxygen tank separates from the seat."

"What about my air?"

"It comes in through the rings on your back," said Kate, "then up through the circulating system in the suit. You can't see them now, but there are two small vents under your chin. It will get a little colder if you have to switch over to your internal air supply."

"We're not already on it?" John asked.

"Not unless there's a hull breach or we manually flip the switch."

The last of the silvery bubbles slipped up over the curved window and disappeared, leaving only a vast expanse of deep green, which darkened to black in the distance.

"Everything good?" asked Kate.

Tom ran a quick test on the systems. "Never looked better," he answered.

"Okay, then. Let's get up close and personal with the torus."

14

"I..." Jeff said, staring at Riley. "You..."

"I'm dead," said Riley. He shrugged. "*Was* dead. Now I'm not, thanks to whatever's down there on the surface." He jabbed his thumb toward Titan.

A soft, reverberating hum coursed through the walls of the command module, overlaid with the faint thrum of an oxygen compressor. With his mind frozen on a half-finished thought, Jeff became acutely aware of every breath, blink, and heartbeat.

Riley burst into harsh laughter. "You're taking it better than I expected," he admitted. "My ex-wife just about died of a heart attack." He shook his head. "Wish I could have been there to see it."

"How did you...?" said Jeff, emerging from his stupor. He swallowed hard and tried again. "What happened?"

Riley grinned and rubbed his square jaw. His face seemed a little less wrinkled—a little less world-weary—than Jeff remembered.

"Washed up on the beach, same as you. Although no girlfriend was there to greet me. I opened my eyes to fifty automatic rifles aimed at my head."

"The Air Force base?" asked Jeff.

"Right in the middle of their top-secret beachfront property," Riley said, nodding. "They thought I was a secret agent scout for some kind of foreign invasion." He chuckled. "Really spun 'em for a loop when they learned the truth."

"When did you get back?"

"Couple of weeks after the torus turned me into soup, near as anyone can tell."

"You remember when it...when it happened?"

He nodded slowly. "I remember *all* of it."

A light flashed on the control panel. Riley reacted out of habit, turning in his chair to press a button that stopped the flashing. His hand froze just over the screen, and he sighed.

"Those bastards wouldn't tell me anything," he said. "They ran enough tests on me to make a lab rat feel neglected. Then they said I wouldn't have to do anything on board the ship...just sit here like a mope the whole time."

"They wouldn't even tell me who the commander is," said Jeff.

Riley grunted. "Well, score one for me. They at least gave me a look at the roster before I climbed into that sleep-tank. One of the commanders, Brighton, seems to know her stuff. The other one, I'm not so sure about."

"Brighton?" Jeff asked. "She?"

"The colonel's daughter. Proof that nepotism will never die."

"Why two commanders?"

"Why not?" Riley smirked. "It's a strange mission, isn't it?"

He scratched the back of his head, at the base of his skull.

"Something wrong?" Jeff asked, watching him closely.

"Just an itch, Dolan," Riley said irritably. "If this were the first mission, I'd tell you to go scrub the oxygen filters. I used to say that to get you out of my hair."

"Good thing it's not the first mission. Still, I'll leave you to your grumbling."

Riley grumbled something as Jeff pulled himself down through the hatch. He drifted aft and climbed down the ladder leading to the rear section, in search of the fabled lemonade.

Elizabeth was asleep in her bunk. He passed her quietly, moving through the stasis section and into what passed for a kitchen.

There had been no way to make it any smaller for the installation of the stasis chambers, but someone had managed to cram a few extra bits of humming equipment in the small closet-like space. Jeff grabbed one of the few remaining sachets of lemonade inside a plastic tub and discovered his profound thirst when the first drop hit his tongue. He finished off two more sachets before belching politely and stuffing the empties into the trash receptacle.

Moving aft, he entered the systems equipment and monitoring ring of the centrifuge. It was in this area on *Explorer I* where he'd spent most of his time. Crawling in and out of the floor to tweak hardware, running constant tests on vital systems—most of that drudgery was eliminated by sleeping his way to Titan. He reflected on the fact that the crew had been extremely lucky none of the automated systems malfunctioned during the voyage.

He rested his palm on the warm surface of a comm relay box as a thin green line moved across the screen: the incoming signal from Earth. Anything picked up by the relay would have been sent about an hour earlier.

On the first mission, being in close proximity to the torus allowed for instant communication between Earth and *Explorer I*. Jeff was left to wonder if that was a characteristic of all tori or if it was an isolated case. In his long list of questions regarding the alien object, the side effect of instant communication was not near the top.

For the time being, at least, the crew of *Explorer II* would have to deal with the delay, and that suited him just fine.

Several voices rose in heated discussion farther aft, talking over each other unintelligibly. Jeff followed them into the laboratory section of the centrifuge. It contained several workstations, cold sample storage, and a new addition since the first mission: a fully enclosed clean room for more sensitive work.

Four people were gathered at the workstation tables, two of them seated and two standing in front of the group. They all fell silent when Jeff approached. He sat on a swivel stool between Will Chapman and Elizabeth McCall.

"Sorry I'm late," he said. "I was…catching up with an old friend."

The two people standing in front of the group shared a brief, knowing glance. The young woman folded her arms and leaned back against a bolted-down table. The middle-aged man to her left flicked through screens on his tablet, ignoring everyone. His broad, truculent face and short, black hair contrasted her sharp features and luminous platinum pixie cut. Both of them were as fit as a person could be for their respective ages.

"You saw Riley, then?" asked the woman.

Jeff nodded slowly. "I did."

She stared at him for a long moment. "Well, good job for not having a mental breakdown. It's the weirdest thing I've ever heard, but I'm glad you can deal with it."

"Um...thank you?" said Jeff.

"You're welcome." She stood up. "You know Chapman and McCall. I'm Commander Brighton, and this is Commander Ward."

The man standing next to her tucked the tablet under his armpit and clasped his hands loosely in front of him, studying Jeff.

Will didn't make eye contact. He adjusted his glasses nervously, then swallowed dryly and stared at his sweaty hands, palm-up on the table. Elizabeth gave Jeff a little smile and nodded. She was pale, but seemed in good spirits.

"I'll catch you up quick, Dolan," said Brighton, "so pay attention."

He sat up a little straighter on his stool.

"We're forty-five hours from Titan," she continued. "The ship's on an automated braking course which will park us in a prograde orbit. This will give our surface sensors enough time to map the area you visited on your first trip, which we believe is in the southern part of the Adiri region."

"That's where the Huygens probe landed," said Jeff.

Brighton nodded. "Even if we can't detect any visitors, we should be able to figure out if anything's moving down there."

"Your sensors can penetrate the atmosphere?" Jeff asked. "Explorer One didn't have anything like that."

"Did you sleep through mission prep?" asked Commander Ward. His deep voice was the same one that greeted Jeff when he first emerged from his stasis chamber.

"There was no mission prep for me," Jeff replied, meeting his eyes. "But you knew that already."

Brighton touched Ward's forearm gently as she looked at Jeff. "We'll get you the necessary docs. But the answer is yes. Our sensors can penetrate down to the surface. Barring any unnatural encounters in orbit, we should have a clear picture of what's down there within two or three days."

"Then what?" Chapman asked in a strained voice.

"Then we'll assess our options," said Brighton. She addressed the small group. "That's all for now."

The two commanders walked quickly out of the lab section, toward the front of the ship.

"I don't think he likes me very much," said Jeff.

"How could you tell?" Will replied.

"He doesn't like anyone," offered Elizabeth, "except Brighton. I think he resents having to take civilians on the mission."

Will opened and closed his hands slowly, staring at them. "My fingers are still numb."

"It takes a while for the effects of the gel to wear off," said Elizabeth.

"How does that work, by the way?" Jeff asked. "Did we breathe that stuff in?"

She shook her head. "We absorbed it. The numbing agent in the gel puts you to sleep after a few minutes. It gets into your bloodstream through your skin."

"I felt like a piece of fruit in a Jell-O mold," said Jeff.

"It's an incredible compound," admitted Elizabeth. "They say you could survive a hundred-story fall if you were inside a glob of it."

"I hope they don't expect us to test that, too."

Chapman clenched and unclenched his fists. "No, they have something else in mind," he said, staring at nothing in particular.

"What's that supposed to mean?" Jeff asked.

"Let's just say we shouldn't get too comfortable." Chapman stood abruptly. "I have to make a call."

He walked away, leaving Jeff and Elizabeth at the table.

"He's still sick from the stasis," she explained.

"I think he's terrified."

"That's not unusual, either."

"But what's he doing up here?" Jeff asked. "He's Colonel Brighton's pencil-pusher, not an astronaut."

"The colonel is...paranoid, for lack of a more intense word," she said. "He spearheaded the mission, hand-picked the crew, but..."

Jeff nodded. "But Will Chapman is *his* man."

"That's right. If you recall, your crew on the first mission quickly went off-book after the torus showed up. Brighton wanted someone up here who would be completely honest in their reports."

"I get the feeling Will wasn't too happy about the decision."

"He's being a big baby, to be honest," said Elizabeth. She covered her mouth and burst out laughing. "I'm sorry. I shouldn't gossip. There hasn't been much chance to really *talk* to anyone since we left."

"Tell me about it," said Jeff. "I was starting to think I'd be the only one on the ship. I felt so…alone."

Elizabeth smiled warmly. "You're not alone. Not anymore."

15

"Visibility's a bit better with daylight," Kate explained. "We usually take the sub out in the morning, but we just came off the tail-end of a nasty storm."

"Surely you don't feel the effects down here," John said.

"That's true. But the Nautica is in constant communication with surface sensors inside the facility and in the water. Too many variables contaminate the data when the weather's pitching a fit. We try to eliminate as many wild cards as we can when dealing with the torus."

Tom flicked on the halogen lamp array under the sub's window. The light illuminated a universe of free-floating particulates, then vanished into darkness five meters from the nose. Electric motors whirred to life, and the sub gently coasted forward.

Behind her, Kate heard John trying to lean forward in his seat. He mumbled a curse under his breath when he couldn't budge.

"Mobility is the only downside to this type of system," she said.

"How do you people scratch an itch?"

Tom smiled. "We ignore it until it goes away."

The sub's motors hummed steadily as Kate stared into the ocean.

"You keep the torus lit up all the time?" John asked.

"Yes, for video documentation."

Far ahead, a faint glow bloomed in the depths—a light shade of green in a black abyss.

"But..." said John, "does it *do* anything?"

"Not a blessed thing," Tom answered. "It just floats there. *Real* fun job."

"Oh, stop it," Kate teased. "Now hand over the controls. I want to take it for a spin."

Tom twisted a dial on his control panel and punched a button. "The stick is yours."

Kate rested her palm on the motor control sphere set into the panel. With a gentle roll forward, the electric motors strained harder, and the sub accelerated.

"Keep an eye on that cross-current, now," Tom warned.

"I know how to read the display," Kate replied calmly, tapping the impeller control stick. "You taught me, remember?"

"Hmph. Just don't make me regret it."

Kate depressed the sphere ever-so-slightly, and the nose of the sub angled downward, aligned with the blooming glow ahead.

"Any second now," she whispered.

A halogen lamp emerged from the murk before them, suspended from a thin truss lined with ballast tanks that encircled the torus. Its light fell on the surface of the artifact, disappearing into it.

Kate piloted the sub under the curved frame.

"We're already closer to the object now than the crew of Explorer One could get without being pulled in," she explained. "We expected *this* torus to have a much broader area of attraction since it's roughly three times as large, but that's not the case. For all intents and purposes, it's dead in the water."

To drive her point home, Kate parked the sub one meter from the outer wall of the torus. Above and below, the exterior hull of the artifact curved out of sight.

Light from the sub's halogen lamps fell into the surface, which reflected nothing back. Nevertheless, intricately-patterned grooves were revealed as light passed by them. The grooves covered every visible inch of the torus.

"Is that some kind of alien language?" John asked as he strained to look up.

"We're not sure yet," Kate answered. "Could be a language, or a schematic, or simply decoration. Could be circuits in a comm relay."

"No," John said, his voice heavy with awe. "It's more than that. I'm sure of it."

Tom smiled. "Ancient cultures painted their pottery."

"This ain't no clay pot, son," said John. "Two of your people went inside the ring, is that right?"

"They went into the torus that was orbiting Titan during the mission, yes," Kate answered.

"How do we get into this one?"

Kate and Tom exchanged a quick glance.

"We mapped the exterior with high-resolution cameras, but we haven't found a door," she said. "Two crew members were pulled inside against their will on the first mission. There are recordings in the facility archives describing what they saw."

"I would very much like to see those recordings," John said, his tone indicating it was more than a request. "You're sure it's safe to be this close?"

"Normally we don't go past the truss," said Tom.

John snorted. "But you wanted to impress me."

"We've been waiting more than six months for any sign of activity," Kate told him. "Noah believes we've entered the 'acceptable risk' period of our investigation."

"What would happen if it activated right now?"

"Well..." Kate said. "We'd either be pulled into a black hole membrane that covered the center of the torus and our sub would be crushed like a tin can... or we'd be sucked inside the ring of the torus itself."

"Hmm," John said thoughtfully.

"That being said," Kate went on, "do you want to touch it?"

Palpable eagerness infused his voice when he said, "I thought you'd never ask."

Kate rolled the control sphere forward with her right hand and worked the impeller stick with her left. The sub climbed sharply, accelerating over the top of the torus. It dropped from view, leaving only dark water ahead. Kate banked to port and tilted the nose downward so they could follow the curvature of the artifact.

A cube slightly larger than the *Nautilus* floated twenty meters above the horizontal torus. A shiny chrome hatch adorned each side of the cube. Thin streams of bubbles flowed from protruding valves in the top four corners.

"Self-stabilizing floating airlock," Kate said as they drew closer. "One of the more impressive toys at our disposal. Just remember to keep your helmet on when we're inside."

"How does it stay in place?" John asked.

"Its systems are linked with the facility's," said Tom. "The facility keeps track of its relative position from the surface and the torus. If you tell the airlock to stay somewhere, it's accurate within a few inches."

"We have to replace the ballast tanks once every three days," Kate added. "Other than that, it's just a matter of keeping the right amount of weight on board."

"Why don't we just use the sub's airlock?"

"It only holds one person at a time." Then she smiled. "And the floating airlock is way more impressive."

John shook his head. "My kids aren't going to believe *any* of this."

Kate glanced sideways at Tom, who rolled his eyes.

"That's probably for the best, Mr. Harris," she said.

Tom gestured toward the console and Kate leaned back, allowing him to take control.

"Hold tight," he said. "This hatch is much smaller than the moon pool at the facility."

Under his guidance, the sub slowed as it approached the cube. Just before impact, it dipped below the cube and came up under it. Tom bit his lower lip as he worked the controls. A moment later, there was a gentle bump and the cabin shook.

"Locked in," he said.

"Releasing oxygen backpacks," Kate said.

She tapped a command into the console and jerked forward as the embedded backpack popped free from her chair. The helmet vents under her chin blew icy cold air for a few seconds before warming up to a mildly uncomfortable cool.

Kate twisted in her seat and smiled at John. "Ready to go swimming?"

16

Jeff sat harnessed in one of the pilot seats, alone in the command module at the front of the ship.

The narrow window over the nose showcased Titan, now a slightly-lopsided orb the size of a tennis ball. A relatively bright point in the empty black behind it was Saturn, its rings barely visible as two tiny notches protruding from the mote of light.

As the minutes crept by, Jeff became increasingly glad to have skipped over the five-month journey to Titan. With both commanders' continued refusal to give him any kind of responsibility, he resigned himself to familiarizing himself with *Explorer II*. Additionally, no one seemed in any hurry to get him the promised documentation highlighting crucial details of the mission.

Jeff began to wonder if he, and perhaps even Riley, had been included on the mission as some sort of publicity stunt—good only for the cameras before being relegated to a vestigial existence on board, haunting the *real* crew like a pair of displaced ghosts. Yet there had been no whiff of press before takeoff; no attempt to garner sympathy from the public for the hundreds of millions in spending to send a few more humans into a deadly vacuum. Jeff thought the government would have wanted their people front and center, waving and smiling, putting a friendly face on the massive dent in the country's budget.

Noah Bell ran security for the first Titan mission with an iron fist, but even *he* knew when to let a little information slide to the evening news. Operating completely in the dark meant raising suspicion, and the people in charge of the second mission couldn't afford to be on the wrong side of public opinion—especially if they might have to ask for more money down the line.

He tapped a command into the console in front of him and got a flashing red screen for his effort. The computer wanted an access password. Jeff typed a half-dozen short insults and got plenty more red flashes.

"Out of the pilot seat, Dolan," said a deep voice behind him.

He turned in his chair. Commander Ward floated over the hatch, regarding Jeff with the same amount of warmth a shark has for its dinner.

"I think both consoles have the same controls," Jeff offered, gesturing to the open seat next to him.

"That's Brighton's," said Ward. His eyes widened. "Get out of my seat."

Jeff unlatched his harness and drifted away from the chair. Ward waited until he was several feet away before pulling himself down into it and strapping in. He glanced back to make sure Jeff wasn't looking over his shoulder, then tapped his password on the console screen.

"Is being a jerk a side effect of stasis?" Jeff asked casually.

Ward's hand froze over the console. He turned around slowly.

"Give me a reason to like you," he said.

"I can't think of any reason *not* to."

Ward's eyes narrowed. "Here's a few." He held up one hand and pinched the tip of each finger with the other as he rattled off his list. "Your knowledge of this craft is redundant. You take up valuable space, weight, and food. You will contribute nothing to the goal of this mission, and worst of all..."

He trailed off with his mouth open, then clamped it shut and spun back around to face the console, shaking his head.

"Worst of all, what?" Jeff asked, heat rising up his neck. "Come on, it was just getting good."

There was a noise from the hatch. Riley drifted into the command module. He turned sideways as he neared the ceiling and grabbed a handhold to steady himself.

"Worst of all," said Riley, "he thinks you're an abomination. That's the word you used to describe me, isn't it, Ward?"

"*Commander* Ward," he corrected, clenching his jaw.

"Yeah, sure," Riley scoffed. "Dolan, got a minute?"

Without waiting for a reply, he pushed off the ceiling and floated back through the open hatch in the floor.

Jeff patted the back of Ward's chair as he drifted down toward the hatch. "Nice chat, Commander."

He entered the passageway connecting the command and crew modules. Riley waited for him near the T-junction leading to the airlock, his arms crossed.

"You hit me with a wrench at this very spot on Explorer One," said Jeff, remembering the helix of blood droplets haloing his head when he awoke.

"You know what they're doing, right?" asked Riley, bulldozing past the reminder.

Jeff looked behind him. "Who?"

"Use your brain for a minute."

Jeff's eyebrows went up slowly.

"I mean think about why we're here," Riley continued. "Despite his attitude, Ward has a point. We're just taking up space that would be better filled by people who were trained specifically for this mission. They left two spots open for us."

"One of the astronauts failed their training," said Jeff. "That's why they asked me to come."

"Baloney. They fed me that same line."

"So why didn't they train us from the beginning?"

"That's what you need to think about," said Riley. "Out here, information equals trust. And we don't know anything. They're purposefully keeping us in the dark."

"You're saying they don't trust us."

He shrugged. "Would you, if you were in their position? We took an impossible shortcut back to Earth, and that raised more than a few red flags. I was dead, for God's sake, and you...well, I don't know *what* happened to you." He ran a hand over his short hair, then shook away a thought and said, "The point is that we're here for a reason, and they don't trust us enough to tell us what it is."

"Maybe we just haven't gotten to the reason yet."

Riley frowned. "What's that supposed to mean?"

"Okay, now *you* think about it. Everyone on the crew has a job. They know the ship like we knew Explorer One. But on the first mission, our knowledge stopped when we got to Titan. Why?"

"The torus," Riley whispered. His vision grew distant, then he blinked and swallowed hard.

"We're the only ones on this crew that have encountered what's out there," Jeff said, pointing toward the front of the ship and at Titan beyond.

"And what do they expect us to do if we meet another one?" asked Riley, his brow knit in confusion.

"I think that's obvious," Jeff said. "They expect us to go in first."

17

Kate sat on the narrow bench that lined the walls of the floating airlock cube. Embedded in the middle of each of the four walls was a circular metal plate. White LED lights shone down from the ceiling, exaggerating her movements in broad shadows on the floor.

John Harris huffed and puffed as he climbed the ladder up from the *Nautilus* and plopped down across from her, a big grin plastered to his face.

Tom came up last. He moved with spider-like grace, two of his limbs in motion at all times, one hand and foot rising simultaneously for the next ladder rung. He seemed to glide up the ladder and onto the bench instead of stomping with each step, the way Kate had done.

Under the bench, she opened a plastic storage locker and pulled out three pairs of flippers. Her feet slipped into them easily, and she turned a dial at each heel until they were comfortably tight.

After the others put theirs on, she gave Tom a thumbs-up. He flicked open the lid of a small panel in the wall behind him to reveal a series of three large buttons: yellow, red, and green. He depressed the yellow button with his gloved fist and the hatch at their feet swung shut.

"Here we go," said Kate.

Tom pushed the red button.

The white LED lights in the ceiling flicked to yellow. With a solenoid *clunk*, the four circular metal plates in the walls turned slowly, and seawater poured in through their edges. John lifted his flippers as the water covered the floor and rose quickly up to Kate's ankles.

"Won't the cube sink when this room fills up with water?" he asked, breathing quickly.

"The walls are filled with water. That's what's filling this room," said Kate. The water level rose up to her shins. "Equal square footage to match the room we're in. The cube swaps the environments."

John looked at her like she was speaking another language.

"The walls fill with air as this room fills with water," Tom explained. "When we get back from our dive, it swaps again. Air in here, water in the walls."

"I see," John said, sounding less than certain. The water climbed up over his belly. "Do I stand up, or...?"

"If you'd like," Kate replied. "Your pack will weigh you down unless you push off, if you want to relax a bit longer."

He stayed on the bench like the others. When the water level reached his neck, he instinctively lifted his chin. Kate could hear his rapid breathing over the helmet intercom.

Soon they were fully submerged. Steady streams of bubbles floated up from their packs to pool under the top hatch.

Tom pushed the green button and the hatch spun in place, then popped outward. The collected bubbles escaped in a rush, making the hundred-foot climb to the surface.

"Step on the bench and you should be able to reach the handhold near the hatch," said Kate.

She went up first to show John how it was done. As she emerged from the hatch into open water, she was once again struck by the endlessness of the ocean around her, and of her own insignificance within it.

Kate suspected it was similar to what Jeff felt during an EVA on *Explorer I*: a deadly void stretching out to infinity in all directions, ready to crush him after the tiniest of mistakes. Yet down here, at least, she was within swimming reach of the airlock cube if things went belly-up.

She kicked to the side to make room for John as he swam up out of the cube. Tom followed after, then closed the hatch behind him.

Kate kicked steadily away from the floating airlock, following the path of the torus from several meters above.

"Try your headlamp," she said. "The control is on your left wrist."

John held his wrist up to his face mask and fumbled at a small black rectangle embedded in the fabric. He continued to kick his fins but veered sideways, heading away from Tom and Kate. A bright light blinked on at the top of his helmet, shining down at the torus in a focused beam.

"Whoops," he said, looking back. He corrected his course and rejoined the others.

They moved slowly over the torus, the light from their headlamps shining down and disappearing into its black exterior.

"Tell me about your next steps," Harris prompted.

It took Kate a moment to realize he was slipping into business mode, and another to adjust herself accordingly. This was only John's third trip to the research station, and it had been a long time since she had to deal with a person who held her job in the palm of their financial hand.

"The facility is ninety percent complete," she said. "We have—"

"Why only ninety?" John interrupted.

"Well, for starters, we're still waiting on an order for a half-dozen dehumidifier systems for the lower levels. We needed to move most of the ones we already had to the equipment room so Tom didn't have to constantly wipe down the mainframe."

"Driest place in the station," said Tom.

"Is that order out of Shenzhen?" John asked.

"Glasgow."

He grunted. "That would be through Global UK's industrial division, then."

"That's right..."

"I play golf with the CEO. I'll give him a call on my flight home."

"That would be very much appreciated," said Kate, cautiously optimistic.

The air in the levels of the facility without dehumidifiers was thick as soup, and Tom had to isolate those electronics from the grid so the moisture wouldn't cause a short-circuit. It turned out to be a bigger problem than the designers anticipated.

"What else?" asked John. "You said there was no door on the torus. When will you make one?"

"Make one?" she repeated.

"To go inside. You're not planning to just crawl over the surface, are you?"

"It would certainly be enough to keep us busy for a long, long time," Kate said, choosing her words carefully. "But I have to admit, getting inside the torus is one of Noah's top priorities."

"Good. I'm in awe of this thing as much as anyone could be, but fascination won't stop the drain on my bank accounts. One patent leased to NASA and we could build ten more research facilities and stuff them with enough dehumidifiers to turn the insides into a desert."

Kate checked the digital readout on her wrist panel. "We need to head back," she said. "Think you got a good enough look?"

"Ms. Bishop," John said, "this has already been the experience of a lifetime. Lead the way, and I will gladly follow."

The torus stretched on into the murk ahead of them. The ring of lights curved into the distance, visible long after the torus was lost to the dark water.

Kate spun around and kicked in the direction of the floating airlock.

It was no surprise to her that John Harris was so eager to get into the torus. At least he stated his intentions as clearly as possible instead of going for subterfuge, which Kate had expected from the beginning. Too many of the elite moneylenders she'd dealt with operated under charitable auspices while angling for rapid private gain. Research cost money. Retaining a staff and maintaining a high-tech ocean facility cost money. John Harris conceded to be a realist, and he was up-front about the cash infusions needed to keep the operation going.

Still, Kate couldn't tell him everything.

Though she had been tempted to give John all the details, Noah had insisted that she leave out the most vital piece of information to date: that her team had already found a way inside the torus.

18

Jeff awoke to the sound of someone whooping for joy at the top of their lungs.

He sat up sharply and cracked his head on the underside of the upper bunk. Wincing and rubbing his forehead, he stepped barefoot onto the cold floor as Elizabeth dashed past him.

"We have contact!" she said. Then she stopped and hurried back to grab Jeff's shoulders. "*Contact!*" She looked down and added, "You might want to put on some pants."

Then she was gone, leaving Jeff to swim up out of his lingering drowsiness and into reality. He reached back into the bunk to grab his pants and bonked his sore head on the upper railing.

"Of course," he whispered hoarsely.

His swimming thoughts cleared as he climbed the ladder leading to the front section of the ship, and he began to realize the implications of what Elizabeth had said.

Contact.

Instead of excitement, fear chilled his belly. He suddenly felt monumentally unprepared for even a bystander's encounter with a torus. What if the commanders asked him to go outside the ship? What if they wanted him to go *inside* the torus again?

Jeff climbed the last few rungs quickly, transitioning into zero gravity as he entered the passageway. He got in line behind Riley, Elizabeth, and Chapman as they drifted up into the command module. Ward and Brighton occupied the two pilot seats, focused on their consoles while Chapman and Elizabeth talked over each other excitedly.

"Alright, alright," Brighton said, raising her voice. "How about some details, if that will lower the volume level a little bit? Scanners picked up an object in a prograde orbit around Titan. The fact that our systems can see it means it's not a torus."

"Unless it *wants* us to see it," said Riley.

Brighton hesitated a moment, then said, "That's a real possibility. Any other guesses?" No one spoke. "Dolan?" she asked. "You have some friends in the area, don't you?"

"It could be Deep Black," he admitted.

"Who's that?" Riley asked.

"A private aerospace company I worked with before this mission."

Ward chuffed. "He gave them technical information about Explorer One that allowed them to build a similar engine."

"They already had the engine," Jeff said. "I helped them make it better."

Brighton looked down at her console. "Here it comes now."

Silence filled the command module as everyone drifted forward, staring out at the hazy surface of Titan which nearly filled the window.

A ship appeared at the left edge of Titan. At that distance, it was no larger than a housefly, yet Jeff recognized the unconventional shape of the spacecraft.

"The Catalyst," he said.

"It looks a skinny black lampshade from one of those fancy home catalogs," said Elizabeth.

"Where's the rest of it?" Brighton asked.

"That's all of it," Jeff replied. "The engine is tucked into the flare of the bell. There's a centrifuge inside, too. It's lined with extra heat and radiation shielding."

Even from so far away, seeing the *Catalyst* in orbit around Titan filled Jeff with a sense of pride. One of the major engineering challenges had been fitting all the equipment inside the slender, bell-shaped housing. He and his team had managed to satisfy most of the design requirements, but two meters of engine-wash shield ended up poking out from the bottom of the bell so the lip wouldn't melt during major burns. There had also been no way to integrate communication equipment inside the shielded hull, so there were several small mounds rising from the smooth shell, some open at the front and some at the back. They looked like small, sculpted caves, and added an organic quality to the overall sterile design.

"How did they build it in space?" Riley asked. "Where's the command module?"

Jeff smiled, pleased to feel useful for the first time on the mission.

"It's sectional," he said. "The front sixth or so of the craft is the command module. It was designed to look like one solid hull after it mated with the rest. I believe they hired a science fiction writer and a concept car designer to draw up the proposal."

Brighton grunted. "Then Deep Black has more money than *we* do."

"The promotional media kit featuring that design landed them ten times the investment capital they were hunting for," Jeff added.

"Proving once again that image really is everything," said Chapman.

Brighton leaned forward and tapped a button on her console. "Let's see if they're listening." She adjusted her earpiece microphone and pushed the broadcast button on the screen. "Catalyst, this is Commander Carol Brighton on Explorer Two. Looks like you beat us to the punch."

There was a brief pause, then a crackling noise from a speaker in the ceiling.

"Sorry for not waiting, Commander. Didn't think you'd be here so soon. This is Commander Manuel Lopez."

"Nice to meet you," said Brighton.

"Hi, Manny," Jeff said loudly.

Ward turned and scowled at him.

"Is that…" said Manny. "Is that *you*, Jeffrey?"

"It's me."

Canned laughter burst through the speaker. "My God! How did you convince them to take you?"

"I didn't. I'm a stowaway."

More laughter.

"That's *enough*," Ward said. "Commander Lopez, this is Commander Ward. If it's alright with you, I'd like to initiate ship-to-ship safety protocols before we enter orbit."

Manny reigned in his laughter and sniffed. "*Government* protocols, you mean?"

"Yes."

"We don't have those, but okay. Whatever makes you feel better."

Jeff grinned.

Ward glanced at Brighton, suddenly uncertain. She suppressed a smile and nodded for him to proceed. Ward clenched his jaw in anger, seemingly aware he had been made the butt of some joke, and began tapping long strings of commands into his console.

"Anything unusual to report?" Brighton asked.

"Well," Manny replied thoughtfully, "there are aliens on Titan."

"Anything *else?*"

"We haven't made contact yet, if that's what you mean. Our sensors can't reach the surface, so we're waiting on word from home base before we progress."

Brighton leaned forward quickly and cut the outgoing signal, then turned to Jeff.

"What's their mission objective?" she asked.

"The founder is an idealist," Jeff answered. "As far as I could tell, their plans don't extend beyond a cross-species meet and greet. But I was kept in the dark about everything except the engine."

"They just came to say hello," Riley grumbled. "What a waste."

"Good thing there's plenty of room for everybody," said Brighton. She reactivated comms.

"We'll fall in with you shortly, Commander, if you don't mind."

"By all means. The more the merrier."

"Until then, if there's anything you need, don't hesitate to ask."

"Likewise," Manny said. "Catalyst, over and out."

The command module was quiet for a brief second, then everyone started talking at once.

Ward and Brighton spoke only to each other, focused and serious. The rest of them, including Jeff, let their enthusiasm and speculation fly. It all culminated in a grand scheme to jump out of the airlock in their spacesuits and board the *Catalyst* for a tour.

"Okay people," Brighton said, waving down the noise with her hands. "Everyone settle. We need to discuss our next steps."

"We'll enter orbit in ten hours," said Ward. "After we run systems diagnostics and verify that everything is in the green, Commander Brighton and I will go EVA to prep the payload. Riley and Dolan, you're coming with us."

Jeff said, "I'm sorry?"

"*What* payload?" asked Riley at the same time.

Will Chapman grinned. "You wanted something to do, didn't you? I'd call this something."

"Don't look a gift horse in the mouth, Dolan," said Brighton. "You and Riley have logged more EVA time than the rest of us combined. We'd be foolish not to make good use of you."

"You want to keep an eye on us, you mean," Riley said. "Worried we'll steal your ship while you're tooling around out there."

She turned to look at him directly. "Yes, Riley," she said, her voice dripping with sarcasm. "*That's* the reason."

His face reddened. Jeff tried and failed to suppress a smile.

"Enough with the conspiracy crap," Brighton continued. "Do you want to go outside or not?"

Riley gritted his teeth, then he muttered, "Fine."

Brighton looked at Jeff. He stared out at the tiny silhouette of the *Catalyst* as it traversed the broad surface of Titan.

"Clock's ticking, Dolan," Ward barked.

Jeff peeled his eyes away from the window. "Okay, I'll go."

"Good," said Brighton. "You and Riley can relax until then. The rest of you...we have work to do."

19

Kate waved her wrist over a dull black tile and the door to the operations room whisked to the side. It was a vast improvement over the door with no handle she had walked through on her first visit to the research facility.

She paused just inside the room, feeling the rush of air as the door closed at her heels.

Noah stood hunched over one of the workstations, conversing intensely with Tom, who made exaggerated hand gestures to emphasize a point he was trying to drive home.

The only other person in the room was Dominic Wright, the theoretical physicist. He sat with his eyes closed behind thin-framed glasses, massaging his temples, bent low over a dimly lit workstation. Scattered notes blanketed his work area. He tugged on his bushy black beard and pounded his beefy fist on the table, then muttered to himself and scribbled a note on a crumpled piece of paper. Noah and Tom paid him no mind.

The three screens at the front of the room showed the same panoramic view of the large torus Kate had come to take for granted over the last six months. She glanced at it briefly as she walked to Dominic's workstation, noting that the sun must be shining because of the increased visibility.

She had looked at herself in the mirror that morning: five shades of pale. Lack of sunlight was an undesirable side effect she hadn't considered when signing up to work in an underwater lab.

"Crack that code yet, comrade?" she asked as she slapped Dominic on the back.

He didn't flinch, he just continued muttering and scribbling notes. After a long moment, he slowly pulled off his glasses and rubbed his eyes, sighing heavily.

"There is no code," he said. "I'm entirely convinced they etched a recipe for Earthling casserole on the outside of their torus."

"Oh, it's not that bad."

Dominic put his glasses back on and looked at her with bloodshot eyes. "It is. It really, really is."

"Tell me."

"Well," he said, leaning over his unstitched quilt of notes. He plucked one from the desk and held it up for her to see. "This chunk of grooves looks like a number string. One vertical line repeats itself in sequence from left to right, but with an extra dash next to it each time."

"Almost like it's counting up," said Kate, intrigued.

"Exactly. Only when you get to the next section of the exterior..." He paused as he hunted for another scrap. "Ah, here it is. The next section changes completely. Instead of vertical and horizontal lines, you get circles and grooves with no outline, like someone attacked the torus with a spoon."

Kate looked over the patchwork of notes.

"Does your gut still tell you it isn't decorative?" she asked.

Dominic sighed. "Yes. Stupid gut. Speaking of which...any of that lasagna left in the galley?"

"Blech," Kate said, making a face. "That stuff never cooks right down here."

He shrugged and slapped his prodigious stomach. "Guy's gotta eat. Might as well do it now." He waved a tired hand over his notes. "Lord knows this stuff isn't going anywhere."

Kate sat on the corner of his desk, arms crossed, looking over the scraps of paper.

"Any progress?" Noah asked from behind her.

"Not according to Dominic," she replied. "But he's accumulating more pieces of paper every day."

Noah smiled. "That's something, at least." He coughed into his hand and swallowed hard.

Kate thought he looked as tired as she felt. The shortage of dehumidifiers had forced all of the crew bunks to be moved out of their private rooms and to the back of the galley, and Dominic snored like a hibernating grizzly bear. Even if he didn't, the simple fact was that Kate went to bed too late and got up much too early. With only four people working at the station, her list of responsibilities grew daily.

"Do I have to mention the assistant you promised me?" she asked.

"You don't *have* to," said Noah. "But since you did...it's going to be a little while yet, Kate."

"Don't tell me it's a money issue. I know Harris isn't the only golden goose on the farm."

"It's not money. It's security. There's a...a situation developing with parties outside my control, and I need to see how it plays out."

Kate studied his face intently, but couldn't decipher the reason for his reticence. His expert-level poker face infuriated her to no end when she wanted information and he slipped back into the role of aloof (former) billionaire.

"Fine," she said with a sigh, letting it go along with the fantasy of getting more than five hours of sleep a night.

"How's our boy doing, anyway?" asked Noah.

Our boy was his slang for John Harris, the most beneficent of his idealistic investors. For as much as Noah seemed to appreciate the steady flow of cash, he left most of the interactions with John to Kate. When she pressed him about his reasons, Noah simply said that John liked her better. Then he would often add, "Heck, *I* like you better."

"He says he can get us more dehumidifiers," Kate replied.

Noah rapped his knuckles on Dominic's workstation thoughtfully.

"I'd like to take the little sub out for another run," he said.

Kate glanced at the viewscreens. The large torus was still out there, taunting them with its inactivity. The remote sub, *Pequod,* had gone out twice in the three months since it arrived in a large shipping container from Singapore. Both glitchy excursions had lasted less than ten minutes, which was barely enough for the torus to show up on the sub's camera. The rest of the time, the *Pequod* had been suspended from a crane arm in drydock because of an issue with its navigation computer.

"Tom, how's our Little Engine That Could?" she asked.

"He's doing just fine," Tom replied from his workstation. He leaned back in his chair and stretched his arms over his head. "The last few tests have all been in the green."

"It has a solid comm link with the station?"

He crossed two fingers and held them up. "Like *this.*"

"Guidance computer in constant contact with our GPS beacon?"

He uncrossed his fingers but kept them close together. "Like this?"

Kate sighed and looked at Noah. "It's your show," she said.

A slow smile spread across his face. "Let's go take a look inside."

20

Jeff floated in the spherical airlock of *Explorer II*, his rapid breath blooming and fading on the inside of his face shield.

Riley was next to him, frowning as he fiddled with the control pad on his left wrist. Commander Brighton checked and re-checked the joint seals on her spacesuit, while Commander Ward busied himself by grinding his teeth and staring coldly at Jeff.

"Interface is different," Riley mumbled, tapping on his wristpad. His voice came through hollow in Jeff's helmet. "Where'd you geniuses hide the comm layout?"

"Hold down the first and third buttons," Brighton answered.

"Ah," Riley said. "No offense, but that's beyond stupid. We should switch it back to the old way."

"You had to push a button twice," said Jeff, "then push another one. How is this worse?"

Riley held up his middle digit in Jeff's direction. "What if there's an accident and you only have one finger left?"

"*Both* of you are going to have an accident if you don't shut up," said Brighton. "I already regret letting you tag along."

The light in the ceiling blinked out and a bright yellow caution lamp flicked on, spinning slowly as it flashed. Jeff and the others watched silently, almost reverently, at the airlock doors as they slowly parted, revealing the blackness of space.

"This is stirring up some very uncomfortable memories for me," Riley murmured.

"It won't be like the last time," Jeff said. "We're all sticking together."

Riley strained to look at him sideways as they floated in the airlock. Jeff was surprised to see sweat beading on his forehead.

"Nice and easy," said Brighton. "Here we go."

She thumbed a small joystick positioned beneath her glove and a thin stream of nitrogen spurted from her pack. Ward followed her, jaw clenched as he focused on his controls.

"Age before beauty," said Jeff, gesturing at the void beyond the airlock.

Riley grunted and shook his head, then coasted outside. Jeff lingered behind, remembering the moment when he first left the relative safety of *Explorer I*. Passing beyond the airlock door of that vessel and into space had made his stomach sink into his bowels. He felt as if he should fall like a stone, but instead he hung there, suspended in the black.

This time there were fewer butterflies in his stomach. As he passed the airlock door and space opened up all around, hesitance turned to excitement and he couldn't help but let out a rollercoaster whoop.

"Control yourself," Ward scolded.

"I didn't think I'd ever get to do that again," Jeff said, smiling.

"You almost gave me a heart attack," said Riley. "Could you please just process your feelings internally, like a normal man?"

Jeff grinned. "Okay, switching over to 'brooding silently' mode."

"For the record, I didn't mind," Brighton offered. "It's too quiet out here anyway."

They moved in a line, the four of them in their bright orange Constellation suits, drifting steadily aft, keeping the hull on their left. Jeff stared at the distant stars: brilliant pinpoints of light, more than he could count in his lifetime.

"That's one of the questions they asked us before the first mission," he recalled. "How well we could handle prolonged silence."

"Not very well, apparently," said Ward.

"I never got your first name, Commander." Jeff waited a few moments, then added, "Hard to get to know someone if you don't know their first name."

"You don't need to know my first name, Dolan. It's not vital mission information."

"Nothing I know about this mission is vital anyway," Jeff replied, "so what's the harm?"

"He's going to hate me for this," Brighton cut in.

"Don't you say it," said Ward.

She ignored him. "It's Clancy."

"*Clancy*?" Jeff repeated. Riley's tin laughter filled his helmet.

Ward sighed, defeated. "My mother named me after one of her favorite authors. Now we're going to drop the subject. You two can call me Commander, or nothing at all. You got that?"

"Sir-yes-sir," Riley said, still chuckling.

"Did everyone forget Riley's first name is Tag?" said Ward.

"Hey, your mom was a reader, mine was a hippie. Lord knows why she picked that name, but I made peace with it long ago."

"Alright everyone," Brighton said. "Time to focus."

Explorer II bulged about a third of the way from the nose, like a snake that swallowed a tin can. Inside was the centrifuge. Jeff and the others followed the tail end of the bulge as it shrank until the hull smoothed out again, bringing them to the hatch of the cargo hold.

"This door is a whole lot bigger than Explorer One's," Jeff said. "Almost twice as long. That would mean..." He trailed off as he looked at the elongated hatch stretching toward the back of the ship.

"The ship's longer, too," said Brighton. "Good eyes, Jeffrey." She gestured at him and Riley. "You two hang back while we open her up." She methodically punched a series of commands into her wristpad. "Ward, you're up."

He nodded and began typing commands into his own pad.

"You need two people to open the hold?" Riley asked.

"On this ship, yes," Brighton answered.

With a tiny burst of nitrogen from his pack, Riley turned to face Jeff, giving him a skeptical, *I-told-you-something-was-fishy* look.

"Open sesame," Ward said as he tapped his wristpad a final time.

Two discs the size of dinner plates set into the hull spun in unison, and a long crack appeared down the length of the hatch. It opened slowly, its four panels hinging outward like the petals of a giant metal flower.

"Okay, so that's a little impressive," Riley admitted.

"Wait till you see what's inside," said Brighton. "Go ahead and take a look."

She and Ward waited while Jeff and Riley drifted past one of the hinged panels and over the open hatch.

Jeff blinked at what lay within, his mind not fully accepting the input.

On the first mission, the cargo hold had been filled with materials to construct a small research station in orbit around Titan, as well as the necessary crew provisions. In the extended hold of *Explorer II*, the only evidence of food and supplies for the crew was a large black crate secured to one end of the cylindrical hold.

The rest of the capacious interior held a flat, snub-nosed craft with a cluster of three bell-shaped engines on the back, two stunted wings with upward-angled tips, and dual dorsal fins that ran the length of the vessel starting just behind the cockpit window.

"That's a..." said Jeff. "It's a..."

"Yeah," Brighton said. "It's a lander."

"But where's the payload?" Riley growled. "Where's the scientific equipment, and the rest of it?"

"This *is* the payload," said Ward. "This is why we're here."

Jeff found himself nodding without knowing why. "So you're, you know, you're..."

"That's correct," said Brighton. "We're taking the lander down to the surface. Beats falling, right?"

21

The drydock room was empty when Kate arrived. A soft, blue-green light glowed from the moon pool. The ripples projected dancing snakes onto the ceiling, and Kate was reminded of one of her many visits to the Monterey Bay Aquarium as a child.

She stood there in the dark, alone, mesmerized by the dancing water, until someone flicked on the lights and made her jump.

"You got here fast," Tom said as he strolled in.

He went immediately to the *Pequod* and began checking the battery levels. The sub dangled from the crane arm secured to the floor near the moon pool.

"Do you think the sub will make it to the torus?" Kate asked.

Tom shrugged nonchalantly as he unplugged a thick cable from the underside of the sub. "No reason it shouldn't. I'm a hundred-percent positive I zapped all the bugs from the system."

"That's what you said last time."

"Yeah, but this time I mean it."

On the other side of the moon pool from the *Pequod,* the passenger sub *Nautilus* sat dark and silent. The spherical front window of the larger sub reflected the drydock room in a bulging fish-eye view, making Kate's head seem absurdly large when she leaned in close.

"I'm worried about losing the signal if the Pequod goes inside the torus," she said.

"*When* he goes in, you mean," Tom corrected, smiling. "And don't be worried. I programmed an emergency evacuation protocol. If we lose contact, he'll retrace his steps automatically until we reconnect. So, even if he's deep inside, he'll know how to get back to open water."

Kate stepped aside as Tom pushed the crane arm, swinging the *Pequod* out over the moon pool. It was a miniaturized version of the bigger sub. The one major difference was that instead of a cockpit with three passenger seats, its interior was dedicated to additional pressure matrices and a telescopic high-definition camera. It could dive much deeper than its larger sibling and send back recognizable photographs taken in darker environments.

Tom cranked a handle on the side of the crane arm which lowered the *Pequod* steadily into the moon pool. When it was halfway submerged, he engaged the locking mechanism on the wench.

"One last systems check and this little champ is good to go," he said. Then he looked at her directly. "You know, Kate, you didn't have to come down here to supervise me. I know my way around the equipment by now."

"I know you do, Tom. It's not that. It's...I don't know what it is. This room is different from the rest of the station. I think I like it down here." She nodded, realizing that's exactly how she felt. "It's quiet."

He chuckled. "Then you must love to dive. Noah says it's the closest we can get to being in space without leaving the atmosphere."

"I didn't expect to like it at all," she admitted. "When Noah said we all had to get our diving certificates, I thought I'd have to quit. I was petrified."

"And now?"

"And now...I love it. I think he's right, about feeling like you're in space." She stared at the *Pequod* a moment longer, lost in some deeper thought. Then she said, "See you up there in a few?"

"Yup, right after splash-down."

Kate's mood slowly shifted toward optimism as she rode the elevator up to the operations level. The *Pequod* would finally make it to the torus and would reveal the technological wonders of an alien civilization. And then...and then she had no idea what would follow.

The door to the operations room whisked open, and her good mood wilted like a flower hit by a flamethrower. Noah was already inside, and he wasn't alone.

Lola Desmond stood beside him, her thin arms crossed casually over her silky blouse, while he spoke animatedly about the imminent excursion.

Kate guessed Lola was somewhere between sixty and sixty-five years old, judging by her silver hair and the dignified face-wrinkles she proudly ignored with her makeup brush. She dressed and carried herself like a much younger woman, and she did it successfully, which did nothing to endear her to most other women she encountered.

Lola was only half-listening to Noah, though she faked it well: a smile halfway to full, a slight nod every once in a while. What gave her away was her raised nose, perpetually stuck up in the air whenever she had to deal with other humans. Her silver hair was pulled back in a bun so tight Kate was sure her face would split down the middle.

And those *heels.*

You can hear her coming down the hall from the other side of the research station, thought Kate. *Who wears high heels in this kind of environment? She must have twenty pairs of them, each one louder than the next—*

"Ah, there she is," said Noah, breaking her reverie.

"Tom will be up in a minute," Kate said as she walked over to him. "He swears his little toy can go the distance."

Lola's smile was made of ice. "That's what he said the *last* time."

Kate looked at her sternly. "This time he means it."

"Mmmm," said Lola, amused.

"What is it you're doing here again?" Kate asked with mock innocence.

Noah coughed into his hand, drawing their attention before Lola could answer.

"As I've said before, Ms. Desmond is my personal financial advisor." He flashed a placating smile. "Let's just focus on the field trip, shall we?"

The left viewscreen switched over to the drydock feed just as the *Pequod* detached from the crane arm and sank into the moon pool. The other two screens showed the torus. Tom gave the camera a thumbs-up and left the room. A few seconds later, all three screens switched to the sub's point-of-view as it self-stabilized in the water.

Kate tapped a command into a workstation console. Small lines of numbers and text scrolled up the left side of the middle screen, like the output of a computer booting up. The scrolling text disappeared and was replaced with a box that displayed critical information such as a proximity monitor and remaining battery percentage. The proximity sensor readout was bright yellow, which meant the sub was within two meters of another object—in this case, the walls of the moon pool.

Tom entered the operations room and sat at a workstation. He surreptitiously rolled his eyes at Kate when he finally noticed Lola. Kate shrugged as if to ask the hypothetical, *What can we do?*

Noah wanted Lola in the facility for whatever reason, and Kate had to deal with it as best she could.

Tom put on his earpiece microphone and logged in to the command interface for the sub.

"Pequod systems are in the green," he said.

"Take her out," said Noah.

"*Him*," Tom mumbled. "It's a *him*."

He pushed a button on his console and the *Pequod* descended. The sub seemed to fall out of the bottom of the research facility and into open water as it left the tunnel. The walls of the facility curved up and away until the screens showed only a solid field of dark blue.

"Here goes nothing," said Tom.

He pushed a small control stick with his thumb, and the *Pequod* accelerated toward the torus.

22

Jeff unzipped the top of his white jumper and sat on his bunk, rubbing his eyes tiredly. He let out a groan as he lay down. Elsewhere on the ship, the others were preparing for the trip to the surface.

"I imagine it's quite a shock." He opened his eyes. Elizabeth stood over him, smiling sympathetically. "I told them it was a bad idea," she said as she sat next to him on the bunk. "They said there was no point in coming back to Titan unless we went down to the surface."

"Is it even possible?" Jeff asked.

"*You* did it."

He grunted. "I fell. And I...well, I didn't exactly have a graceful landing."

"All of us signed on knowing the risks."

"I didn't."

She hesitated. "You're not going down."

He sat up slowly, swinging his legs over the edge of the bunk until his bare feet touched the cold floor.

"But Riley is?" he said at last.

She nodded.

"I guess that makes sense," Jeff continued. "Otherwise it would be all their eggs in one basket. Who else is staying?"

"Me…and Ward."

Jeff grimaced.

"Don't worry."

"It's not me I'm worried about. What if a torus shows up? That would be a pretty quick end to this expedition."

"We just have to hope it's not interested in us."

"Hope," Jeff repeated.

"That's right. You have some, don't you?"

He sighed. "Working on it."

"Good." She stood up and patted his back, then walked away.

Jeff forced himself up and went off in search of Riley. He found him in the lab section of the centrifuge, standing in front of a rack-mounted EKG machine. Two wires ran from the machine to suction cups on his temples. He stared intently at the readout of spiky lines on the monitor. When he heard Jeff's footsteps, he quickly yanked off the suction cups and switched off the machine.

For a moment he looked like he was about to yell at Jeff for interrupting him. The moment passed, and he sighed.

"Yes, Dolan. I have one in my head, too."

"Do you know what it is?"

"Been trying to figure that out. The eggheads back home could only guess. Worthless bunch of..." He clenched his fist and trailed off. "What if it's a bomb? What if we're just walking around one day and BOOM!"

"Well," Jeff said thoughtfully. "At least it'll be quick."

"That's a real comfort," said Riley, rubbing his neck.

"Maybe you'll find out on Titan."

Riley looked at him. "I'm sorry you're not going."

"You can tell me all about it when you get back."

He grunted. "Right. Listen, Dolan. I was thinking. If one of those...things...shows up, you and I are probably the only ones that can get between it and the rest of the crew."

"What do you mean by 'get between'?"

"I mean we're alive for a reason. If it looks like a torus will attack the ship, you and I need to be ready to...to...you know...jump out in front."

Jeff burst out laughing. "You're not serious," he said.

Riley looked at him without a hint of amusement.

"You *are* serious! Why would you do that? Ward's been a pain this whole mission. He's like you used to be, but worse."

"He's not the only member of the crew. Like I said, we're here for a reason. I think we might be a link between humanity and...and whatever *they* are."

"You think they won't hurt us?"

"They can't hurt me more than they already did," said Riley. "I think we could delay a torus long enough for the crew to have a chance, if it came down to that."

"That's a pretty grim thought."

"It's the only kind I have these days." He grabbed Jeff's elbow and pulled him closer. "Promise me, Dolan. Say you'll do it."

Jeff was surprised at the earnestness in his eyes. "I promise."

Riley seemed enormously relieved. "Good," he said, nodding. "Good." He clapped his hands together. "Now if you'll excuse me, I have to fly down to a horrifyingly dangerous ice moon for no reason other than to tempt fate on the off-chance I can shake hands with murderous aliens, all while praying those eggheads on Earth designed a lander capable of returning to orbit."

"So, just another day," Jeff said.

"Just another day. Take care of yourself, Dolan."

Jeff looked at the blank EKG display and tried not to think about the little sphere tucked neatly into his brain.

Ward's tinny voice spoke from a nearby embedded wall speaker. "Commander Brighton, please report to engineering."

Hearing him gave Jeff an idea. He passed Brighton on her way aft as he walked toward the front of the ship. He saluted and she rolled her eyes, but not without a trace amount of good humor.

As he suspected, the command module was empty. Jeff drifted to Ward's seat and pulled himself into it. He buckled in and looked out through the narrow window. Titan lay to starboard, only a sliver of it visible at the very edge of the window. A small gleam in the distance caught Jeff's eye—the sun's old light reflecting off the *Catalyst*'s hull. He cycled through menus on the unlocked control screen in front of him until he found the button layout he was looking for, then he activated ship-to-ship comms.

"Explorer to Catalyst, come in," he said. After a moment, he added, "Manny, are you there?"

A burst of static on the line, then: "Jeffrey?"

"It's me. Is this a private channel?"

There was a pause, then a click. "It is now. What's up?"

"I never gave much thought to it at the time, but I finally figured out the reason for the oversized cargo hold on your ship."

Commander Manuel Lopez was silent for a long moment. "And?"

"And it contains a lander, just like the one on this ship."

"Not *just* like it. Ours is prettier."

"Manny...it's not safe."

"But of course not, my friend! If it was safe, there would be a hundred other ships already here, ready to go down. Instead, there are two. We are the pioneers, Jeffrey."

"When are you launching?" Jeff asked.

"When are *you* launching?"

"As far as I can tell...within the hour."

"Ah, how unfortunate for your team. I am going to the lander as soon as this conversation is over. I will try to save some discoveries for you, yes?"

"I'm not going down, Manny."

"They are keeping you on the ship? They would not be here without your help!"

"I thought the same thing when your boss fired me."

Manny *tsk*ed. "Alas, that is true. I am sorry, Jeffrey. Sorry you came all this way to be stuck up here."

"Can you do me a favor?"

"Anything that is possible."

"Stay close to my team if you can. I don't know exactly where they're landing in the Adiri region, but it won't be too far from the construction site I saw on my last trip."

"If they don't interfere with my team, they are more than welcome to tag along."

"Could you just...would you please make that offer when they arrive?"

"Of course, Jeffrey. You have my word."

"Be safe, Manny."

"Always."

The line went silent.

Jeff unclipped his belt and drifted toward the window. Titan filled his vision, blocking out the void beyond. Nothing marred the hazy surface of that pale orange atmosphere. It was still and silent... indifferent to their presence. Yet the stillness beckoned. Jeff longed to part the orange haze and reveal what was happening down on the surface. He wanted clarity, and so far he'd only been offered more questions.

Brighton's voice came over the ship's intercom. "Flight team, report to the airlock. EVA in five."

Jeff pushed himself away from the window and went to help the team prep for their departure.

23

"Passing the halfway point now," said Tom.

Kate sat next to him at the workstation, eyes glued to the viewscreens at the front of the room. Dominic sat at his own station, completely devoted to whatever he was scribbling.

While the sub made its way to the torus, Noah entertained Lola with stories about previous companies he'd started and failed to get off the ground.

Of all the so-called outsiders Noah brought to the station, she alone would stay a few days at a time. Her extended visits ran counter to his mandate that no one who wasn't directly involved with the project remain there overnight.

There was also the separate, nagging question of why Lola had been told there was a way inside the torus, and why John Harris—their prime investor—was being kept in the dark.

"*Et voilà!*" Noah said, spreading his hands wide as the torus appeared on the viewscreen. "No surface scans this time, Tom. Head straight for the opening."

"You got it, boss."

With a twist of the control stick, the *Pequod* veered left, heading for one side of the torus ring instead of its center.

Kate glanced at the sub's information panel on the viewscreen. Battery levels wavered at just over ninety percent. They dropped steadily instead of brick-like, as they had during the last two error-filled outings.

Tom positioned the *Pequod* a few meters above the torus. The artifact stretched into the distance like a black highway.

"You expect to get inside that thing?" asked Lola.

Noah smiled, refusing to reveal the details of his secret. Lola turned to him, impatient, and he motioned toward the screen.

"There's your answer," he said.

Farther ahead, a new shape faded into view as the sub continued on: a torus much smaller than the nearby horizontal giant. It floated vertically, motionless in the water, aligned with the larger torus like a ring that was too big for a finger—except where the little torus met the bigger one, the larger one simply ceased to exist.

"Did part of it break off?" asked Lola.

"It's only seventy-five percent complete," Noah answered. "Both open ends of the large torus are perfectly flat edges, like cross-sections, as if sliced off by a single, clean stroke."

Lola took a step closer to the screens as the sub drew closer to the small torus.

"What happened?"

Kate looked at Noah, and he nodded.

"We believe the smaller one was in the process of constructing the larger one," she said. "On Titan, these objects were observed with a black membrane that filled the middle of their hoops. You can see that it's missing from both of these. Alien structures emerged from this membrane as if being forged on demand, then embedded themselves into the ice."

After a moment to let that sink in, she added, "There's no way to know why this one stopped."

"But none of the ones Jeff saw on Titan were building another torus," said Noah. He gave Tom's shoulder a squeeze. "Show us the opening."

Tom obliged, piloting the sub past the vertical torus, then swinging it around in a wide arc to face the way it had come. The smaller torus encircled the larger one with a small gap between them, reminding Kate of a two-dimensional view of Saturn's rings around the gas giant.

The open side of the large torus was a perfect cross-section, as Noah mentioned. Details were hazy at that distance, but she could discern several circular layers within the outer shell, like the rings of a great tree. The center was murky—a wide, unwelcoming black hole.

"And you're going to send that little submarine inside?" asked Lola.

Noah rubbed his hands together. "You bet we are. Tom?"

Tom worked the controls, and the *Pequod* sped toward the opening. He throttled back at the threshold, and the sub drifted slowly inside, swallowed instantly by darkness. Tom tapped his console and the viewscreens flashed white, then gradually adjusted as the camera compensated for the sub's bright halogen lamps.

The gritty image showed a flat floor extending away into the black. The walls curved up to form a wide, low arch. They came together directly overhead, meeting at a segmented, spine-like tube that paralleled the floor as far as the sub's cameras could see.

"Are we recording?" asked Noah.

Tom nodded. "Gettin' it all in high-def. Might lose some quality deeper in, though."

"Something tells me that won't be the case," muttered Noah.

The halogen lamps created a ring of light on the walls and floor as the *Pequod* progressed farther into the torus. The video feed rippled wherever the light hit a solid surface, like rainfall on a still pond.

Kate squinted and leaned forward, trying to make sense of the image.

"I think the walls are translucent," she said.

The sub's lamps swept over a wall, and light glimmered off a barely-visible patch of dark water.

When the lamps moved away, the wall seemed to solidify in their wake.

"Cut to the wide view," said Noah.

Kate switched to one of the external camera feeds on the truss of lights encircling the large torus.

"I'll be dipped," Tom said. "Would you look at that?"

The halogen lamps on the *Pequod* were visible through the walls of the torus. They could see exactly where it was inside the curving black tube, moving slowly and steadily along. Wherever light hit the interior wall, a shimmering patch of translucence bloomed on the outer hull, partially revealing the dim outline of the sub.

Lola whistled in appreciation. "Now *that* is something."

"Talk about a super-material," said Dominic. "I can't wait to check that out up close."

"You can go as soon as the sub comes back," Noah said.

"Movement sensors are twitching," said Tom.

Kate switched back to the sub's video feed. In the darkness beyond the light's reach, a wall of what looked like silver coins flashed and then disappeared.

"What *is* that?" she asked.

A school of small fish burst from the darkness and swam past the *Pequod*. The sub's microphone array transmitted a flurry of gurgling and thumps as the fish brushed against its hull.

Tom nudged the sub forward again.

Noah frowned. "We're a little far from shore for bait fish."

"Could be like an artificial reef to them," Tom offered.

"Or they were drawn to it by something else," Noah said. "They sure were in a hurry to get out."

"I think I see why," said Kate, pointing at the screen.

Deeper in the tunnel, at the edge of light cast from the *Pequod*, the tunnel glowed.

Kate leaned toward the screen as the light intensified.

"I think there's something on the ceiling," she said, pointing up at the screen, "back a little ways, near the—"

There was a burst of light and the screen crackled with static. Tom eased off the accelerator and the remote sub floated in the center of the passage.

The light began to pulse.

"Reverse slowly," Kate said. "Get back to open water."

"It's just getting good!" said Lola.

Tom engaged the sub's reverse thrusters and eased it away from the pulsing light.

A dark blur shot out of the light, passing the sub and leaving a streak of silvery bubbles in its wake.

"Whoa!" Tom shouted as the image tumbled sideways.

The sub hit the interior torus wall with a clang. A steady stream of bubbles leaked into view from the bottom of the screen.

"Anyone get a look at it?" asked Noah.

"Turn the sub around," Kate said.

Tom fiddled with the controls. The sub jerked left, then right, then shuddered as it swung around to face the other way.

"Servos are damaged," he said, shaking his head, "along with who-knows what else. Need to bring him back for repairs."

"It's coming back!" Lola shouted, pointing at the screen.

The dark object appeared at the very edge of the sub's visual range, approaching quickly.

"Move it, Tom!" Kate said.

He jammed the control stick and the *Pequod* sped forward. More bubbles streamed up past the camera from some broken part of the sub.

"It's gonna hit," he said.

The dark blur was in the distance, and then it was *there*, filling the screen. There was a rush and gurgle of water and the screen went black.

"Can you get the image back?" Kate asked.

Tom worked quickly, his hands flying over his control station. "No incoming signals of any kind. Not even a ping-back."

"What does that mean?" asked Lola.

Kate slowly sat down. "It means we lost our sub," she said.

"Not only that," Noah added. "It means there's something inside the torus."

24

Jeff sat behind Ward in the command module, watching him work. Elizabeth had excused herself to go about her daily maintenance duties, leaving Jeff alone with a man who seemed perfectly content to ignore him. The silence suited Jeff just fine for the moment. He was finding it more than a little difficult not to brood over the fact that he had been left behind.

As Ward navigated a plethora of menu screens on his console, Jeff watched the camera feed streaming from inside the lander. The angle was fixed on the cockpit interior. Commander Brighton, wearing her spacesuit, sat in the pilot seat, carefully tapping commands into her console with gloved fingers as she went over her pre-flight checklist. Three more seats had been crammed into the rear of the cockpit, two of which were occupied by Will Chapman and Riley.

Riley twisted in his seat, trying to get comfortable within his bulky suit, and asked, "How long is this going to take?"

Brighton didn't turn around as she said, "As long as it takes."

Riley then turned to look at Chapman. "I'm surprised you didn't stay on the ship."

"As if I had a choice," Will said, more to himself than anyone else.

In the command module, Jeff cleared his throat. "There are two civilians and a pilot in the lander," he pointed out.

"So?" Ward barked.

"This is a scientific mission, and you're not sending any scientists down to the surface."

Ward chuckled and shook his head. "Think you know it all, do you?"

"What am I missing?"

Ward muted the comm channel and pointed at Commander Brighton on the camera feed. "That woman got a degree in molecular biology, then went *back* to get a degree in evolutionary biology, *then* decided she wanted to be a pilot. She's smarter than the rest of us combined."

Jeff nodded. "In other words, you have the science part covered. I stand corrected."

Ward abruptly spun his chair around to face Jeff.

"Speaking of your lack of knowledge," he said, "we sent two probes toward the surface when we first arrived in orbit."

"Okay…" Jeff replied with hesitation.

"They fizzled out before landing. At my insistence, you and Riley were the only members of the crew who weren't given this information." He paused meaningfully. "In your report of the first mission, you mentioned large objects in the clouds. You said they looked like tumbling skyscrapers."

Jeff remembered them vividly. When he had emerged from the lower reaches of Titan's hazy orange atmosphere, he had seen hints of the massive structures hiding in the mist. They moved with no apparent friction, stopping instantly and reversing spin, as if there was no mass to them at all.

"Yes, that's right," said Jeff.

"Did you ever see any offensive apparatus on them?" Ward asked. "Something that could attack one of the probes?"

"I never really saw them in their entirety. I mostly saw corners and edges, but every surface I caught a glimpse of was completely smooth."

Ward nodded to himself and looked away.

"They're still going down?" Jeff asked, nodding toward the camera feed from the lander. "Even though you lost contact with the probes? How do you know the lander won't be any different?"

"The probes didn't have extra shielding," said Ward as he swiveled his chair around to face his console, "or a human pilot. So yeah, they're still going down. That's the job." He frowned at his console. "Sensors are getting fuzzier by the minute."

"Some kind of interference?"

"Can't tell."

Jeff watched him work for a moment longer, then said, "Did you want to go down to the surface instead of Brighton?"

Ward hesitated, and Jeff didn't think he was going to answer. Then he said, "I don't think any of us should be here in the first place."

"But that's the job," Jeff quoted.

Ward nodded. He reactivated the comm link with the lander, but its occupants were silent.

A green, rectangular button pulsed to life on Ward's console screen and he quickly tapped it. An unfamiliar voice spoke through the command module speakers.

"Explorer, this is the Catalyst. Anyone still on board?"

"This is Explorer," Ward replied. "Who am I talking to?"

"Ah, you must be Commander Ward. I'm Dex Hollander, engineer over here on the Catalyst. Nice to make your acquaintance." After a moment of silence when Ward didn't reply, Hollander continued. "Had ourselves a bit of a launch delay, but now we're back on track. My commander asked me to check in with you to keep a line of communication open. He wanted me to say he'll be landing just north of Lake Dolan at Adiri."

"Lake Dolan?" Jeff asked.

Ward muted the feed by holding down the green button. "Don't let it go to your head. When you're the only one who's been to a place, you tend to get something named after you. Nothing else required."

He took his finger off the mute button. "We'll be in the same neighborhood, Catalyst. Tell your commander that if they hit a snag down there, my people would be happy to help."

"Likewise," said Hollander. "Over and out."

The channel went silent.

"Private company monkeys," said Ward, shaking his head. "Who knows what they're up to down there?"

"You think they might interfere with the mission?"

"It's just an extra variable we don't need. The colonel tried to nix their launch but couldn't justify the authorization in time. Congress passed a whole slew of new laws regarding planet exploration after the first Titan mission, but the ones that allow private space companies to operate without oversight in situations like this are still under review. Whoever's running their show must have friends in very high places."

"You know," said Jeff, "you're being a lot chattier than usual."

Ward grunted. "Don't get used to it."

After that, his wall went back up, and the conversation was over.

The comm line from the lander crackled, and Brighton said, "We're ready to go here."

"Copy that," Ward replied, tapping his console. The interior camera feeds switched to an external feed from *Explorer II,* looking aft down the length of the ship. A long telescoping arm had extended from the cargo hold. The lander was attached to the end of the arm, ten meters from the hull of *Explorer.* "Routing docking clamp control to the lander. Safe journey."

"I'll keep the line open," said Brighton. "And away we go."

Explorer II shuddered as the lander detached. Several bursts of nitrogen pushed the lander gently away. Its nose swung around, and with another small burst, it drifted toward Titan.

25

Kate stared at her workstation monitor, the glow of the screen casting a kaleidoscope of blues and whites upon her face as she re-watched the video recording from within the large torus. She played it through in fast-motion as the *Pequod* moved down the long curving hallway, until a silvery light appeared ahead. She slowed down the playback as a school of fish shot past the sub, swimming away from the light.

Then there was a flash. A blur of light charged at the camera faster than the sensors could visually process the movement. The screen went blank.

Kate tapped a key several times to reverse the recording frame by frame, stopping at the moment right before the screen went black. The still image was a pixelated blur with a starburst of static in the middle. All she could discern was a streak of shadow and light passing the sub on the left.

She tapped another key and the camera angle switched to a feed from outside the large torus, recorded from one of the monitoring clusters attached to the truss of lights encircling the artifact.

The walls became translucent as the *Pequod* traversed the interior of the torus, its lights glowing through the hull, creating a kind of x-ray cutout that moved along with the sub. The rest of the torus was dark, until a few moments later when a small silvery light bloomed some distance ahead of the *Pequod*. The bloom intensified and shot past the sub. Kate toggled between the two still video frames. In the first frame, the silvery light was at least thirty meters from the sub. In the second frame, it was right next to it. After that, the hull of the torus was solid again, and the lights were gone.

She sighed and tiredly rubbed her eyes. The facility had lost one sub, and she wasn't any closer to finding a reason for the torus to be on Earth.

Kate glanced across the control room at Dominic, who sat at his desk, eyes closed, chewing on the end of his pen while rocking gently in his chair. He seemed to sense her staring at him and opened his eyes.

"Any progress?" she asked.

He took the pen out of his mouth and stuck it behind his ear, then scratched his bushy beard thoughtfully.

"Everything's still hypothetical," he said.

"You mean theoretical?"

"Har, har. Like that didn't get old the first dozen times you said it."

She pretended to look hurt. "And here I thought you physicists were renowned for your senses of humor."

"Do you want to see what I'm working on, or not?"

"God, yes. I'm driving myself crazy watching this."

He spread out his arms magnanimously, and said, "Come, then, and be enlightened!"

She shook her head as she walked over to his desk and sat on the edge of it, surveying the chaos of his research. Every inch of his desktop was covered with scribbled notes, open books detailing various esoteric topics within the field of theoretical physics, and empty coffee cups.

Dominic picked up a sticky note with a simple circle drawn on it, and a question mark within the circle.

"We know they float," he said. "Or hover, or whatever you want to call it. They have propulsion from an unseen source. Based on what you and Noah have told me about Diamond Aerospace's first mission, they can enable instant communication across vast distances. On top of that, they seem impervious to direct sensor probes. We can only detect them by their absence in the matter surrounding their exteriors." He set the sticky note back on his desk and steepled his fingers. "Now, in the first two cases, these are emissions. The torus has to give off some kind of energy in order to hover or transmit communications signals. But in the third case, with sensor obfuscation, what is it?"

Kate thought about it a moment, then said, "Absorption?"

Dominic nodded. "At first glance it seems as if its exterior is absorbing all of our sensor probes and giving nothing back." He shuffled some papers around on his desk, then found a printout that looked more like a child's scribbling than useful data. Jagged red, green, yellow, and blue lines zigzagged across the page. Kate couldn't sense a pattern, then she tilted her head and noticed the lines were tracing the outline of a three-dimensional torus. "We've been battering that thing with every kind of sensor at our disposal," he continued. "Nothing sticks. Like you, I thought that was because the object was absorbing all of our signals. Then I started running spectrograms across every possible wavelength of light, and I found this." He pointed at the sheet of paper. "Our sensors aren't being absorbed by the hull. They are being bent *around* it. When the sensor probes reach the other side of the torus, they continue without a fraction of measurable distortion. It makes the object completely invisible unless you're looking right at it."

"That's incredible."

"It's some kind of shell," said Dominic. "A deflection shield which also might explain how they move about so effortlessly. There's no friction on the hull because it's surrounded by this invisible shielding." He tossed the sheet of paper back onto his desk and sighed. "For the life of me, I can't even *begin* to guess at its method of propulsion."

"Well," Kate said, patting his back, "nobody's perfect." She looked over the notes on his desk once again, and asked, "Do you have any guesses about who built them?"

"Only that they must be shorter than the hallways inside a torus. You said a couple of crew members from the first mission went through a door on the outer hull."

"All they saw was a shadow on the exterior. They couldn't gauge the size of the door, but Jeff said the hallway was at least twice his height."

"And that was one of the smaller tori," said Dominic. "More like the little guy out there in the water than the larger one that it's building."

"Is this hallway bigger?" she asked, pointing at the image of the large torus on her own monitor.

"Hard to tell from the Pequod footage alone because we don't have anything to measure it against for scale."

Kate sighed. "So whoever or whatever built the tori come in all shapes and sizes, or it has nothing to do whatsoever with their height. It's all coming together, isn't it?"

"Oh sure," said Dominic, smiling as he leaned

back in his chair. "We're really cracking this thing wide open."

There was a loud beep from Kate's workstation. She walked over and pushed a blinking alert button on her monitor.

"What is it?" asked Dominic.

"Proximity sensors have picked up something in the water."

He sat up in his chair. "What is it?"

Kate cycled through all of the available video feeds outside the facility, searching for the anomaly. She gasped when she saw it.

"Kate?" asked Dominic.

She sent the video feed to the center viewscreen at the front of the room. It showed a wide view of dark water, stretching to black in the distance. Floating right in the middle of the screen, thirty meters from the facility, was the *Pequod*. Its spherical front window housing the camera and sensor array seemed to be looking directly at the facility.

Behind the sub's window, a glimmering ball of light gently pulsed.

26

Jeff and Commander Ward sat silently in the command module while the lander moved farther and farther away from *Explorer II*. Ward busied himself by tapping commands into his console and constantly checking the monitor feeds from the lander's equipment. All reports were in the green, but he watched every piece of incoming data like a hawk.

"All systems nominal," said Brighton from the lander. "Initiating approach procedure."

A moment later, the lander rotated until, from Jeff's point-of-view, its stubby wings were vertical. Then it banked away from *Explorer*. Ward switched to a different camera feed that showed a wider view of Titan. The lander appeared as a dark speck on a wide field of orange.

"Approaching the upper atmosphere," said Brighton. "No change from the sensors. Equipment looks good. Proceeding."

"Can you route their camera feed to these monitors?" Jeff asked.

Ward tapped a few commands on his console. The wide view of Titan from the exterior of *Explorer* switched to a closer view of the moon's hazy atmosphere from a sensor array embedded in the hull near the lander's nose. The view was simple: a thick fog of pale, grainy orange with no discernible characteristics.

"We're in it now," said Brighton. There was a slight distortion in the signal. "Can't see a thing."

Then she gasped. Ahead of the lander, something moved in the dense clouds. The corner of a multi-sided geometric structure emerged from the haze, twisting and tumbling, and disappeared just as quickly.

"That was *big*," Brighton said. "Sensors aren't picking up any of this."

Jeff leaned forward in his seat. "If it's anything like the tori, it would be able to hide from the sensors."

"That would be a useful piece of technology," Ward muttered.

"There are more of them," said Brighton, a slight edge of worry creeping into her voice.

The camera feed from the nose of the lander, which Jeff thought offered a narrow field of view, was actually wider than he expected. As the small ship penetrated deeper into Titan's atmosphere, more of the massive geometric structures became visible in the mist. Soon the lander was surrounded by them.

"I'm having to use manual control to avoid collision," Brighton said.

"Your trajectory looks good," said Ward. "Stay on that heading and you should be fine."

Brighton grunted as she swung the ship away from a tumbling slate-gray skyscraper that shot across her path.

"That was too close," she whispered through clenched teeth.

Ward glanced at Jeff, but said nothing. His console beeped and he tapped a button, then frowned.

"Something's wrong," he said.

"Say again," said Brighton. "Lost you on that last transmission, over." Static popped over her words, chopping up the signal.

Ward pulled up the lander's trajectory on his console, from the point that it detached from *Explorer* to the moment it was supposed to land. It wasn't expected to break out of Titan's thick, gauzy atmosphere until much closer to the surface, yet his sensor readings were telling him the lander was about to hit clear skies.

"Either my sensors are going haywire," he said, "or the floor of Titan's atmosphere is about two miles higher than it should be."

Brighton's voice was a symphony of pops and static when she replied. "It's not—sensors. We see—initely a barrier—an't tell what—"

"You're breaking up," said Ward. He wiped sweat from his forehead. "Say again, over. Do you need to abort?"

"—ort—want to try the oth—ang on, there's somethi—"

The camera feed went dead.

Ward sat back in his seat abruptly, his eyes wide. He tried to raise Brighton on comms, but the line was silent. He quickly cycled through all of the available camera feeds, but they all showed the same thing: a black screen.

"We lost them."

"We lost their *signal*," said Jeff.

"That's what I meant!" Ward shouted. He was breathing hard, and Jeff realized he was terrified.

"Commander, what do we do now?"

Ward took a few moments to calm down, then said, "We give them time. They could've hit a patch of atmosphere that blanked out their sensors, along with their comms. Maybe one of those floating buildings triggered an EMP. I don't know. Whatever happened, we give them time."

"How long do we wait?"

"As long as we have to."

Jeff unclipped his seat harness and pulled himself toward the hatch.

"Where are you going?" Ward asked, suddenly suspicious.

"To tell Elizabeth. She needs to know."

Ward seemed to consider it for a moment, then nodded reluctantly and turned back to his console.

Jeff drifted down through the hatch, past the airlock T-junction, and into the passageway that connected with the crew module. He gripped a handhold on the wall and stopped his forward motion. There was a tightness in his chest, and he closed his eyes as he tried to steady his rapid breathing.

We knew the risks, he told himself. *We knew the risks and we came anyway.*

Yet that thought did nothing to comfort him. When he opened his eyes, his hands were still shaking.

Elizabeth was at the top of the ladder at the end of the passageway, staring at him.

"Is it bad?" she asked hesitantly, as if she were afraid to hear the answer.

Jeff nodded. "It's bad. We lost contact with the lander. There's no evidence that they were attacked…or that they crashed. But we lost the signal."

Elizabeth kicked off from the ladder and floated over to him. "They're still alive," she said. "Don't you worry about that. Any number of things could've interfered with our communications. What did Ward say?"

"He said to give them time."

"Then that's what we should do. Commander Brighton is smart, and she's capable. If there's a way to send us a message, she will."

"So we're just supposed to sit up here and twiddle our thumbs?"

Elizabeth gestured toward the back of the ship. "I got some oxygen filters that need scrubbing. Might help keep our minds off the situation." She wiggled her eyebrows up and down. "Wanna get dirty?"

Jeff couldn't help but smile. "Absolutely."

27

"It's just floating there?" asked Noah.

Kate nodded. "It hasn't moved since the sensors first picked it up."

"It doesn't look damaged," said Tom.

He stood closest to the viewscreens, squinting up at the enlarged view of the *Pequod*. The sphere of light behind its bulbous front window spun rapidly and then slowed, then reversed direction, seemingly at random.

"Any movement from the big torus?" asked Noah.

"Nothing new," Kate said. "Still dead in the water."

Noah pointed at the sub on the screen. "Have you tried talking to it?"

Kate looked at him. "What do you mean?"

"Have you sent it a message? Something is obviously inside of it. Maybe it wants to talk."

Tom walked over to his desk and typed quickly on his keyboard. "Here's my opening salvo of greetings," he said. "Everything from 'Hello' in binary to the Fibonacci sequence."

They all waited after Tom stopped typing, staring at the screen. There was no noticeable change in the behavior of the sphere of light within the sub.

"You know," said Kate, "that looks an awful lot like what Jeff and Gabriel described seeing inside the torus that was orbiting Titan. They said it moved along a track in the ceiling, and it spoke to them by constructing sentences from their recorded voices."

"It's not talking now," said Dominic.

Noah was silent for a moment, then he said, "Let's go get it."

"What?" Kate asked.

"Let's bring it inside. We're not going to get any answers while it's out there."

Dominic cleared his throat. "The Trojans said the same thing about that big horse, if you'll recall."

Noah smiled. "Thank you for the reminder. Tom, how's the Nautilus holding up?"

"Shipshape," Tom replied.

"Want to take her for a spin?"

"Absolutely. I'll bring home our prodigal son."

"Wait just a minute," Kate said, holding up her hand. "We don't know anything about what we're dealing with here. What if we bring it on board and it takes over our computer systems and sinks the facility, or fries us with radiation?"

Noah seemed to consider it for a moment. "How long would you say Jeff's encounter lasted inside the torus near Titan?"

She shrugged. "Based on his description, no more than a few minutes."

"That should be more than enough time to determine if it means us any harm," Noah said.

"Or enough time to sink us." Kate shook her head. "I don't like this policy of poking the hornet's nest to see if anybody's home."

"I understand," Noah said. "But sometimes you have to poke the nest to find out what's inside. Tom?"

"I'm on it."

He left the room just as Lola entered.

"What's going on?" she asked.

"We have a visitor," said Noah.

She looked at the viewscreens. "Is that the missing sub?"

He nodded. "With a little something extra."

"Is Tom going to get it?"

"Oh, you're quick," Kate muttered under her breath.

"We'll leave it in the drydock room for now," said Noah. "Tom will get it hooked up to his equipment and we can start running some diagnostics, maybe figure out what we're dealing with."

"You'll want to keep it hidden away as long as possible," said Lola.

Noah turned to her with interest.

"I just got off the phone with a contact on the mainland," she continued. "You all have been so busy looking below the surface that you haven't taken the time to look above it."

Noah turned to Kate. "Would you please check the surface feeds?"

Kate pulled up the feeds on her monitor and sent them to the three viewscreens, cycling through them quickly. The sky was overcast and there was a slight chop to the water. The impossible bowl-shaped dent in the water looked the same as before.

She stopped on one view that showed a cluster of large ships in the distance, approaching the facility.

"Ah," said Noah.

"Who is *that?*" Kate asked.

"That," said Noah, "would be the US Military. Looks like they found us after all."

28

Jeff slid the last oxygen filter back into place after scrubbing it clean. Contributing something to the mission gave him some small sense of purpose. He was about to ask Elizabeth if there was anything else he could do when Ward's voice came over the intercom.

"Dolan. McCall. Report to the command module."

Jeff and Elizabeth stood in the aft section of the ship, staring at each other while they waited for more information. Then Elizabeth shrugged as she wiped her hands on her white shirt, streaking it with dark gray filter dust.

Ward was waiting for them impatiently when they arrived, drumming his fingers on the arm of his chair. As soon as Jeff had cleared the hatch and floated into the command module, Ward tapped his console and said, "Explorer to Catalyst. Everybody's here."

"Right," said Dex Hollander from the other ship. "Hi, everyone. I wanted you all to hear this at the same time."

Ward twirled his finger and rolled his eyes, silently saying *Get on with it.*

"Several minutes after our lander left for the surface, I lost contact," said Dex. "After waiting the requisite time for a message and receiving none, I am prepared to concede that the worst has happened."

"Then you give up too easily," Ward cut in.

"However," Dex added sharply, "that doesn't mean we can't continue the mission."

"Short of jumping down to the surface in our suits," said Ward, "I think that's *exactly* what it means."

"Mr. Dolan," said Dex. "What is the approximate volume difference between the cargo holds of our two ships?"

Jeff frowned as he thought. "Without being able to measure the exact cubic footage of Explorer's, I would guess that the Catalyst's is roughly twice as big."

"Almost *exactly* twice as big," said Dex. "And what did you carry in your cargo hold?"

"One lander," Jeff replied quietly.

Ward leaned forward. "You brought two."

"That's correct, Commander. We could afford a good deal of redundancy on this mission. The landers were designed to be operated remotely, if necessary. I could send the second one to the surface unmanned to try and make contact with my crew, but I've decided to go down myself. I wanted to offer you the chance to join me."

Ward cut the line. He leaned back in his chair slowly, his eyes darting around the cabin as he considered the proposition.

"Explorer can maintain orbit on its own," he said. "The only issue is reestablishing contact for docking when we return."

If we return, Jeff almost said out loud before stopping himself. It took him another moment to realize exactly what Ward had just said.

"All of us would go," he said, looking at Ward for confirmation.

"At this point, it's best for the mission if we stick together."

"Commander," Jeff said carefully, "there's a very real possibility that both landers have been destroyed. The likeliest outcome is that the same thing will happen to us."

Ward stared at him. "Have you always been a coward?"

"I'm afraid to go down there," said Jeff. "Of course I am, because I know what happened to me last time. And I know what happened to Riley. A torus turned him inside-out. I was the lucky one. But you can't re-create luck like that. You can't count on it. So yes, I'm afraid to go down to the surface, but I also came all this way for the chance to do it. You two have nothing to lose by staying on the ship, but you could lose everything if you get in that lander."

The three of them sat in silence for what seemed like a long time.

"I'm staying on board," said Elizabeth at last.

Ward opened his mouth to protest, but the look she gave him brooked no argument.

"Don't worry," she continued. "I'll have the ship ready for you when you get back."

Ward sighed and tapped the comms button.

"—happening over there?" Dex was saying. "Hello?"

"We're here," said Ward. He looked at Jeff. "Two for pickup. Come and get us."

29

Kate hurried down to the drydock room, hoping to catch Tom before he got the *Nautilus* in the water. He was already in his dive suit and had just released the sub from the crane arm when she ran into the room. He turned to look at her, surprised.

"Got room for one more?" she asked, breathing hard.

He smiled. "Always room for you."

He swung the crane arm away from the moon pool. The *Nautilus* floated peacefully in the circle of water.

Kate donned one of the dive suits hanging from an equipment rack.

She followed Tom into the sub, putting in her earbud as she took her seat. She hooked her suit's oxygen system into the sub's and felt a chilly blast of air from the helmet vent under her chin.

Tom worked the controls, prepping for departure.

"You really think it's a good idea bringing that thing inside the facility?" Tom asked.

"I think we can minimize the risk as much as possible," Kate answered, trying hard to convince herself.

"What if it's a bomb? The ball of light, I mean. What if it's some kind of alien C-4?"

Kate thought about it for a moment. "Then it could probably destroy us from outside the facility just as easily. I'm not exactly comfortable with bringing it inside, either, but I'm less comfortable with whoever's on board those ships getting to it before we can take a look."

"Not everyone in a government suit is evil," said Tom.

"That's true," Kate agreed. "But it's safer to know who you're dealing with before you decide to trust them completely. The same goes for anyone."

"Descending," said Tom, flipping a switch.

He blew the ballast and the *Nautilus* dropped out of the bottom of the research facility, sinking at one meter per second. The sub leveled out when it cleared minimum safe distance from the facility, then Tom flicked on the forward halogen lamps and gave it minimal thrust, coasting forward toward the *Pequod*.

The smaller sub floated like a ghost in the murk, the sphere of light spinning and pulsing like a beacon.

Kate manipulated her controls, and two robotic arms slowly extended from the front of the *Nautilus*. Each arm was fitted with a simple articulated grasping claw. Tom slowed as they approached the *Pequod*. The robotic arms reached out until they bumped ineffectually against the hull of the smaller sub.

"Hang on a sec," said Tom through pursed lips. He muttered to himself under his breath as he pulled back from the *Pequod* to readjust his approach. He managed to line the robotic arms up perfectly with one of the bottom rails of the smaller sub, and Kate grabbed it with both claws.

"Secure," she said. "Nice work."

Tom leaned forward in his chair to look out through the convex front window.

"Well," he said, "if it was gonna try anything, now would be a good time."

"Let's head back," said Kate. "I want to get this thing secure before our guests arrive."

"Copy that," Tom said.

Later, in the drydock room, Kate waited as Tom hoisted the *Pequod* out of the moon pool with the crane arm and swung it carefully onto a flat pushcart. Kate knelt at the front of the sub while Tom went about securing the *Nautilus*.

Rainbow-colored light danced across her face, almost as if the surface of the glowing sphere was water itself, reflecting light from an unseen source. She gazed into the sphere, hoping to see something within. After a moment, staring into it became too painful and she had to look away. She blinked hard and rubbed her eyes to clear away the bright after-image.

While Tom lifted the *Nautilus* out of the moon pool with the crane arm, Kate rolled the cart with the smaller sub to the far side of the drydock room, as far away from any operational equipment as she could. In case the sphere had any kind of visual sensors, she faced it away from the moon pool so all it could see was a blank wall. Then she went about setting up a makeshift barrier to hide it from casual view. She stacked several storage crates to form a low wall so that anybody entering on the other side of the room would only see a pile of random containers. She laid out a tarp next to the front of the sub, intending to cover it up when she left so the light wouldn't attract attention.

Tom walked over, rubbing his wet hands on his T-shirt. Kate looked up at him and smiled. She hadn't noticed the shirt he was wearing earlier. It said *Hippies do it whenever, man.*

"I like your shirt," she said.

"Thanks. I changed when I heard we were gonna have visitors. First impressions, and all that. You want me to hook this thing up to the computer?"

"Not yet. Let's get a camera on it. I want to watch it for a while first. Send the feed directly to one of the tablets. I don't want anyone putting this on the screens in the control room."

"Want me to encrypt the signal?"

Kate nodded. Tom went away to find a camera, and Kate sat on the cold floor, arms wrapped around her knees, studying the light patterns the sphere cast upon the wall.

Pale blues, purples, yellows, and oranges moved in seemingly random waves, as if a multicolored light were reflecting off the disturbed surface of the moon pool. Kate cocked her head to the side and noticed that, after a few seconds, the patterns reset with a blink, as if the projection of light was a video that snapped back to the first frame once it reached the end.

It's scanning the wall, she realized. *It's trying to interact with it.*

She slowly held out her hand, moving it into the light until the waves danced across her palm. It could've been her imagination, but she thought she felt a slight warmth.

The pattern on the wall shifted from random wavy lines to more of a sunburst, with her palm as the center of the sun. The light seemed to flow toward her hand, and the warmth on her palm intensified. She quickly pulled her hand out of the light, and the previous wavy projections resumed.

Within the domed window of the *Pequod,* the ball of light floated indifferently, spinning slowly in one direction, then abruptly stopping to spin the other way.

"What are you?" Kate whispered.

The glowing sphere continued its slow spin.

30

Jeff hadn't expected to be back in his spacesuit so soon.

He stood in the airlock next to Riley, looking up at the slowly spinning yellow hazard light above him. The small monitor screen on the wall showed a camera feed of the command module. Elizabeth sat in one of the pilot seats, nervously watching a feed of the airlock. She was constantly monitoring the comm channel for any signal from the lander, but so far there had been only static.

Jeff reached for the wall and gently tapped it, turning himself around so he could wave at the camera. They had spoken in private after Dex offered for all of them to join him on the second lander. Elizabeth said that while part of her wanted to go, a bigger part was perfectly fine imagining the answers to all of Titan's questions instead of risking her life to solve them. Jeff had joked that if none of them made it back to the ship, she could finally stop worrying about who was drinking all of the lemonade sachets and leaving only the orange juice. She had tried to smile, but her heart wasn't in it. Then they hugged, and she held on to him for several long moments.

In the airlock, Jeff thumbed his control stick to let out a small burst of nitrogen from his pack so he could face the airlock door. Ward floated next to him, still as a statue. Jeff would have had a hard time believing someone was inside the spacesuit if it wasn't for the sound of his steady breathing over the comm system.

The door split down the middle silently, the two sides drawing apart to reveal a widening black rectangle dotted with the pinpoint brilliance of distant stars. A moment later, a small area of that rectangle shifted, seemingly bending the trace amounts of light around it, until Jeff realized it was the approaching lander from the *Catalyst*. The small craft was perfectly black, and its cockpit window had a matte coating, preventing light reflections.

Its design was similar to *Explorer II*'s lander, with a snub nose and two stubby wings, but it only had a single stabilizing dorsal fin running down the middle instead of two.

According to Dex, the lander's hardwired safety protocols would only allow him to pilot the craft within forty meters of *Explorer II* if he wasn't intent on docking. Ward had offered the use of *Explorer*'s docking arm, but Dex said it would be faster to spacewalk and use the airlock on the lander. It would mean that Jeff and Ward had to travel away from their ship without any sort of safety tether, but neither of them had objected.

Jeff followed Ward's lead as they left the airlock, slowly drifting out into open space. The lander briefly engaged its forward atmospheric thrusters, keeping it at a steady forty meters from *Explorer II* and matching its orbital trajectory.

Ward tapped a command on his small wristpad screen with clumsy gloved fingers.

"Catalyst lander, do you copy?" he asked.

"Loud and clear," Dex answered. "Swing around toward the back. Airlock's on the port side, just behind the wings."

"Roger that."

A steady stream of nitrogen jetted from Ward's pack as he accelerated toward the lander. Jeff matched his speed, staying a few meters behind him. Off to his right, Titan nearly filled his field of view. As was the case since *Explorer II* began orbiting the moon, he kept expecting a torus to emerge from the hazy atmosphere at any moment and swallow him. Imagining that scenario led him to the same question every time: would it kill him, as it had Riley, or would it send him back to Earth again?

He wasn't in a hurry to discover the answer.

Ward shifted his course and veered to the lander's port side, drifting past one of its stunted wings. The airlock door opened slowly as he and Jeff approached. They turned into it and bumped gently against the inner wall, grabbing onto handholds to steady themselves as the hatch closed.

"Give me a minute," said Dex. "I'm not as good at these controls as the others."

Ward gave Jeff a skeptical look.

A moment later, the ship's atmosphere blasted into the airlock through large wall vents, and the red lights in the ceiling flicked to a sedate green.

"There we go," said Dex. "Come on in."

There was enough space on the wall to hang their helmets and spacesuits, but in silent agreement, they had decided to remain fully suited.

Ward gripped the circular handle in the center of the hatch and turned it ninety degrees. A set of three rectangular buttons next to the hatch lit up white, and Ward pressed them in sequence until each one glowed green. There was a deep metallic clunk from inside the hatch, then it swung inward.

Dex Hollander was floating on the other side to greet them, smiling a bit sheepishly from behind his own helmet's face shield. Jeff recognized him from the Deep Black facility back on Earth, though they had never actually spoken.

Jeff wasn't surprised to see that Dex had also decided to leave his spacesuit on. Without knowing what faced them ahead, it was best not to trust that the ship's atmosphere would hold.

Dex had a boyish face and red cheeks. Jeff guessed he was no older than twenty-five.

"Permission to come aboard," Ward said formally.

"Permission granted, Commander," Dex replied. "Happy to have you."

"Jeff Dolan," said Jeff, extending his hand. Dex did his best to shake it through the bulky gloves.

"This way," Dex said, spinning around to face the nose of the ship.

He led them through a short cylindrical passageway, past another hatch, and into the cockpit.

"I understand you're quite the pilot, Commander," he said.

"I have some experience, yes," Ward admitted.

"In that case, I think we'd all be better off if you took the front seat." Without waiting for a reply, Dex maneuvered himself down into one of the two passenger seats at the rear of the small cockpit.

Jeff sat next to him and buckled in. It had been impossible to gauge Dex's height while floating in zero-gravity, but now that they were seated next to each other, Jeff could tell the other man was about a head shorter.

"If it's possible to make it to the surface," said Ward, "I'll get us there." He strapped into the pilot seat and fiddled with the lander's controls for a couple of minutes, then said, "This control scheme is remarkably similar to our own."

"Yes, well, that tends to happen when someone poaches our engineers during every stage of the design process," said Dex. "We were able to convince most of them to stick around on principle alone, but there are always those who can't resist the siren song of cold hard cash."

Ward grunted. "I'm surprised we were able to pull anybody out of the private sector. Convincing someone to work for the government again after they spend time with the yahoos on your side of the fence is an exercise in madness."

"I'll take that as a compliment," said Dex. He turned awkwardly in his seat to face Jeff. "So, one of your crew decided to stay on the ship."

"That's right," Jeff answered. "She'll keep the fire burning for us."

Dex settled back into his seat. Then he said, "I'm being honest when I say there's something extremely comforting about that."

Jeff smiled. "I was just thinking the same thing."

Ward reached over his head and flicked a switch, then settled his gloved hands over the controls.

"Okay," he said. "Let's get this show on the road."

cleared the landing platform, heading back toward the ships.

Noah leaned toward Kate. "Looks like we won't be getting rid of them so easily."

He smiled as the older man leading the group stopped and looked at them, frowning.

"Colonel Brighton," Noah shouted. "I expected you to get here sooner."

The colonel's stern face grew harder. "I would've gotten here much earlier," he said, "if the Vice President hadn't gone to college with one of your biggest investors."

"John Harris went to Yale?" said Noah. "That's news to me."

"I'll bet it is," Brighton growled. "You mind if we continue this inside?"

Noah pretended to think about it for a moment, then he nodded behind him.

"This way."

He led them into the small wet room which connected the outer docks to the inner facility. Kate peeled off her jacket and hung it on a hook while the soldiers stomped their boots and brushed off their sleeves.

"There are no bad guys inside, Colonel," said Noah. "Your men can leave their weapons here."

The colonel looked at his men with hesitation, then nodded at them. They unstrapped their rifles and leaned them against the wall. Kate noticed the colonel made no attempt to remove his own pistol.

Noah walked briskly down the hallway leading away from the wet room, bypassing the expansive window he had shown off to Kate when she first arrived. The floating lights which usually illuminated the exterior of the larger torus had been switched off. Nothing was visible in the inky blackness outside the facility.

They marched in silence, and Kate didn't want to be the one to break it. She had no idea where this was headed, but something told her it couldn't be good. Diamond Aerospace had successfully avoided government involvement during the first Titan mission, but it seemed now as if they could no longer operate without oversight. The most likely outcome, as she saw it, was that she would have to pack her bags and leave. Then she would be back at square one, looking for another job that she didn't want, loaded down with a truckload of questions she could never answer.

The colonel and his crew crowded into the operations room along with the employees of the research facility. Noah, Kate, Dominic, and Tom stood off to one side, while Brighton and his men stood on the other. Lola leaned against the wall at the back of the room, watching everything with a calm demeanor.

"So," Noah said, breaking the silence. "How can we help you, Colonel?"

"You can start by telling me why no one at this facility has been answering our *repeated* calls."

Noah shrugged. "Reception out here is kind of fuzzy. Between the weather and the distance, we're lucky to get the occasional email."

Brighton clenched his jaw, but let that comment pass. "You know I'm in charge of the mission to Titan."

"One of them, yes," Noah replied.

Kate gaped at him. He had never mentioned anything about a return to Titan. It had never occurred to her that anyone would be in a hurry to go back.

"What you're doing out here," said the colonel, "on your own...you're gathering information which might be critical to our mission. Not to mention crucial for the safety of this planet. This is *not* the type of situation that is best left in civilian hands."

"We're doing okay so far," Tom said.

"So far," said Brighton, "you are doing just fine. But there are elements in play of which you know nothing about."

"Care to share some information?" Noah asked.

"I'm not here to share information. I'm here to make sure you don't endanger the future of our species."

"That's a bit dramatic," said Noah.

"Bell," said the colonel, "if you think this is about anything less than that, you are more naive than I feared. Are you going to cooperate or not?"

Noah crossed his arms. "And by cooperate, you mean hand over the operation to you and your men?"

The colonel stared at him.

"I don't think so," said Noah.

The colonel nodded, as if he had been expecting that response. "In that case, we'll make it official. I'm seizing this facility in the name of the United States Government, in the interest of national security, and for the safety of my fellow citizens. We'll be back shortly." He addressed the young man in his retinue, saying, "Call the helicopter."

As he turned to leave with his men, Noah held up his index finger and said, "There's just one little problem with your plan, Colonel."

Brighton stopped and slowly turned around to glare at him. "And what's that?"

"This facility isn't owned by an American company."

"Excuse me?"

"You're not on American soil. I know you can only claim eminent domain and take over in the interest of national security if you're dealing with property owned by Americans. Which you're not. You're inside a two-square mile region previously owned by the Cuban government."

"Explain yourself!" said the colonel. Kate could tell he was struggling to contain an outburst.

"Forty-nine percent American-owned," said Noah. "Fifty-one percent...who was it, again?" he asked, looking at Lola.

She referenced a small black journal that she pulled from her pocket. "The Independent Republic of Banaba," she answered. "This area was gifted to the nation twenty-five years ago after its successful bid for independence. When oil rights negotiations broke down with the United States, Cuba gave it to the first crown prince as a way to stick it to our President."

"Bit of a space buff, surprisingly," Noah said. "The majority of this facility was financed through his personal savings. I'm afraid you'll find his signature on every official document."

Brighton clenched his fists until his knuckles were white.

"This isn't over yet," he growled.

As he turned once more to leave, Noah said, "Colonel Brighton."

The colonel stopped but didn't look back.

"That doesn't mean we can't come to some kind of arrangement. Ms. Desmond here is my lawyer. She's drawn up some papers for your team to look through. I think you'll find my conditions very agreeable for everyone involved."

Brighton looked across the room at Lola, who gave him a small grin. Then he nodded at her and stormed out of the room, his entourage trailing behind.

After they had gone, Noah let out a sigh of relief. "That went better than I expected," he said.

"But you *were* expecting it," said Kate.

"I knew it was only a matter of time before they showed up. We got away with it on the first mission, before anybody knew what was on Titan. I expected they would be watching me a lot more closely."

"I've heard of the Republic of Banaba," Kate said. "Cyclone Jacob bulldozed every square inch of that island several years back. It's on the list of the world's most impoverished nations. The crown prince lives in a straw hut and there's no way he could bankroll this kind of facility."

Noah grinned. "There may have been some creative solutions involved. What matters is that, when Brighton convinces his superiors to buy out the prince's stake in this facility, his fifty-one percent will net his little island nation enough money to rebuild their entire infrastructure, and then some."

"So Brighton is going to end up in charge no matter what?" Kate asked.

"They would find a way to run the show eventually," said Noah. "I knew that as long as we were the ones negotiating the terms of the handover, we'd be able to stay in the game."

Kate shook her head. "I just can't figure out how they learned so much about the first mission."

"The takeover of Diamond Aerospace was rather...how shall I put this?" said Noah. "*Abrupt.* They got their hands on a mainframe full of mission reports and ship designs. Not to mention there were forty-seven people working for me at the time. Their non-disclosure agreements expired after I was removed as CEO."

"Okay, then," said Kate, no less overwhelmed than before. "What can I do to help?"

"You're already doing everything you can," Noah replied. "Lola will keep the colonel's lawyers running in circles for as long as possible, but it won't be forever. That means we have a lot of work to do, and not much time to do it."

32

Ward gave the lander minimal thrust, and it drifted toward Titan.

Both the *Catalyst* and *Explorer II* were holding prograde orbits around the moon, keeping them in a position more or less directly overhead of where Jeff fell to the surface on the first mission. Scanners were still unable to penetrate the full depth of Titan's atmosphere, which hadn't been the case when the ships first arrived.

Something had changed.

"Does this vessel have a name?" Ward asked over his shoulder.

"Lander Two," said Dex.

Jeff turned toward him. "That's the best you could come up with? I thought you guys had a budget."

Dex tried to shrug beneath his seat harness. "We spent all our money on designers."

"Explorer," said Ward, "this is Lander Two."

"I hear you, Commander," Elizabeth said over the channel.

"We'll maintain contact as long as possible. If we go radio silent for more than two days, you are ordered to collect what data you can and return home. Is that understood?"

There was a long pause, then Elizabeth said, "Understood."

Jeff swallowed hard. Even if they survived the landing, but lost comms, they would only have two days to signal Elizabeth that they were okay.

He mentally filed that with the thousand other things he was struggling not to think about, like how he should have tried harder to stay together with Kate. He should have been less distant. She was right about him: he hadn't been the same since he got back from Titan. It felt as if a part of him was still there, and he didn't think he would ever be whole again unless he went back to find it. But now, sitting in that seat on the lander, getting exactly what he thought he'd wanted, there was a peculiar clarity to the realization that he had been so very foolish.

"Approaching upper atmosphere," said Ward. "Minimum visibility in twenty seconds."

The only thing Jeff could see through the lander's cockpit window was a field of orange haze.

"Ten seconds."

Visibly, nothing changed. Jeff couldn't tell if they were five meters from the atmosphere or a thousand. There was nothing by which to gauge their proximity. Then a shudder ran through the walls of the vessel.

"We're in," said Ward. He calmly worked the controls, and Jeff discovered that he was immensely grateful to have someone else flying the ship.

Dex leaned forward in his seat, straining against his harness.

"There," he said pointing ahead of the lander.

In the orange haze, a massive dark shape slowly drifted away.

More shapes became visible as they penetrated deeper into Titan's atmosphere. Many of them seemed to be stationary, tumbling slowly or quickly in place, rotating on a random axis. There appeared to be no identifiable pattern to their placement, nor to their motions.

All three of them jumped in their seats when a flash of purple lightning arced between two nearby objects, leaving behind a fading afterglow. Jeff tried to rub his eyes but his glove bumped against his face shield.

"Maybe that's what hit the other landers," said Dex.

"That would certainly be enough to fry a comm array," Ward admitted.

"It would fry everything it hit," Jeff said. "There would be nothing left."

"Two minutes from blackout barrier," said Ward. "According to your readings, Hollander, both our vessels lost contact at the same altitude."

"I'm still with you," said Elizabeth. Her voice was tinny and distant, laced with distortion.

"Two days," Ward said. "Don't forget."

"I won't."

The shudder coursing through the walls of the lander increased the closer they got to the blackout barrier.

"One minute," said Ward.

Jeff's vision began to shake. There was a rattle from somewhere inside his helmet.

The orange fog parted briefly ahead of the lander to reveal a gargantuan, multifaceted black object tumbling in their path.

Ward cursed and brought his fist down on the console to activate manual control while he grabbed the flight stick with his other hand. Jeff was pushed down into his seat as the lander rose sharply. His shaking vision darkened at the edges as he teetered on the edge of passing out.

The object filled the cockpit window. Dex yelled something unintelligible and Ward roared with exertion as he fought the stick.

Then they were clear, and all that lay ahead of them once more was a field of endless orange.

Ward gently maneuvered the ship back onto its original trajectory, and the three of them let out a collective sigh of relief. Just when it felt like they finally had something to celebrate, Ward said, "Ten seconds to blackout barrier."

Jeff squinted at the pale orange expanse ahead, certain that he had seen something shimmering in the haze. The lander suddenly emerged from the orange cloud and into clear sky, and Jeff could see what lay before them.

Stretching in all directions as far as he could see, several miles above the surface, was a translucent blue barrier that crawled with snakes of purple lightning.

"Pull up!" he shouted, but it was too late.

The lander shot through the barrier. Ward's console went blank and the walls stopped shuddering.

"What just happened?" Jeff asked, his voice loud inside his own helmet.

When no one answered, he turned to face Dex, who was shouting something at him. Jeff couldn't hear a thing. The barrier had knocked out their comms.

The lander slowly began to dip, and as Jeff's stomach sank with it, he came to the horrible realization that the barrier had knocked out *all* the systems.

The ship was dead weight, falling toward the surface.

Above the lander, the shimmering barrier extended downward in all directions, forming an enormous, translucent dome over some of the surface. The dome crawled with purple lightning and blocked out Titan's thick atmosphere.

Without knowing what else to do, Jeff pushed himself as far back into his seat as he could and tightened his harness until he could barely breathe.

Ward furiously worked at the controls, trying to get the lander to respond. Then he stopped mid-movement and just sat there. Jeff shouted at him to do something, and he could tell by Dex's frantic movements he was doing the same thing. Suddenly, irrationally, Ward unbuckled his safety harness and crumpled to the floor under the pressure.

Jeff looked out the cockpit window. The surface of Titan was spinning in the distance ahead, growing rapidly closer, a vast swath of brilliant white peppered with tiny black specks. Off to one side, a pillar of dark gray smoke billowed into the air.

Ward slowly pulled himself to his feet, struggling against the forces pushing him down. Jeff reached out to help him but Ward swatted his hand away as he moved toward the rear of the cockpit. Jeff craned his neck to see what he was doing.

Ward twisted two handles embedded in the wall and yanked off a rectangular metal panel. He threw it behind him without looking, then reached into the cavity, his arm vanishing up to his elbow.

Gravity shifted, and Jeff was pressed against one side of his chair as the lander began to spin. Now the cockpit window revealed an alternating view of white and orange and white and orange as the craft tumbled toward the surface. Ward braced himself and yanked on something within the wall, then fell backward and slammed into the back of his own seat.

Jeff felt something beneath the floor break free of the lander, as if an explosive charge had pushed away a section of the vessel. He was compressed into his seat again, and an instant later slammed upward against his harness as the lander tried to right itself.

With obvious effort, Ward pulled himself back into his seat and strapped in. He grabbed the flight stick, and this time it seemed to respond. He strained to get the nose of the craft aimed at the surface. Jeff was shocked to see how close they were.

Once the lander had stopped its chaotic spin and was now more or less heading straight for solid ground, Ward pulled up on the stick. The lander shuddered, but complied, and the white surface below slowly drifted down out of view.

Jeff crossed his arms over his chest and grabbed his harness as they descended. The nose dipped briefly and he saw they were seconds from impact. The sound of his own scream was deafening inside his helmet as the bottom of the lander hit the surface with a crack.

He slammed forward against his harness and lost his breath, then an invisible semi-truck hit him and he crashed back, banging his head against the inside of his helmet.

The lander drifted sideways as it slid across rough ice. Jeff's teeth rattled and he barely had the strength to clench his jaw.

A plume of white shot up and covered the window. The vessel steadily lost momentum until it bumped into something solid and finally stopped.

Jeff sat slumped in his seat with his arms hanging down, like a puppet whose strings had just been cut. The only thing he was able to do in that moment was catch his breath.

Dex was the first one to unbuckle his own harness. He fell out of his seat and hit the floor with a dull thud. Then he crawled to the front of the cockpit and slowly stood up next to Ward, who wasn't moving. Dex turned and said something to Jeff, but their helmet intercom system still wasn't working. Jeff managed to glean the gist of it from Dex's motions, so he unbuckled his own harness and stumbled forward. He felt a warm wetness on the back of his head and knew he was bleeding.

Ward was unconscious in his seat. A line of blood ran down one temple from above his hairline. Dex motioned again and Jeff nodded. He unbuckled Ward's harness and the two of them pulled him from his seat and down to the floor, where they laid him out, slightly propped up by his oxygen backpack.

Dex walked to the rear of the cockpit and motioned for Jeff to follow him. They went into the small airlock and Dex sealed the hatch behind them. He patted the outer hatch and shrugged at Jeff.

Want to have a look around? he seemed to be asking.

Without power to the ship, they had no way to flood the airlock with Titan's native atmosphere for the transition. Jeff knew the pressure was roughly sixty percent greater than that of Earth's. It wouldn't crush them, but it would feel like moving beneath fifty feet of water.

Jeff glanced at his wristpad and was relieved to see it was still operational. He tapped a few commands, checking seal integrity and oxygen levels. All readouts were in the green. He gave Dex a thumbs-up, then helped him pull the manual override for the hatch. They strained to push it open, then stumbled out onto the surface of Titan.

33

Jeff stepped into a world of white.

As far as he could see, nothing but white. He turned around to look at the lander to make sure it wasn't his eyesight that had failed. The vessel was battered, resting with its nose slightly in the air against a large boulder of ice, but it was still in one piece. One of the landing sleds had snapped off, and the remaining sled rested at a crooked angle. Several gleaming, dented scrapes marred the pitch-black exterior.

Jeff took a few hesitant steps on the hard ground. It had a texture like sandpaper, and seemed to be covered by a thin layer of white powder. While the ground was made of ice, it wasn't smooth. Its surface was jagged and sharp, as if someone had chipped away at it with an ice pick.

Jeff knew something was off right away. He tapped Dex's shoulder and waited for him to turn around.

"The pressure is wrong," said Jeff loudly, hoping Dex could read his lips. "Should be harder to move."

Dex didn't look as if he understood. Jeff shrugged, motioning for him to forget it.

He took another step, then awkwardly flapped his arms as if he were doing jumping jacks as fast as he could. Titan's surface pressure should have been one-hundred-and-sixty percent of Earth's, yet Jeff felt no extra weight. With his eyes closed, he wouldn't be able to tell if he were walking around on Earth or on Titan.

He searched for a horizon line in the distance, staring at one spot in the vast sheet of white, but could see nothing. There was no way to determine where they had landed. Jeff only knew of two landmarks on the surface by which to judge his location: the lake he had fallen into and the alien construction site, and neither of those was visible. He tapped Dex on the shoulder again and motioned that he was going to walk around to the other side of the lander. Dex nodded and followed him.

Jeff stopped to look inside the thrusters. They were filled with ice. He tried to scoop some out with his gloved hands, but it was frozen solid against the interior wall of the boosters.

"Dunno how we're gonna get this thing off the ground," he muttered.

He and Dex stopped again after they walked around to the other side. In the distance, a single column of dark gray smoke rose into the sky.

A hand fell on Jeff's shoulder and he jumped in his suit. He spun around to see Ward bent over, hands on his knees, breathing hard, fogging his face shield. Ward stood upright and said something to Jeff, then grew impatient when he realized Jeff couldn't hear him and motioned for him to turn around. Still confused, Jeff obeyed, turning back to face the distant column of smoke.

He could feel Ward manipulating something on the back of his oxygen pack. A moment later, the tiny speaker in his helmet crackled with static.

"Guess nobody read the manual but me," Ward said over the suit-to-suit intercom system.

Jeff turned around to look at him. "You never *showed* me the manual, remember?"

Ward smirked. The blood on the side of his face had dried. His left eye was bloodshot, but other than that he seemed okay. He went over to Dex and reactivated his comm system.

"Much better," said Dex. "Thanks."

"What's the plan?" Jeff asked.

"Lander's computer fried on the way down," said Ward.

"Can you reboot the system?"

"No, it melted the hardware." Ward looked back at the damaged lander. "Not that we could take off anyway. Comms aren't penetrating that barrier we hit. We need to reestablish contact with the rest of the crew."

"Isn't there a portable radio on Explorer's lander?" Jeff asked.

Ward nodded. "If it hasn't been damaged, it might have enough juice to reach the ship." He studied his wristpad for a moment. "If the wristpads are still working, maybe the radio is, too. But I'm still not picking up the location beacon from our lander. Oxygen reserves will last us a couple hours. Let's grab what we can from this site and head toward the smoke."

Ten minutes later, they walked single file away from the lander, each carrying as many spare oxygen packs as they could manage.

"What did you do to the ship when we were falling?" Jeff asked. "You left your seat."

Ward trudged ahead of him, walking in a straight line toward the rising smoke.

"I blew the atmosphere out through the bottom vents, popped the landing sleds, and overrode the automatic aileron controls."

Jeff thought about it for a minute. "That's all?"

Dex laughed. "I'm sorry," he said, still chuckling. "It feels wrong to laugh, given the circumstances."

"It's perfectly natural," said Ward. "Laughter is healthy when the only other option is weeping."

Jeff looked at the column of smoke up ahead. Now he could discern a dark shape on the ground at the base of the column. If it was a vessel of some kind, it sure didn't look like one.

"Do you think that's Brighton's lander?" he asked.

"I'll tell you what I do in situations like this," Ward said. "I don't think about it until I get there."

They walked without speaking for another fifteen minutes. Jeff checked his wristpad and noted that he had used up a quarter of his oxygen during the trek. Unless they found more oxygen packs, the three extras that he carried would only last him six hours...maybe eight if he sat down and breathed as slowly as possible.

"It's mine," Dex said as they drew closer to the source of the smoke. "Oh God, it's Lander One."

He dropped the packs he was carrying and hurried as fast as he could to the wrecked lander. The vessel had broken into two pieces on impact, its contents spilling across the hard, frozen ground. Smoke billowed from the rear section.

Dex moved frantically around the crash site, muttering, "*Ohno ohno ohno...*" to himself quietly as he searched the wreckage. He stopped dead in his tracks when he found the two suited figures in the forward section of the craft.

One of them sat on the floor, propped against the back of the pilot seat. It was a young woman with tan skin and short, dark hair. Her eyes were closed and her forehead rested against the inside of her face shield. Jeff didn't recognize her from his time working for Deep Black.

She cradled the other suited figure across her lap. The inside of the occupant's cracked face shield was coated with blood.

Dex seemed to snap out of a trance. He looked around the broken cabin.

"There were three," he said. "There were three of them."

"Over here," said Ward.

Jeff and Dex left the forward section and walked over to where Ward was standing, ten meters from the crash site on the far side of the lander. A solitary figure lay sprawled on the ice, a trail of blood leading from the spacesuit back to the vessel.

"He crawled here," said Dex. He knelt down and touched the figure gingerly. "It's Carlo. Carlo Moretti. Second in command."

Dreadful realization crept into Jeff's mind. If the man on the ground was Carlo, and the other suited figure was a woman, that would mean...

He walked back into the forward section of the lander and knelt down next to the woman. He gently moved her arm from across the other figure's chest, revealing a name badge.

"Manny," he said softly. "I'm sorry, my friend."

The woman's body jerked. Her eyes popped open and she slammed her head back against the interior of her own helmet. Jeff leaped up and stumbled backward, then bumped into one of the passenger seats and plopped down.

"Piper!" Dex shouted as he ran into the lander.

He stumbled to her side, tripped, and fell down next to her. He quickly sat up and grabbed one of her hands, forcing her attention onto him. Her gaze ricocheted between her crewmate and Jeff, until she finally seemed to understand her situation. She slowly looked down at her commander's body and swallowed thickly.

Jeff and Dex helped move Manny to the side of the cockpit so Piper could stand up. She turned to Dex and began speaking rapidly, her hands gesturing wildly, but they couldn't hear her. Dex held up a finger for her to wait while Ward went around to the back of her pack and reactivated her comm system.

As soon as she knew everyone could hear her, she made a visible effort to calm down.

"Where's Carlo?" she asked, staring at Dex. Her voice carried a faint hint of French accent.

Ward caught Jeff's eye and motioned for them to go outside. He held up his wristpad as they walked to show that he had switched to a different comm channel. Jeff did the same.

"Best to let them work through this part on their own," said Ward.

"What do we do after that?" Jeff asked.

Ward studied the featureless landscape. "We find the others," he said. "Then we figure out how to get a message to the Explorer. We collect as much data as we can, then we get off this rock."

34

While Noah and Lola kept Colonel Brighton and his lawyers busy following their return to the facility, Kate went down to drydock.

The door was usually kept wide open, but since their guests had arrived, Noah asked Tom to install a hasty security keypad so that only the facility employees could gain access. She quickly typed in the code and pushed open the door, then sealed it behind her, making sure it was locked.

Tom and Dominic were on the far side of the drydock room, next to the *Pequod*.

It hadn't taken long for Dominic to adopt the space as his own. His scribbled notes and empty coffee cups had grown to fill the area like a goldfish growing to fit the size of its container. He sat on an overturned crate, his legs bouncing up and down restlessly while he studied the colorful light playing across the wall.

Tom stood next to him, arms crossed and brow furrowed.

"Anything new?" Kate asked as she walked over to join them.

"Infuriatingly, no," Dominic admitted. "The pattern of light changes based on what you put in front of the sphere, but nothing beyond that. I agree with your hypothesis that the light is some kind of scanning mechanism, but the 'how' and 'why' of its function eludes me."

"How's the boss doing with our visitors?" Tom asked.

Kate sat on an empty crate next to Dominic and shrugged. "I have no idea what they're discussing in that room. Of course, I had no idea Noah had planned on handing the operation over in the first place. And I *definitely* had no clue there was another mission to Titan. I feel like I'm the last person to ask about what's going on around here."

"It's not that he was planning on handing it over from the beginning," said Dominic. "It's that he knew the takeover was inevitable, and he tried to control it as much as he could."

"Still," said Kate, "it feels like we were all kept in the dark."

Dominic patted her knee sympathetically. "If you get into bed with an eccentric, you should expect weird things to happen."

"How 'bout that Lola bein' his lawyer?" said Tom. "Didn't see that one coming."

"I assumed she was another investor," Dominic added.

Kate stared into the glowing sphere of light as long as she could before it became painful, then looked away.

"It hasn't made any attempt to communicate?" she asked.

"Not that I can tell," said Dominic. "Of course, my tests are limited without being able to use any of the facility's equipment."

"Could we isolate it from the network? Create a locked system so that even if the sphere did take control, it couldn't get into the mainframe?"

Tom scratched his head thoughtfully. "I could encrypt a closed network, set up a mobile equipment rack with all the toys and a laptop to run all of it. Wouldn't be as powerful as tapping into the facility systems, but it would be a whole lot safer."

"How long would that take?" Kate asked.

"With anyone else, all day. I'll be back in a jiffy."

He left the room whistling.

"What I like best about him is his humility," said Dominic.

"Yeah, he really puts us all to shame in that category," Kate agreed.

She watched Dominic's face while he studied the patterns of light on the wall in front of the sub.

"Do you ever regret taking this job?" she asked.

A slow smile crept across his face. "Are you kidding me? My former colleagues are still reading from books and squinting into telescopes, trying to unravel the mysteries of the universe." He gestured toward the glowing sphere. "And look what I have right in front of me." He shook his head. "No, even with all the frustration, the lack of answers...I wouldn't change a thing."

"Even if we never get more out of this ball of light than patterns on the wall?"

"No question about it."

"You know," she said thoughtfully, "the first time we encountered one of these things, it spoke to the astronauts using the recorded voices from our communications between Earth and Titan. The message didn't make much sense, but it proves they were trying to communicate. Do you think it's alive?"

Dominic's eyebrows went up at the question. "You mean organic?"

"I mean sentient. Is this thing," she said, nodding toward the ball of light, "is it the infamous 'them'? The ones that built the tori?"

Dominic considered the question for a long moment. "The tori, and the structures Jeff described seeing on the surface of Titan, strike me as being extraordinarily complex machines," he said. "Elegant, but complex. Unless this little ball of light had some way to physically manipulate the world around it, I don't see how that's possible. Then again, a year ago if you would've asked me if any of this was possible," he added, gesturing at the facility around him, "I would've said not a chance." He smiled. "I guess the moral of the story is that it never hurts to keep an open mind."

"There were human drones on Titan," said Kate. "Human-*shaped* drones, anyway, doing all the legwork."

Dominic frowned. "I didn't read about that in the reports."

"For various reasons, Noah thought it was best not to disclose every detail, and I agreed with him."

After a moment of consideration, he nodded. "I understand. What were they doing?"

"Building. Or helping to build. Jeff described it as a city under construction on the surface of Titan. The drones seemed like construction workers, he said, crawling in and over all of the newly-built structures. There was this room inside the torus. Jeff said the walls were covered with material samples, organic and inorganic. There was a human eye, and it looked at him."

"Sounds like a collection of building blocks," said Dominic. "The tori might be able to synthesize complex molecules and form them into shapes, or even into other life forms."

"That swings us back to my original question," said Kate. "Did this ball of light build the tori, or was it the other way around?"

The heavy door to the drydock room banged open and Kate jumped in surprise. Tom waved apologetically as he lifted a teetering equipment rack over the lip of the entrance and rolled it into the room.

"Sorry," he said. "Trying to keep this thing from falling over."

Kate stood up. "That was fast. Think you crammed enough in there?"

"Hey, you said you wanted equipment. I got you equipment. Between all this junk you should be able to figure out something."

Kate slid out the laptop tray and lifted the lid. "And this system is totally isolated from the facility?"

Tom nodded. "One-hundred percent disconnected. You won't be sharing any data with the mainframe, so if you fry this rack, you lose everything. Just keep that in mind."

"It's worth the risk," said Kate. "Thank you, Tom."

He blushed and tipped an invisible hat in her direction.

"Now," Kate said with a sigh, turning back to the laptop. "Let's get a closer look at our little friend here."

35

Jeff salvaged what he could from the rear section of the wrecked *Catalyst* lander. He found four more oxygen packs, then he joined Ward on the ice as the commander was checking his own oxygen reserves.

Ward glanced back at the lander.

"I'll give them another minute," he said.

As if on cue, Dex and Piper emerged. Ward motioned to Jeff, and they both switched back to the public comm channel.

"We need to get moving," said Ward. "We have limited resources, and limited time."

Neither Dex nor Piper made any sign they were going to move. Piper crossed her arms and looked at Dex.

"Tell them," she said.

"Commander Lopez said not to," Dex replied. He shifted uncomfortably in his spacesuit.

"We are in this together now," she continued. "Tell them."

"Tell us what?" Jeff asked.

Dex sighed. "Carlo was like you," he said.

"How so?"

"He died on the first mission and...and he *came back*."

Jeff knew that only two people had 'officially' survived the first mission to Titan, and both of them had been safely aboard *Explorer I*, his own ship.

"He was on the North Star," Jeff said.

"Washed up on the beach, just like you," Piper said, "and like Commander Riley. Only he came to Deep Black first. We gave him the chance to return here." She stamped her boot on the ice. "He just wanted answers. And now he will never leave this place."

"I'm sorry," said Jeff.

"It does answer one question we had about him," said Piper, "and you."

"What's that?"

"Whether or not you're immortal."

Jeff chuckled, thinking she was joking. He saw the look on her face and realized she was not.

"How could we be possibly be *immortal?*" he asked incredulously.

She shrugged. "How could you *possibly* return from the first mission? Carlo himself posed the question to us before we entered stasis. He knew he died on the ship in orbit around Titan. If he had been remade, why couldn't he be made better? These were his thoughts."

"They healed me and sent me home," said Jeff. "I didn't die."

"How can you be sure?" asked Piper.

Jeff didn't have an answer.

"We need to move, people," said Ward.

Piper turned around and pointed into the distance. "We saw the construction site as we fell to the surface," she said. "It's that way, more or less."

"That's a better lead than we have," Ward admitted.

"What do you have?"

"Nothing."

He started walking in the direction she indicated, followed by Dex and Piper. Jeff hoisted the extra oxygen packs, distributing the weight as best he could, then joined the procession. If the pressure on Titan's surface had been what it was supposed to be, carrying the packs would have drained every last ounce of his strength.

Following that same line of thinking, he asked, "Has anyone tested the air?"

"No," said Dex. "Why?"

"The atmospheric pressure is far below what we were expecting," Jeff said. "I was curious if anything else was different. Air composition, radiation levels, that kind of thing."

"We would need to use a sensor array on one of the landers for that," said Ward.

"Based on the fact that none of us are shivering inside our suits," said Dex, "I would guess the temperature is higher than usual. The lowest tolerance of the Constellation series is just barely enough to keep us alive on the surface under normal conditions. There's also the smoke from the lander."

"What about it?" asked Ward.

"If the surface was as cold as we expected, the smoke would freeze," said Piper.

Ward glanced back at her. "Did those goons at Deep Black hire you two straight out of college, or what?"

Dex grinned and shared a knowing look with Piper. "The best and brightest," he said. She reached out and squeezed his gloved hand with her own.

Jeff looked past them, toward the blank white canvas beyond. In the sky far above, he caught a glimpse of a tumbling skyscraper-sized object in the dense organonitrogen haze. He slid his reflective gold sun visor down over his face shield to cut out some of the glare.

"I think I see something up ahead. A mountain, maybe."

"Yes," Piper said. "The construction site was near the base of a mountain."

"Did you see a lake, too?" Jeff asked.

"You mean Lake Dolan?" He could tell she was smiling. "Yes, we saw it."

"Not exactly the legacy I was hoping for," said Jeff.

"Well," Dex said, "it's not like they have any libraries out here to name after you."

The top half of the looming mountain was fogged over. As they drew nearer, the fog cleared to reveal that the entire top third had been ripped away, leaving most of one side a jagged ruin.

"Has your team detected any volcanic activity?" he asked.

"No seismic activity of any kind," said Dex. "We had the same bad luck as you did scanning the surface."

"How are you going to find the other lander?" asked Piper.

Ward took a moment to answer. "If I don't get a ping from their location beacon, they'll have to find us. I don't have enough resources to perform a proper search."

Jeff could tell it was hard for Ward to admit he was mostly helpless, especially when it came to the safety of his crew.

"If they saw the construction site on their way down," Ward continued, "it's the first place they would go."

"I'm sure we will find them there," said Piper.

Ward shifted the thick bundle of oxygen packs to his other shoulder and did not reply.

It took another half an hour of marching across the ice until they saw the outline of an object in the distance. From that far away, it was a tiny black hoop on the horizon.

The four of them stopped.

"Is that what I think it is?" Dex asked, looking to Jeff for confirmation.

"Yes," Jeff replied with dread. "It's a torus."

36

Jeff began to relax a little as they drew nearer to the torus when it became obvious it wasn't moving. It faced their direction like some kind of sentinel, thirty meters in diameter, hovering just off the ground as it watched their approach.

And it was only once they were standing right next to it that they realized it was fully encased in ice.

The frozen ground beneath the torus had cracked open, spewing a plume of water that had frozen instantly. The wall of ice in which the torus was stuck had erupted at an angle, imbuing it with a sense of violent motion, frozen in mid-launch. The top edge of the crystal-clear wall was like a line of ice daggers stabbing toward the sky.

Jeff looked up at the mountain in the distance.

"That's a cryovolcano," he said. "Recently active, would be my guess."

"So this is water?" Piper asked, nodding toward the nearby wall of ice.

"Could be methane," Jeff replied. "Either way, I wouldn't touch it."

"Let's keep moving," said Ward.

They gave the frozen torus a wide berth as they continued in the direction of the cryovolcano.

More dark objects became visible in the distance.

"That's the site," said Piper, pointing ahead. "That's what we saw on the way down."

"What are we supposed to do when we get there?" Dex asked.

"You can do whatever you want," said Ward. "I need to collect some viable data for the lab techs back on Earth, then I'm getting out of here."

Jeff turned to Piper. "What are your mission objectives?"

"Make contact," she said. "Learn what we can. Offer to swap technology, if possible."

Ward shook his head. "Greedy little private space monkeys."

"And what will your government do with the information you bring back, eh?" Piper shot back. "Give it to the people? Make it free for everyone? You are here for the same reasons we are. The only difference is that we are not pretending to be here for anything else."

"I don't need to pretend, sweetheart," said Ward. "Top Brass said to bring back samples, so I'm going to bring back samples. What they do with that information is above my pay grade. If it helps them make a stronger glue or a faster bullet, then good for them. I'll be too busy spending my paycheck on Oahu to care. You want to talk about pretending, let's talk about the false notion of nobility that seems to plague every corner of the private space industry. You seem to think that just because you're not working directly for a government that your goals are more pure, and that by simply being outside the system you are above it. Here's a bit of news you may have missed. Everything comes down to money, no matter how it's packaged. Every single thing."

"You have a very cynical view of humanity," Piper said quietly.

"Yeah, well, experience is the best teacher."

A short time later they stopped to swap out their nearly-depleted oxygen packs. The quartet had remained mostly silent since the exchange between Piper and Ward.

As they drew nearer to the outer edge of the construction site, Piper said, "I'm sorry I got so heated back there. I didn't mean to insinuate you were a bad person just because you work for your own government. I feel like my brain is having a hard time keeping up with my emotions in this place."

"I'm sorry, too," said Ward. "At least you have a decent excuse."

"What's yours?" she asked.

"I was born mean."

Jeff smiled.

"Look," Dex said, pointing at the sky.

Jeff glanced up, and it took him a moment to realize what Dex was referring to. In the distance, the sky next to the jagged side of the cryovolcano shimmered with light.

"It's ice," said Piper. "A massive wall of ice."

The edge of the wall was nearly invisible against the bright haze of Titan's lower atmosphere. Jeff could trace its outline from the point where it emerged from the interior of the cracked-open cryovolcano, along its jagged arc through the sky, and to the point where it tapered down to the ground.

"That thing's half-a-mile long," said Ward. "Or longer. It must've been some eruption."

They walked past the first object at the edge of the construction site: a twenty-foot-tall black pyramid jutting from the ground at an odd angle.

Piper walked up to it and slapped its surface.

"Hey!" Dex shouted.

She turned back and looked at him as if to say, *What's the problem?*

"Just, you know," he said uncertainly, "be careful."

"I will slap it more gently next time."

"How are you supposed to take a sample of that?" Jeff asked.

Ward considered the pyramid for a minute. "I have no idea," he admitted. "Assuming the other lander is still in one piece, and assuming we can get its computer system working, we'll blanket the whole area with scans and call it a day. But if you see anything pocket-sized, feel free to bring it along."

"There's more of them up ahead," said Jeff.

They walked past two more pyramids before the structures began to offer a little more variety. A large cube hovered over the frozen ground. Piper tapped one corner and it tumbled slowly in place.

"What could be the purpose for this?" she mused. "Do you think they are all connected to each other? Like pieces on a circuit board?"

No one had an answer.

"I would very much like to talk with whoever created this," she continued.

"Are you a linguist?" Jeff asked.

Piper nodded. "I speak seven languages, and I can read ten."

"I guarantee you that whatever built these things doesn't speak any of them," said Ward.

"Most of my equipment was damaged in the crash," she said with regret. "I helped design an artificial intelligence that can break down every known language to its roots in less than a minute with only a minimal word bank. It could have given us a start."

Next they came to a wide black arch, its ends buried in the ice twenty meters apart. Over the apex of the arch hovered two humanoid figures wearing older-model Constellation spacesuits. Their black sun visors were pulled down, hiding their faces.

"No company I know of issues black sun visors," said Ward.

He walked slowly past the arch, keeping an eye on the two figures floating above. They didn't turn to face him as he moved.

Piper stopped and fished a small white box from a pocket on her thigh. She tapped on the box's small screen, then looked up at the hovering, suited figures.

"Can you hear me?" she asked.

Jeff and Dex stood next to her, watching. Ward stopped walking and turned back.

"What are you doing?" he asked.

"It's an external comm speaker," Piper replied. "I'm saying hello."

The two humanoid figures floating above the arch did not react. Piper tapped on her wristpad and pushed a button on the side of the white box.

"What's happening?" Dex asked.

"I'm broadcasting a greeting in twenty-eight different Earth languages. Also binary, Morse, and every machine language that can be translated into an audio stream."

"We don't have time for this," said Ward.

"This is why we're here, is it not?" Piper replied. "To make contact. To study and learn."

"Sure, that was the plan," Ward admitted. "Then we passed through the barrier and crashed. First we need to secure a way off this moon. *Then* we can chat with the locals."

He turned and walked away from the arch. Piper sighed and stuffed the box into her pocket.

"Any response?" Jeff asked.

"Not that I could hear. But that doesn't mean they were silent."

With Dex at her side, she reluctantly followed after Ward.

Jeff looked up at the two silent guardians. They seemed to be frozen in mid-air, completely motionless.

"Careful here," said Ward from the front of the group. "The ground is cracked."

Jeff left the arch behind and hurried to catch up with the others. A spiderweb of black lines coursed through the rough, icy surface.

"Oh my God," said Piper.

Jeff bumped into her while still looking at the ground and excused himself. He followed her gaze and stopped dead in his tracks when he saw what lay ahead.

An enormous torus, easily three times wider in diameter then the ones Jeff had previously encountered, hovered parallel to the ground near the center of the construction site. They had been approaching it side-on, so that at first glance it looked like a wide black bar floating in midair.

The ground beneath the massive torus had cracked wide open, creating a broad chasm. An enormous spear of ice had erupted from the pit and encased more than half of the torus.

"It isn't complete," said Piper. She pointed at the angled tower of ice. "Look. There is a little one stuck inside, straddling the big one."

The group stopped a good distance from the edge of the chasm, then walked parallel to the drop-off. Piper was right. About a quarter of the large torus was missing, the empty space filled with ice. The smaller torus hung suspended around one open end of the larger, frozen in place.

"Looks like they were in the middle of building that giant one when the cryovolcano erupted," said Dex. "Bad timing."

"Why can't it melt the ice?" asked Piper.

"Maybe it uses heat as an energy source."

Piper smiled. "If so, *mon choupinou*, then Titan is maybe not the best place to build a vacation home."

A high-pitched chime sounded within Jeff's helmet, and Ward quickly looked down at his own wristpad.

"Our lander's location beacon just activated," he said. "He spun in place until he got the bearing, then he pointed away from the large torus. "It's this way."

He set off at a brisk pace. Jeff, Dex, and Piper hurried to keep up.

37

"Nothing," said Kate. "Absolutely nothing."

She stood at the equipment rack next to the *Pequod*, reading the results of Dominic's latest battery of tests.

"It doesn't absorb any signals, it doesn't *emit* any signals, and it doesn't respond to external stimuli. I feel warmth on my hand when I hold it in the light, but the heat doesn't register on our equipment."

"It must be on a wavelength we can't measure," said Dominic. He wiggled his fingers at her dramatically and added in a fake-stage voice, "Or it's in another dim-*ennnn*-sion!"

Kate offered him a wry smile for his trouble. "But if it's in the visible spectrum, we should be able to detect *some*thing."

"It's a ball of light from outer space," said Dominic. "We might have to admit we're not going to learn anything useful."

She groaned with frustration. "I refuse to believe that."

He smiled gently. "Then we'll just have to keep trying."

Kate smacked the side of the equipment rack and bit back a scream.

After she had taken a few deep breaths, Dominic said, "You know, if you think about it, we didn't start with the basics."

"What do you mean?"

"I mean we're trying to communicate with this thing, or at least glean some kind of data from it, and we've been going about it like we're expecting it to know what we're up to. We haven't even so much as shaken its proverbial hand."

She knelt down in front of the ball of light. "Hi," she said. "I'm Kate. Nice to meet you."

"That's not quite what I meant," said Dominic.

She rubbed her eyes harshly and swiped a hand through her frazzled hair. "I'm sorry," she said. "I'm tired. I'm frustrated."

kate meet, said the sphere. *nice n-nice nice.*

It was her own voice played back at her in a flat monotone.

"Oh my God," she whispered, covering her mouth with her hands.

Dominic barked laughter and slapped his leg. "Eureka!" he shouted.

kate meet, the sphere said again.

The light playing across her face shifted patterns, swirling slowly like a miniature hurricane.

"Why are you here?" she asked.

After a long pause, Dominic said, "*Why* is a very human concept."

"What am I *supposed* to ask it?"

"Maybe nothing. I don't know. This is my first time as well."

She put her hand to her chest and looked into the sphere. "Kate," she said. Then she pointed at Dominic and said his name. The light pattern on her face shifted again, reversing direction, but the sphere remained silent.

"Well," Kate sighed, "it's a start."

She stood up and stretched her back, watching the colorful light dance across the blank wall. An idea struck her suddenly, and she picked up the tablet linked to the sphere's video feed.

"What are you up to?" asked Dominic.

She swiped through the menus on the tablet and pulled up the video feed of the sub, then she held the tablet in front of the sphere.

The unformed splash of light on the wall instantly shrank to cover only the surface of the tablet. The video feed on the tablet screen went blank. Then, as if the device were malfunctioning, the screen began to flash far too quickly for Kate's eyes to fully track, cycling through every possible screen from every possible menu and program installed on the tablet. The screen flicked to black. The dancing light that had been focused solely on the tablet expanded back to its previous amorphous configuration on the blank wall.

"I'd call that something," said Dominic.

Kate reactivated the tablet screen and browsed through the menus. Nothing looked out of place. There were no glitches. She lowered it slowly and tapped it against her thigh, thinking.

"When I first asked if you had learned anything about who built the tori, you said they had to be shorter than the hallways."

Dominic nodded. "That's right."

"This ball seems to be able to manipulate its environment using only light," Kate said. "What if the hallway inside a torus wasn't designed *only* to be walked in?"

He rubbed his beard and looked at the ceiling. "That's interesting. The hallway is one long control room, and the controls are the walls, the floor, and the ceiling"

"Exactly. Jeff said the floor illuminated with different colors as he walked on it." Kate pointed at the ball of light. "One of these things was contained in a track in the middle of the ceiling."

"To use a crude metaphor," said Dominic, "the ball of light is a CPU, and the empty hallway is the motherboard."

"We manipulate our computers by typing on a keyboard," said Kate. "Maybe these spheres manipulate the tori by projecting different patterns of light on the interior."

"That," said Dominic, lowering his gaze from the ceiling to look at her, "would be quite the discovery."

"Not that we'd be able to do anything useful with it," Kate said. "There's no way to apply that knowledge."

"Not yet, anyway. This ball of light came to us for a reason. Whether or not it was out of mild curiosity or part of its programming, we can't stop trying."

Kate sighed. "Right. In that case, we'll need more coffee."

She set the tablet on the equipment rack and walked away.

"Um, Kate?" said Dominic.

She glanced back and stopped. The light on the wall had changed from dancing, wavy lines, to a solid rectangle of white light.

"What is that?" she asked.

Dominic shook his head. "I have no idea. It changed as soon as you left."

"Is that a video feed?"

She walked back to the wall and knelt down in front of the projection. Someone stepped into view from outside the frame, and Kate jumped back, startled. The person wore an orange Constellation suit—the same type worn by the astronauts on the first Titan mission. Shadows covered the occupant's face.

The feed was distorted, as if the camera were looking through melted glass. The suited figure looked up at the sky, then down at the ground. It shifted to one side, and Kate saw several other suited figures walking away into the distance. The world beyond them was so bright it appeared solid white.

The nearest suited figure stepped toward the source of the video feed and held its gloves up to its face shield, blocking out the oppressive glare.

When it stepped back, Kate caught a clear glimpse of the name badge sewn onto its chest.

It read, in big bold capital letters, DOLAN.

She stared dumbly at the image on the wall, then said, "Jeffrey?"

38

Jeff whipped around when he heard his name over comms.

That sounded an awful lot like Kate, he thought.

His eyes darted across the massive boulder of ice he had been inspecting, and the frozen torus within. He and the others had discovered this one not long after Ward had picked up the location beacon from the third lander. This torus was not completely frozen. Only the bottom half was encased in ice, cementing it to the cracked ground from which the liquid erupted.

Jeff thought he had seen a shimmering light from within the bottom half of the torus, so he had waited behind to take a closer look. And now, just when he turned away to join the others, he was certain it was Kate's voice that spoke his name.

He knew he shouldn't be able to hear anything but the loudest external noises from inside his helmet, and certainly not a solitary word spoken at a normal volume, yet he couldn't deny he heard *some*thing.

He turned back to see if any of the others had stopped, but they were still walking in the direction of the other lander's beacon.

Am I finally going crazy? he wondered.

"Comms check," he said.

Dex was the first one answer. "Working fine."

"Quit fooling around, Dolan," said Ward.

A moment later, Piper chimed in. "I read you."

Jeff turned back to look at the torus. He held up his wristpad and changed his comm frequency so the others couldn't hear him.

"*Am* I going crazy?" he asked the frozen alien artifact.

He was about to turn away and switch back to the other comm channel when Kate's distorted voice said, "If you're not crazy, then we're both stuck in the same dream."

Jeff walked up to the ice and put his gloved palm flat against it. He hadn't been entirely certain before, but now he was sure multicolored light emanated from inside the torus, shining through black walls that had become translucent.

"What...?" he started. "How...where are you?"

"Earth. You?"

"Surface of Titan."

"I figured."

His vision blurred unexpectedly with tears, and he squeezed his eyes shut to let them spill down his cheek. "It's good to hear your voice," he said. He didn't realize how true the words were until he spoke them out loud.

"Likewise."

"How is this possible?"

"Do you remember the ball of light you saw in the ceiling of the torus near Titan? I'm talking into the one of them. It possessed our remote sub."

"Remote sub? Are you underwater?"

"Noah set up a research facility in the ocean."

"Bell is there with you?"

"Not in the room, no. But he set the whole thing up so we could study..."

Her voice trailed off and Jeff thought he had lost the connection. "Are you still there?" he asked.

"Study what?"

Kate seemed to hesitate, then she said, "The big torus here on Earth."

After a long moment, Jeff quietly asked, "There's one on Earth?"

"Two, actually. The smaller torus is about the same size as the one you encountered in orbit around Titan. The larger one is a little over three times its size. But it's incomplete. It seems as if the smaller one was in the process of building the larger one when it stopped. We haven't been able to figure out why."

Jeff looked back at the other members of his crew. They had turned around when they noticed he wasn't with them and were waving their arms. He looked up at the boulder of ice in front of him, and at the torus within.

"I know why," he said.

"What?" Kate asked. "Jeff? You're bre—ing up. Say th——st—rt aga—"

Her voice clipped off, and Jeff could only hear static. He shouted her name and pounded on the ice in front of him, but she didn't respond. The light inside the torus dimmed.

"No," he whispered. "No, no, no. I just got her back."

He suddenly remembered he was on a different comm frequency and switched back to be greeted by a flurry of cursing from Ward.

"—are you *doing*, Dolan?!"

"Something just happened," said Jeff.

"Yeah," Ward said. "You caused an unnecessary delay. If anything bad happened to the lander crew while we were standing here staring at our belly buttons, I'm holding you personally responsible."

"I just talked to someone on Earth," he said, walking in their direction.

"Come again?" said Dex.

"Somehow our comm equipment became linked while I was standing near that frozen torus."

Ward turned away from him and continued walking. "Fascinating," he said, obviously not believing a word of it. "Learn anything new?"

"Yes, actually. There's a huge torus in the ocean on Earth. Partially constructed, just like the one here."

Ward stopped again. "You really talked to someone?"

"I really did."

"So we can't talk to our own ship in orbit but you can talk to Earth?"

"Apparently."

"Think you can make it happen again?"

"I don't even know how it happened in the first place."

Ward thought about it a moment, then nodded. "Then we keep moving. But if the magical long-distance phone call fairies pay you another visit, you might consider mentioning our situation."

Dex caught up to Jeff as they resumed their march in the direction of the lander beacon.

"Who did you talk to?" he asked.

"Kate Bishop."

"Your ex-girlfriend?"

Jeff glanced at him sideways. "How do you know about that?"

"Sorry. We know a lot about most of the people who worked on the first mission."

Jeff picked up his pace, leaving Dex trailing behind. He didn't really feel like thinking about anything other than Kate at the moment, and even those thoughts were in a chaotic jumble.

Dex scrambled to catch up. "It's just that, well, Mr. Kemp said—you know Richard Kemp? Human Resources?"

"Yeah, the guy that fired me."

"Right," said Dex. He glanced back at Piper, as if for reassurance. Then he said, "Well, it's just that Mr. Kemp advised my boss about Noah Bell."

"In what capacity?"

"Kemp was very good at digging up dirt on people. He could find out secrets about your own past that even *you* had forgotten. Anyway, my boss was trying to find something he could use against Bell when both companies were up for the big Grumman contract. You know, back before he lost Diamond Aerospace."

Jeff glared at him. "What's your point?"

Dex cleared his throat. "It's just that, um, well... Noah Bell is dying."

39

Jeff stopped and looked at Dex. "Dying?"

"Yes," said Piper. "Brain tumor."

"And what exactly am I supposed to do with that information?"

"Right," said Dex. "Okay. Mr. Kemp said that Noah was prone to making irrational decisions long before he was diagnosed, even when he was healthy. I just thought you might want to tell Ms. Bishop to be careful."

"She knows how to take care of herself," Jeff said. "Wouldn't have made it so far if she didn't." Then he added, "But thank you for letting me know."

"Getting close," said Ward, consulting his wristpad. "Still can't raise anyone on comms. Another hundred meters or so."

Jeff looked ahead. They were still in the thick of the construction site, with alien structures dotting the landscape all around, no two of which were alike. Occasionally they would pass a hovering humanoid figure wearing a spacesuit, but the figures never acknowledged their presence. Some of them seemed stuck in mid-operation, as if they had been reaching out to grab a structure and then were frozen in place.

"Just past that big egg," said Ward, picking up his pace.

Half-buried in the ice ahead of them was indeed a black egg the size of a minivan, its tapered end pointing up at the sky. It was made of the same non-reflective material as the rest of the structures, and seemed to suck in the surrounding light.

They jogged around the base of the egg and stopped when they saw the lander from *Explorer II*.

Like the lander from the *Catalyst*, *Explorer*'s had slid to a stop on the surface, arriving undamaged except for deep scarring on its underside. Commander Brighton had either been unable to deploy the landing sleds in time or had chosen not to, which meant the belly of the craft had absorbed most of the impact. It also meant the vessel still had a chance of taking off, provided the sleds could be coaxed from the hull.

The hatch was wide open.

Jeff stayed close behind Ward as the commander jogged to the lander and ducked inside. A moment later, he hurried back out.

"Empty," said Ward. "No interior damage. No blood." He looked down at the frozen ground and scuffed it with his boot. "And no footprints."

"Now what do we do?" Dex asked.

He nearly jumped out of his spacesuit when someone walked out from behind the back of the lander.

It was Will Chapman.

He carried a metal briefcase in one hand and gestured wildly with the other while he talked a mile a minute. Jeff couldn't hear a word he said. Chapman banged the side of his helmet in frustration and continued his silent rant.

Ward went around to the back of his equipment pack and reset his comm system.

"Did it work?" asked Chapman.

"We can hear you," Jeff said.

"Good. I thought I'd be here forever. They told me to wait in case anyone else showed up. I just got that stupid beacon working, too." He stopped and looked at Jeff and Ward. "So how'd you two get down here? Did you take the second lander from the Catalyst?"

"You knew about that?" Jeff asked.

Chapman shrugged. "I work for the colonel, remember?"

"Was anyone injured?" Ward asked.

"What? No. No, everyone's fine." He looked at the group and seemed to realize there were fewer people than there should have been. "Oh," he said. "I'm sorry. I didn't mean to be so nonchalant. Besides the equipment failure on the ride down, we've had it pretty easy."

"What happened?"

"We hit some kind of electrical barrier and everything shut off. I had my eyes closed for a good part of it. One time when I opened them I could have sworn I saw Riley laughing." He took a quick breath. "I'm rambling. Sorry. I'm supposed to tell you that Riley and Commander Brighton went that way." He pointed to the opposite side of the construction site from where Jeff and the others had approached.

"Why?" Ward asked.

"To find a way to call the ship. We were communicating in gestures, but I think that's what they said."

"What about that radio?" asked Ward.

Will gave the metal briefcase in his hand a shake. "It lost power when we passed through the barrier."

Ward looked in the direction Will indicated, then he sighed. "It'll be nice when their comm systems are back online. Chapman, grab as many spare oxygen packs from the lander as you can carry."

"Right." He ducked back inside the ship.

Ward turned to Piper. "Do you have any objection to our crews sticking together for the time being?"

"None whatsoever," she answered quickly.

"I'm staying with the lander," said Dex.

"Are you sure that's a good idea?" Jeff asked.

"Well, if the flight computer isn't burnt to a crisp, I might be able to get the system back online. Since the beacon is working, maybe I can reboot some of the other systems."

"Call us if anything happens," said Ward. "Good or bad."

"Will do."

Ward marched away from the lander as soon as Chapman reemerged, laden with spare oxygen packs. Piper took a couple from him and added them to her own collection.

As they walked toward the center of the construction site, Jeff didn't want to say what he figured everyone else was thinking: that the lander which had the biggest chance of making it back into orbit only had four seats. It was rated to carry the weight of five passengers at the absolute maximum, but that meant only the pilot had any room to move.

When he and the others caught up to Riley and Commander Brighton, there would be seven people who wanted a one-way ticket off Titan.

40

Kate plopped down on an overturned crate, her eyes staring at the blank wall in front of her.

"Are you okay?" Dominic asked hesitantly.

She shook her head to clear away her trance.

"Yeah, I…I'm fine. I just wasn't expecting…*that*."

The projection of Titan had vanished from the wall and was replaced by the water-like reflection of colorful wavy lines that Kate now thought of as "normal" for the ball of light.

"How's it going down here?"

She turned at the sound of Noah's voice.

"Kate just had a video chat with Jeff Dolan," said Dominic, "…on the surface of Titan."

Noah walked over and knelt next to her, studying her face with something akin to wonder.

"How extraordinary," he whispered.

"You don't seem surprised," said Kate.

"I'm afraid I don't have time to be surprised by our discoveries," he explained. "I just want to understand them. What was Titan like?"

Her brow creased as she recalled the details.

"It was white. Endless white, except for a faint orange hue in the sky."

"Was Jeff alone?"

She shook her head.

"Then at least some of the crew survived. Remarkable." He stood up. "How did you make the connection?"

"I'm not sure," said Kate. "The video feed just popped up on the wall. I saw Jeff's name tag and we started talking."

"This isn't the first time we've experienced instant communication between Earth and Titan," said Noah. "During each occurrence, at least one of the parties was in close proximity to a torus." He rested his hand gently on the *Pequod*'s front window. "Or in this case, close to one of these fascinating little guys."

He bent down until his face was bathed in the light emitted by the slowly-turning sphere. The undulating waves shifted away from the wall and seemed to scan his features. The light condensed over a small area just above his left eyebrow, swirling more and more quickly, then glowing brighter.

Noah stood abruptly, a sad smile touching the corners of his mouth.

"Like I said. Extraordinary."

Dominic cleared his throat. "So, how's it going up there?"

"Surprisingly well," Noah admitted. He stuck his hands in his pockets and paced behind the *Pequod*. "Lola is performing her job better than I could've hoped. She has Brighton's lawyers chasing their own tails so effectively even *I* couldn't tell which direction they were facing. When they leave that room, however, they'll have reached an agreement, and we need to be ready for the changes that are coming."

"Why didn't you tell us?" Kate asked.

He stopped pacing and sat on a crate next to her. Once again, she was struck by his paleness. Dark circles hung below his eyes, and his cheeks had a sunken appearance that made him look as if he hadn't eaten in days.

"When I first started this project," he said, "I made a vow to be more transparent with the people who put their trust in me. I was so obsessed with secrecy on the first mission that it damaged some very important relationships. I didn't want that to happen again. Yes, it's necessary to keep some things off the mainframe, so to speak. I just...I just didn't want you thinking that I would give up so easily. Especially not when we were first getting started."

"What is the colonel getting out of the deal?" Kate asked.

"If he buys out the majority share, he'll get full control of this facility."

"What about us?"

"We stay on as independent contractors. From what I could tell during the negotiations, he's content to let us continue operating as if nothing has changed. The colonel is turning out to be more clever than I anticipated, and, for whatever reason, more than a little sympathetic." Noah looked at Kate. "He seems to know the value of surrounding oneself with smarter people."

"And what do *you* get out of it?"

He smiled. "Diamond Aerospace."

Her eyebrows went up. "He's giving you back your company?"

"Whatever's left of it. Apparently, one of the tori has made short work of the Mars mining facility. Most of the equipment is gone. It makes me wonder if there are other tori here on Earth, gathering materials. Perhaps one is sucking up all the sand in the Gobi Desert as we speak."

Kate looked at him suspiciously. "That was your plan all along, wasn't it? To put yourself in a position with enough leverage to win back your company."

"I knew government intervention was a foregone conclusion this time around, so I took the necessary steps to ensure they wouldn't be holding all the cards."

"And this has *nothing* to do with proving everyone wrong? All those people who said that without your father's money you would be nothing."

"People say that?" he asked, feigning ignorance.

"Pick up a magazine," said Dominic.

"I made my own money," said Noah. "I built my own company. But I don't want this to be about me. I want it to be about *us*. I want it to be about discovery, about the pure joy of unraveling a mystery greater than ourselves. Not because it benefits us in some obvious way, but because it's begging to be unraveled. And if I get to shove our success down a few throats while we're at it, I'll jump at the opportunity. Getting Diamond Aerospace back out of their greedy claws is simply the icing on the cake."

She stared at him for a long time. "I believe you," she said.

"Now I understand how you convinced all those investors," said Dominic. "That was some speech."

"Every word of it was true," Noah replied.

He stood up and stumbled forward, reaching out to Kate for support. She grabbed his forearms to keep him from falling.

"Are you okay?" she asked.

"I'm fine," he said quickly, patting her arms and gently breaking her grip. "I'm just tired, that's all. I haven't slept in…I can't remember how long."

"Maybe move that to the top of your agenda," said Kate, hesitantly stepping back.

Noah nodded and smiled weakly. "Just as soon as all the paperwork is signed. In the meantime, try to figure out a way to reopen communication with Titan. I have a hunch they might know a little bit more about what's going on outside this facility than we do."

41

Jeff and Piper walked behind Ward and Chapman, their boots crunching over the frozen ground as they searched for Brighton and Riley.

"What do you think it means?" Piper asked. "That they would build a torus of such a size here, and also on Earth?"

Jeff had been pondering that very question ever since his conversation with Kate.

"I think it means that whoever built the tori wants to move something between the two locations," he answered. "Something big that needs a lot more space than the smaller torus can accommodate."

"Something big?" she repeated.

"Well, if they just wanted to transport smaller objects, or some of their human drones, they wouldn't need such a large portal."

"Wait," said Ward. "Hold on a minute. What's this about a portal?"

"It's just a guess," said Jeff. "Two similar setups at two identical stages of construction. They must be linked in some way."

"But are they bringing something here," said Piper, "or sending something to Earth?"

"What could they want from Earth?" Chapman asked. His gloved hand tightly gripped the handle of the briefcase radio.

"Maybe water," Jeff suggested. "They are building the torus in the ocean, after all."

"Bringing all that water here would make no sense," said Ward. "It would freeze almost instantly."

"Unless Titan isn't the final destination," Jeff said.

"You mean they want to funnel it someplace else," said Chapman.

"They might be constructing some kind of intergalactic transit system. They're building portals on Earth and Titan. Who knows where else they built them?"

"And what if they *are* sending something to Earth?" Piper asked.

"Then," said Jeff, "there's a very strong possibility that it's from outside our own solar system. Maybe even beyond our own galaxy."

"Wonderful," Ward said grimly. "We *have* to get a message to Explorer. McCall needs to warn them."

"Warn who?" Jeff asked.

"The colonel. The military. Anybody. Whether or not these things are gonna steal all our water or drop some kind of alien bomb into the ocean, somebody needs to know about it."

He stopped suddenly and held out a hand toward the others, signaling for them to wait.

"That was a close one," he muttered, looking down at the ground.

Jeff walked forward slowly, then stopped next to Ward. They stood at the edge of a narrow chasm which ran across their path like a lightning bolt. It zigzagged through the alien construction site, disappearing from view in the direction of the large, unfinished torus.

The opening had been impossible to see from a distance because the walls of the chasm were as white as the frozen surface. Even standing at the edge, it looked like an optical illusion, and Jeff had a hard time telling where the other side of the chasm ended and the frozen surface continued.

"Can we jump it?" asked Piper.

"What is that, about four feet?" said Ward. "Maybe it narrows at some point."

He set off, walking parallel to the chasm.

Jeff traced the line of the opening, searching for a safe place to jump across. A small heap of cloth and tubes rested on the ground nearby, at the very edge of the drop-off.

He hurried past Ward and bent down to pick it up.

"It's an oxygen pack," he said, showing the others.

It took him a moment to realize what that could possibly mean, and he slowly looked out over the edge of the chasm, and down.

He saw both of the suited figures about six meters below, on a wide shelf that connected both sides of the chasm. To either side of the shelf, the ground dropped away into darkness.

One of them was standing, but the other was lying face down on the ice shelf.

The one standing up had been probing the wall, perhaps searching for a safe way to climb it. It was

Commander Brighton. She looked up and noticed Jeff and the others peering over the edge. She waved her arms at them, then pointed down at Riley.

Ward held up a finger, telling her to wait.

"If it isn't one thing, it's another," he grumbled under his breath. Then he turned to Piper. "There's some rope in the aft storage bay of our lander. Contact Dex and tell him to meet you halfway with it. Dolan, you scout ahead and see if there's a way to get across."

"Will do," said Jeff.

"Chapman, you stay here with me," Ward continued. "I want to try that radio again." When he didn't hear a response, he looked up from the chasm. "Chapman?"

Jeff turned around, looking for Will. "He's not here."

"Where *is* he?"

"There," said Piper, pointing.

Will was at least fifty meters away from them, jogging in the direction of the large torus. The briefcase radio bounced against the leg of his spacesuit as he moved.

"Chapman, what do you think you're doing?!" Ward barked.

No response.

"Dolan, go after him! He's up to something, and he's got our radio."

"What are *you* going to do?"

"I'm staying here."

"But—"

"I'm not leaving them down there! Now go. Go!"

Jeff took off at a jog while Piper hurried in the other direction, back toward the lander.

42

Kate stood in the control room of the research facility with her arms crossed, staring up at the dark video feed of the torus.

She and Dominic had been banging their heads against the wall, trying to tease another revelation out of the mysterious ball of light. So far, since her conversation with Jeff, it simply remained in the *Pequod,* silently spinning, casting its indifferent light against the wall.

Noah sat in a chair nearby, leaning back with his eyes closed. It was a habit he had picked up recently. When Kate asked him about it, he replied that it was a centering technique useful for keeping his head clear. To Kate it looked like he was just taking a nap.

A door leading to a small side room opened and Lola stepped out. She smoothed down the front of her blouse and looked at Kate, giving a quick sigh as if to say *I can't believe that's finally over*.

Noah stood up and went over to her.

"Is it finished?" he asked.

"It is," she replied. She took off her glasses and tapped them against Noah's chest. "And I dare say you came out better than expected, so be grateful."

He surprised her by giving her a big hug. She smiled despite herself, then politely extricated herself from his grasp.

"Alright," she said, "alright. Calm down."

"And what about the other thing?" he asked.

Her eyes flicked briefly over to Kate. "Yes, that too."

"Excellent. I can't thank you enough."

"Don't I know it," she said cheekily. "Now," she added with a tired sigh, "I can finally leave this floating zoo."

"Do you want me to call for a helicopter?"

"The colonel was generous enough to offer me his," she said.

Noah's eyebrows went up with interest. "Is that right? You *do* work your magic, don't you?"

She placed her palm on his cheek and stared into his eyes. “Promise me you will take care of yourself.”

“I promise,” he said quietly. “Give my love to Uncle Walter.”

She smiled again, this time more sadly. “He’ll be glad to hear it.” She nodded at Kate. “Ms. Bishop.”

“Ms. Desmond.”

After she left, Colonel Brighton emerged from the small side room, his aide nipping at his heels. Three stiff men in gray suits were next, following after Lola.

“Remarkable woman, your aunt,” said Brighton. “I’ve never seen my lawyer sweat before, but by God, she made it happen.”

“Quite remarkable, indeed,” Noah said. “How did everything shake out?”

“I suspect you already know the answer to that question. Needless to say, this facility is now the property of the US Government, and you got your company back.”

“I suppose that means we’ll have to make space for all the men with guns you’ll be bringing over,” Kate said.

Brighton frowned. “But I thought you said there were no bad guys inside.”

Noah chuckled. "I'm glad they sent someone with a sense of humor, Colonel. You're going to need it."

"Why is that?"

"There's something in the drydock room we need to show you."

Kate glanced at him.

"The sub is his now, after all," Noah added.

"Alright, then," Kate said. "It's this way, Colonel."

She led him down to the bottom of the facility and into the drydock room. Tom scrambled to his feet from next to the *Nautilus* when they entered and made a valiant effort to shield the barrier of crates on the other side of the room.

"Hello, Colonel! Nothing going on here."

"It's okay, Tom," said Kate. "We work for him now."

"Oh, crap," said Tom. "I mean, hi, Boss!" He offered a greasy hand and Brighton shook it.

"Yes, well," said the colonel, frowning at his own shiny palm. "Always good to meet the, uh, the, you know..."

"The brains of the operation," Tom finished.

Brighton hesitated, then said, "Okay."

Kate walked around the side of the *Nautilus*, stepping over Tom's scattered tools. Dominic stood up from an overturned crate as they approached.

"This is Dominic Wright," said Kate. "Theoretical physicist."

"I've read some of your papers," said Brighton. "It's good to have you on the team."

Dominic glanced at Kate uncertainly. She got the feeling he had been expecting to dislike the colonel from the start.

"Thank you," he said guardedly. "Forgive the mess," he added, gesturing to the clutter of papers and coffee cups strewn across the floor.

"Don't mention it. I learned long ago that it's best not to interfere with the creative process." He couldn't help but look at the floor again. "Encouraging people to work in their own, uh, natural environment tends to provide the best results."

Kate walked over to stand next to the *Pequod*. "This is why I brought you down here."

She pulled a tarp off the front of the sub to reveal the spinning ball of light within.

Brighton stepped toward it slowly, eyes wide, mouth slightly open.

"Has this been down here the whole time?" he asked quietly.

"It's a fairly recent addition," Kate said.

As he studied the undulating light projected upon the wall, it shifted over to his startled face.

"Don't worry, that's normal," said Kate.

"Yeah, don't shoot," Tom added.

Brighton leaned in closer. "What's it doing?"

Kate smiled. "Saying hello."

The light flicked off suddenly and the sphere went dark. Brighton stepped back in alarm.

"*That's* new," said Kate.

A focused beam of light extended from the sphere and touched the wall. Moving images played across the surface of the narrow beam, as if it were a rolled-up television screen.

"We don't understand," Kate said to the sphere.

The beam flicked off, and the sphere was dark a few moments more. Then it lit up again and the entire back wall of the drydock room was bathed in a soft, pink light.

Kate and the others stepped back so they could see the whole canvas.

"I take it this is new as well," said Brighton.

Kate nodded. "If I didn't know any better, Colonel, I'd say your arrival has made it more talkative than usual."

A sequence of images flashed against the wall as quickly as if they had been shot from a machine gun, then disappeared.

"I saw an elephant," said Tom.

"I saw a whale," said the colonel.

Each image had only lasted a fraction of a fraction of a second, but Kate had been able to identify a giraffe and a small rodent, maybe a mouse or gerbil.

A few seconds later, another burst of images hit the wall and disappeared.

"Are you recording this?" asked the colonel.

Kate nodded, not taking her eyes off the wall. In the second barrage of images, she had been able to pick out a house cat and a human female.

"Is it trying to communicate?" Brighton asked.

"I get the distinct feeling this isn't a two-way street," said Dominic.

"How do you mean?"

"It seems more like it wants us to *know* or understand something. There's no sense of it asking a question, which would indicate the desire to have a conversation. It's showing us images from our native planet, instead of its own, so it's not trying to tell us about where it came from. I think it's trying to tell us something about our own world."

Brighton gave the drydock room a more detailed look.

"Smart move keeping it isolated from the facility's network. If you wouldn't mind the help, I'd like to have my team go over what we just experienced. And before you say anything, I won't ask them to come here and step all over your feet. I'm perfectly fine keeping them on my ship for the time being. But I will need a few of my staff here moving forward."

"Are you asking us or telling us, Colonel?" said Kate. She knew he could do whatever he wanted now that Noah had signed over the facility. Yet if the colonel was willing to play nice, then she would follow that path as long as she could.

"I am politely informing you about how things are going to proceed."

Kate hesitated, then said, "You'll have to excuse my cynicism, but it surprises me that your first reaction isn't to shut us down and dismantle the torus piece by piece."

"Or blow it to smithereens," Tom added.

Brighton nodded, as if to say he understood the sentiment. "I think we should all be grateful that I was put in charge of this assignment. Not everyone I work with feels the way I do about our visitors."

"Which way is that?"

"Cautiously hopeful."

Kate made eye contact with Tom and Dominic. Dominic nodded, and Tom shrugged and turned away.

"We'll set you up with an access code," she said. "Welcome to the team, Colonel."

43

Jeff breathed quickly as he jogged after Will, the slim oxygen packs bouncing over his shoulder.

Moving at any kind of decent speed while wearing a spacesuit on Earth would have been taxing. Wearing a heavy Constellation-class suit on Titan while carrying several oxygen packs was exhausting. His only saving grace was that the pressure within the translucent, dome-shaped barrier had been artificially lowered by whatever built the tori, or by the tori themselves.

"Chapman!" he shouted between breaths.

Jeff switched comm channels and tried again. Will had ignored all of his previous attempts, and Jeff didn't expect that to change now. He was gaining slowly, but Will had enough of a head-start to reach the large torus first.

If that's even where he's heading, Jeff thought.

There didn't seem to be any other landmarks ahead except for the varied alien structures dotting the landscape. Chapman ran past these without slowing, so Jeff had to guess he was heading toward the unfinished torus. What he could possibly hope to accomplish once he got there was another question entirely.

Jeff hurried past the smaller frozen torus through which he had communicated with Kate earlier. He looked at it longingly until it vanished behind him, then focused once again on Will.

Jeff switched comm channels and tried to contact him again.

This time Chapman turned around, and Jeff knew he had heard him. Will stumbled when he looked back and realized he was being pursued. He regained his footing and jogged faster.

Jeff cursed. If the ground wasn't opening to swallow him, and if his ship wasn't crashing, and if a torus wasn't trying to turn him inside-out, then one of his own crewmates was running off with their own secret agenda.

Will made it to the large torus and dropped to his knees. He set the radio briefcase on the frozen ground in front of him and popped it open. A small chrome multi-tool flashed in his hand.

"Chapman," said Jeff breathlessly as he jogged toward him. "Will, what are you doing?"

Will panted hard over the comm system, but he didn't answer. He muttered something to himself that Jeff couldn't understand at first, until he realized it was a sequence of instructions.

"Step one, remove the cover, step two, separate the green wire from the housing..."

He glanced over his shoulder just as Jeff dove for him. Will spun away at the last second, and Jeff hit his shoulder instead of the middle of his equipment pack as he'd been intending.

Jeff landed face down on the hard ground, and Will sat on top of him, straddling his equipment pack and keeping his arms pinned down by his sides.

"Hold still," said Chapman.

Jeff tried to grab Will's boots to pull him away, but couldn't wrap the fingers of his gloves around them.

Will picked up the radio briefcase and set it on Jeff's back, then resumed muttering technical instructions to himself.

Jeff grunted and pushed himself off the ground with his hands and legs. Will jumped up and came back down hard in the middle of Jeff's back, slamming him against the ice.

"I said *hold still!* Almost finished. There we go."

He snapped the briefcase closed, then stood up and jogged away, heading toward the open end of the large torus where the smaller one hung suspended in ice.

Jeff groaned and slowly got to his feet. Pain radiated from the middle of his back, and his knees hurt from where he'd banged them against the ice. He resolved to give Will Chapman a swift kick in the stomach when he caught up with him, and that was just for starters.

Jeff stumbled after him, picking up speed after the first few painful steps.

Will had stopped beneath the smaller torus. He looked at the metal briefcase in his hand, then up at the torus, suspended vertically in the air ten meters above him. The ice that had erupted from the ground beneath it formed a jagged slope leading up to a point in the air high above. Chapman looked back, and Jeff thought he detected hesitation.

"Whatever you're gonna do, Will, you don't have to do it."

Will seemed to make up his mind. He ran toward the base of the small ice mountain and started grabbing for handholds in the jagged surface.

Jeff made it to the base of the ice mountain as Will drew parallel to the center of the smaller torus farther up. He brought the briefcase back with both hands and slammed a corner of it against the ice, chipping away large chunks that tumbled down the slope.

Jeff threw his spare oxygen packs off his shoulder and began to climb up after him, struggling not to slip off the wet outcroppings. He hugged the wall of ice every time a large chunk bounced past from above.

He had covered about half the distance when Will hit the ice with the briefcase one last time, then brushed away several chunks with his gloves. He wedged the dented case into the wall of ice, spun around, jumped, and slid down the slope on his back.

It was not a graceful slide.

He hit an outcropping and tumbled sideways, screaming as he fell. Jeff glanced below to see if he could safely jump off the wall of ice, but it was too late. Chapman smashed into him, knocking them both into the air.

Will hit the ground first and Jeff landed on top of him with a crunch. He rolled off slowly, groaning from the pain.

"Have to...get away..." Will panted.

He tried to stand but fell back down.

Jeff sat up and let out a yell as a sharp pain stabbed him in the side.

"Bomb," said Will.

Jeff looked up at the wall of ice behind him, and at the metal briefcase lodged near the vertical torus. He forced himself to his hands and knees, then crawled over to Chapman. He pushed the face shield of his helmet against Will's.

"You stay close," he hissed.

Then he got to his feet and yanked Will off the frozen ground.

"As if we didn't have enough to deal with already," Jeff spat as he half-pulled, half-dragged Will behind him. "As if we didn't have a hard enough time—"

The bomb detonated.

The blast launched Jeff into the air, spinning him end over end like a rag doll. The world outside his helmet tumbled so violently he couldn't tell ground from sky. The question was answered for him when he smacked into something hard and everything went black.

44

Kate was with Dominic in the drydock room when it happened.

She had been staring at the screen of her tablet, re-watching footage from earlier, when brilliant white light blasted from the window of the *Pequod* like a flash bomb.

She screamed and dropped the tablet to shield her eyes from the blinding light. Dominic yelled something from across the room, where he had been typing up his notes into a computer terminal.

As Kate's vision slowly returned, the sphere spun like a pulsar within the *Pequod*'s domed front window. She covered her ears as a painful, high-pitched whine filled the air.

Wind hit her face, pushing back her hair. The faster the ball of light spun, the stronger the wind became. Dominic's scattered notes blew away to the far corners of the room. He shouted at Kate as he tried to walk away from the computer terminal, but the wind was blowing so strongly he fell back against the wall and couldn't peel himself off again.

The high-pitched whine cut off with a snap. The ball of light exploded out of the remote sub and shot across the drydock room, blasting through the hull into the open ocean.

Seawater gushed in.

Red lights flashed in the ceiling. Dominic was swept off his feet in the rush of water and slammed into the side of the *Nautilus.* The sub snapped off the crane arm and scraped across the floor toward the moon pool, which had begun to overflow.

The flood of water kept Dominic pinned against the sub. He struggled to hold on to an external light array. Kate hurried toward him, sloshing through cold, ankle-deep water.

She looked over at the door leading to the rest of the facility.

It was still open.

Surely the others must realize what's happening by now, she thought. Would they come down and seal the door, locking her in? She was gripped by a sudden and terrible fear that she would drown, and for a moment she froze in place, staring at the open door.

Dominic shouted her name, and she snapped back to reality. The *Nautilus* hit the ledge of the moon pool and remained there. Water erupted around Dominic as he clung to the sub.

Billions of gallons of water out there, she thought, *and all of it wants to get into this little room.*

She hurried toward the sub. The water had reached her knees.

Dominic grabbed for her outstretched arms, and she pulled him from the rushing water.

"We have to close the door!" she shouted.

He wiped water from his face and nodded. He was shaking and soaked to the bone, his dark hair plastered to his forehead.

Holding each other for support, they carefully avoided the moon pool and walked slowly toward the door as the water rose around them. The main jet of water flooding through the hole in the wall was aimed at the center of the room, and once they cleared it, they were helped along by the force of water pushing toward the walls.

The metal wall groaned, and with a sound like a gunshot the hole cracked open wider. The stream of gushing water became a torrent, picking up the *Nautilus* and crashing it against the far wall. The fragmented remains of the smaller *Pequod* roiled next to it violently.

Kate was the first to reach the heavy metal door.

She reached out for Dominic and pulled him the last couple of feet, then pushed him past her and into the flooding hallway. Together they grabbed the door and pulled. Their hands slipped on the small handle and Kate fell back.

The water had risen to her waist.

"Need more leverage!" she shouted.

Against Dominic's protests, she waded back into the drydock room. She turned around and put her back to the door, then braced her feet against the computer console built into the wall and heaved.

Dominic didn't realize what she was doing until the door was only a few inches from closing. He yelled something as it clanged shut. Before he could push it open again, Kate slapped the lock control switch next to the handle on her side. He furiously tapped on the control panel in the hallway, and she could tell he was trying to input the unlock code. She held her thumb on the override button until it turned red.

Dominic banged against the slender window with his fist, and Kate turned away. The water rose to her neck and her feet left the floor.

Great move, Kate, she thought. *Now what?*

She was four feet from the ceiling, and rising quickly.

Think! she yelled at herself. *Think, or die.*

Of course I'm going to die, she thought. *The only way out is through the moon pool, and I'd never make it to the surface before I ran out of air.*

Kate breathed faster as the water pushed her higher. Even though the water wasn't freezing, her teeth chattered and her body shook uncontrollably. She put her hand against the ceiling, willing it to rise along with her.

I could make it if I had more air, she realized. *The suits! Where are the dive suits?*

She looked around frantically. Everything in the room had been pushed out of place by the rushing water. Some of the crates that were stacked by the *Pequod* now floated like wreckage on a stormy sea. But the suits wouldn't float. The balanced weight would keep them exactly where they were, hanging on the rack near the computer equipment.

Underwater.

Her head bumped against the ceiling. She tried to take a deep breath and swallowed liquid, then hacked and sputtered.

Using pipes and shielded electrical cables bolted to the ceiling, she pulled herself to the other side of the room. Water splashed up over her mouth. She crammed her nose against the ceiling, took a great lungful of air, and dived.

The water around her was nearly black. Several dim lights glowed from the moon pool, but the perimeter of the drydock room was lost to darkness. Kate reached the wall right above where the rack of hanging dive suits should have been. Using protruding computer equipment as handholds, she pulled herself down. A distant part of her mind warned her about electrocution, but more pressing fears overruled it.

She saw a glimpse of silver in the murk and grabbed for it. Her hand smacked against the equipment rack. Kate scrambled to find a dive suit, feeling along the pole from which they usually hung. She reached one end and started back toward the other. Her brain couldn't quite process the input when she hit the other end of the rack empty-handed.

Dead, she thought. *This is how I die. No suit no oxygen no help no air—*

There's air in the sub, she remembered.

The Pequod is in a million pieces, another voice inside her contradicted.

Not that one, dummy, said the first voice, *the other sub.*

Nautilus.

Kate spun in place and planted her feet against the wall, then pushed off across the room. The current carried her swiftly to the far wall, and she turned before her back slammed against it.

She felt a burning pressure in her chest and knew she couldn't hold her breath much longer. The instinct to suck in air would soon overpower her will to keep water out of her lungs.

Despite that, she forced herself to wait. She looked around, searching for a hint of the *Nautilus.*

Then she saw it.

In the dim light from the fixtures near the moon pool, she could just barely make out the silhouette of the three-person sub.

She grabbed for the propeller and pulled herself to the sub, unable to feel what her own hands were doing. They banged against the hull of the *Nautilus* as she moved upward, grabbing onto whatever she jammed them against to reach the top.

The sub was pressed up against the ceiling.

Kate wiggled her arms into the narrow space, then shoved her shoulder in, then her whole body, then she pushed the sub downward.

She coughed out an involuntary burst of bubbles and her head swam with dizziness. She grabbed what she thought was the sub's airlock hatch and turned the wheel.

Mercifully, it spun on the first try.

The hatch flipped open and a rush of silvery bubbles exploded upward, pushing Kate back into dark water.

Stupid stupid stupid, she cursed herself. *Of course it would have been filled with air.*

She pulled herself back to the top of the sub and down through the open hatch. Without closing it behind her, she kicked deeper into the airlock. A red button glowed brightly near the floor. She reached for it, expecting to black out at any second, and punched it.

Turning back, she watched the silhouette of the hatch as it automatically sealed. There was a rush of bubbles all around her as she floated in the airlock.

Fear slipped away, replaced by a deep calm.

She could no longer fight the urge to breathe. Kate opened her mouth to draw seawater into her lungs, and she was no longer afraid.

She was ready. This was it.

This was the end.

And she had been so close.

45

When Jeff opened his eyes, he saw the hazy, orange sky of Titan. He couldn't be certain, but if he squinted, he thought he could discern tiny arcs of purple lightning forming a curved barrier that blocked out Titan's upper atmosphere.

He closed his eyes and sat up slowly, with no small amount of pain, and waited for the expected dizziness to wash over him. It hit him like a rolling ocean wave, and he wanted to vomit and lie back down, in that order. Instead, he brought his knees up to his chest and leaned forward until the moment passed.

Will lay on the ground a short distance away. His wristpad flashed yellow, which meant he was almost out of air.

“Hey,” Jeff croaked. He took a sip of water from the straw sticking up at the interior base of his helmet and cleared his throat. “Hey, Chapman. Wake up.”

Will didn’t move.

Jeff sighed, then rolled sideways until he was on his hands and knees. The urge to vomit grew stronger, but he swallowed hard and forced himself to his feet. He patted his shoulders but the spare oxygen packs were gone. He vaguely remembered throwing them somewhere before climbing up the hill of ice after Chapman.

Jeff turned around and saw the result of Will’s bomb.

An enormous chunk of ice had exploded outward from the bomb site. Boulder-sized chunks were lodged half-buried in the icy ground at the end of long trenches they had gouged into the surface. The boulders fanned out from the bomb site in all directions, and it did not escape Jeff’s notice that he and Chapman were extremely lucky not to have been smeared across the surface of Titan by one of those ice boulders.

He thought he had left the oxygen packs at the base of the ice mountain, but all that remained there now was a large crater. Above the crater, the smaller torus hovered vertically, completely free of ice. Icy fingers still reached up from the ground to touch the base of the larger horizontal torus, but Jeff didn't think it would be enough to prevent the smaller one from completing its job.

As he watched, a black film spread across the hole of the smaller torus, completely filling the inside of its hoop. The middle of the black hole distorted, as if it were being pulled into the distance from behind. Still breathing hard, Jeff limped slowly to the other side of the smaller torus. The black hole was indeed stretching to meet the open end of the larger torus, feeding into it like a funnel. Lights like falling stars flowed down the funnel from the smaller torus to the big one.

Slowly, almost imperceptibly, the larger torus grew.

Jeff heard a beep from Chapman's wristpad, relayed over the comm system as a warning to others. He forced himself to look away from the tori and searched the ground for an oxygen pack. The first two he found were damaged beyond use, but the third and final one merely had a torn strap. Jeff pushed the test button on the outside of the pack and got a green light, so he carried it over to Will.

He got both hands under Will's back and flipped him over onto his stomach. Then Jeff disconnected the oxygen feed from Chapman's suit pack, and alarms blared inside his helmet. A moment later, he sealed the connection from the spare pack to Chapman's suit. He pushed Will's arm through the one good strap and secured the broken one to a small fabric loop near his shoulder.

Exhausted, Jeff plopped back to sit on the ice and contemplate his current predicament.

Both missions to Titan had gone belly-up from the start. The remarkable thing to him was that anyone would be crazy enough to go back a second time, yet here they were. While the first mission barely had a chance to bring back anything that could be considered useful data, he and the others now on Titan were smack in the middle of the most incredible event to ever touch humanity. Returning to Earth empty-handed would not only be irresponsible, it would be a tragedy. Yet what could they bring back? Eyewitness accounts and some audio recordings were all they had at the moment. Jeff wasn't convinced anything useful could be derived from those, perhaps other than golden excuses for more defense funding and yet another reason to return.

He found himself confronted by the question of how the mission could benefit anyone other than those who were funding it, and he couldn't think of an answer. Unless the aliens were using a better kind of Velcro that Jeff could smuggle back inside his spacesuit, he didn't see how the astronauts' presence on Titan could be exploited to benefit humanity.

Once more he thought of Kate, and once more he knew beyond any doubt that he should have remained on Earth.

Chapman let out a long groan as he slowly sat up. He noticed his new backpack right away and stared at one of the straps in confusion. He looked over at Jeff, then up at the smaller torus.

"Hey, it worked," he said weakly.

"No, it didn't," said Jeff. "The torus is still in one piece."

Chapman grunted as he lay back down. “Wasn’t trying…to destroy it. Just trying…to break the ice.”

Jeff hadn’t been expecting that. “Why?”

“Orders. Facilitate whatever the aliens were doing here. Help it along, if I could.”

“Why would you do that?”

“You’d have to ask Colonel Brighton. But I would guess he wants to trade technology. Space travel, immortality, the usual.”

“In exchange for what? Teeth whitener? Genetically modified corn?”

“I agree it’s a bit naive, but what are you gonna do? He’s the one in charge.”

“Was there ever a radio in that briefcase?”

“Yes,” said Will.

“How did you turn it into a bomb?”

“They taught me all sorts of neat tricks before I left Earth.”

“Yeah, well, your ‘neat trick’ put the crew in danger.”

Chapman looked over at him. “If you hadn’t chased me, I’m the only one who would’ve been hurt.”

"You destroyed our radio, and possibly our only chance at getting back to the ships."

Will waved a gloved hand up at the sky. "Signal can't penetrate that electrical barrier anyway."

"The situation could change."

"Look around. It's out of our hands, wouldn't you say?"

Jeff saw the crater left behind by the bomb. "I don't know if that's true," he said. "You sure seem to have made a difference."

Will sat up again and took a moment to catch his breath. Then he said, "Don't tell me you're not interested in seeing what they're up to. That's the whole reason we came down here in the first place, isn't it?"

"I'll feel better about asking those kinds of questions once I know we have a guaranteed way out of here."

Jeff suddenly remembered he had switched comm frequencies when he was chasing after Will. He quickly switched back.

"Is everyone okay?" he said. "I found Chapman."

"Found him too late to make a difference, you mean," said Ward.

Will realized Jeff had switched comm channels and followed suit.

"We are okay," said Piper. "And you?"

"Just a little banged up. What about Riley and Brighton?"

"What *about* us?" Riley grumbled.

"We're fine, Jeff," said Commander Brighton.

But Riley wasn't finished yet. "It's not enough to just fall into an ice canyon, we have to survive a bomb going off as soon as we crawl out of it?"

Jeff smiled. "Glad to hear you're both okay."

"You two stay put," said Ward. "We're headed your way."

"Gladly," said Jeff, leaning back to rest on his elbows. His wristpad beeped and flashed yellow. "And if somebody could remember to bring an oxygen pack, I'm almost out."

"You can take Chapman's," said Ward.

Will frowned, then looked up at the sky. Jeff lay back and did the same, breathing as slowly as possible to conserve his air until the others arrived.

46

Kate's eyes popped open and her first thought was, *I'm not dead.*

Her second was, *I can't breathe.*

She rolled onto her side and coughed up a long stream of seawater. She sucked in air and did it again. After she cleared the water from her lungs, she stood up slowly in the cylindrical airlock of the *Nautilus*, her legs quivering like jelly.

A gash on the back of her left hand dripped blood onto the floor grate. Her right knee felt like someone had used it to test a sledgehammer. Slowly, she straddled the hatch by her feet and pried it open.

Kate found the first two grooves in the molded ladder of the passageway leading down, but missed the third and slipped.

She fell into the sub's dark cockpit, landing half on one of the seats with a scream.

The sub rocked from the force of the water current swirling around the drydock room. Kate thought about lying there a while longer until she could regain some of her strength. Then, without making the conscious decision to do so, she raised her shaking arm and found a handhold, then pulled herself up into the seat. Her pants squished wetly on the fabric. She dripped water everywhere.

For one terrifying moment, she forgot how to operate the sub. She stared blankly at the controls, focusing on a glowing yellow warning screen telling her she could not power on the motor until her dive suit was connected to the sub's air system. Kate swiped the screen to acknowledge and bypass the warning, then keyed in the sequence to activate all systems.

Recessed lights flicked on around her, illuminating the red mess her wounded left hand had made on the console. There was a hum from the back of the sub as the motor kicked into idle.

She opened a comm channel to the control room.

"I'm in the Nautilus," she said.

She heard screaming on the other end of the line, and was certain they were all suffering a horrible death as seawater flooded into the facility. Then she picked out Dominic's deep laughter and realized they weren't dying, they were celebrating.

"Thought we lost you, Ms. Bishop," said Noah, his voice heavy with relief.

"You almost did. You still might, if I can't get out of here in one piece."

"How can we help?"

"Ask Tom what he was working on inside the sub earlier."

A moment later, Tom's voice came on the line. "Nothing critical," he said. "Just running maintenance on the starboard impeller. Your lights are out on that side, but everything else is working just fine."

"There's a whirlpool current inside the drydock room," said Kate. "Any suggestions on how I get to the moon pool?"

"If you slip into the stream," said Tom, "you should be able to use your impellers to drift closer to the pool, kinda like spinning down a drain. I'd go easy on the throttle, and let the current do most of the work."

“Copy that.”

She rested her hands on the controls and gently guided the sub down and away from the ceiling. The walls of the sub shuddered briefly as the impellers spun faster to compensate for the current. She let the moving water turn the sub until its nose was moving forward, then eased off the aft propeller. The current was strong enough to push the sub in a wide circle around the moon pool. Her forward lamps illuminated bits of debris floating in the water like drifting snow. She nudged the controls and swirled closer to the center of the room.

Tom’s voice came on the line again. “When you’re right over that sucker, just mash that stick and you should shoot right out the bottom of the facility.”

The controls vibrated under her grip as the current fought to keep her closer to the ceiling of the drydock room. Leaning forward in her seat, she could no longer see the moon pool below her, so she jammed the control stick forward and the sub nosedived.

Rushing water roared around the sub and the walls shook. Kate was slammed sideways in her seat as the *Nautilus* hit the lip of the moon pool on its way past.

The sub shot into open water, and everything went still.

"I made it!" she said, only half-believing it herself.

She sat back in her seat and wiped tears from her cheeks as she listened to the excited hoots and hollers from the control room.

When the noise quieted down, Noah said, "We'll be waiting for you topside."

Kate didn't trust her voice not to shake when she answered, so she simply nodded and reached for the controls. As she was preparing to ascend, she had a different idea. She swung the sub around to face the torus.

It floated in the distance, only a small portion of its exterior dimly illuminated in the murk. Kate was sure the ball of light had gone back inside of it. She couldn't see the smaller torus in the dark water, but it *felt* like something had changed.

Her most pressing question was whether or not the colonel would take the sphere's violent exit as an act of aggression and sink both tori to the bottom of the sea. While she had nearly died when the ball of light burst from the facility, she had never caught a whiff of malicious intent.

But she knew there was another side to that argument. A pet dog could be sweet for years until the day it woke up and decided to attack a neighbor. It would be irresponsible to excuse the dog's behavior, though the behavior was instinctively natural to the dog. If the ball of light had a habit of smashing through walls, and even if that was a function of its normal behavior, a fragile little thing like a human being didn't stand a chance at surviving.

Kate worked the controls, swinging the sub around and guiding it toward the surface.

Noah and Colonel Brighton stood waiting for her on the helicopter landing platform when she popped open the top hatch. The sun made a valiant effort to peek out from the gray clouds overhead, and mostly failed. A light mist blew across the surface of the ocean.

The colonel offered his hand and helped Kate jump to the platform.

"Don't worry," he said. "I'm not going to nuke it yet."

"So you can read minds," she said.

"It certainly helps."

Noah squeezed her shoulders. "Are you okay?"

She held up her injured hand and shrugged. "Could be worse."

He smiled. "That's the spirit." He sighed with relief and shook his head. "I hope you don't regret coming back to work with me."

She looked at him curiously. "Of course not."

"Good. We never would've gotten so far without you." He looked into her eyes a moment longer, a funny face smile on his face, then said, "Colonel, would you mind accompanying Ms. Bishop safely inside so she can get warmed up? I need to see about securing the Nautilus."

"My pleasure," said Brighton, sweeping an inviting arm toward the facility entrance. "I can take a look at that hand as well, Ms. Bishop. I was quite the field medic back in the day."

They walked into the wet room together, and Kate turned to look back. Noah was alone on the platform, still staring at her, that same funny smile touching his lips.

The door closed, and he was gone.

47

Jeff's low oxygen indicator was flashing red by the time the others showed up. Piper gave him a fresh pack. Riley helped him to his feet and slapped his shoulder by way of a greeting, causing him to stumble sideways.

Nobody helped Chapman get up. He did it on his own, slowly, breathing hard through clenched teeth. He held one arm close to his body, cradling it delicately with the other.

Ward approached him quickly. "How's that arm?"

Will tried to back away, but Ward grabbed his elbow and twisted his arm, eliciting a howl of pain.

"Hmph. Not broken, unfortunately," Ward grumbled.

Jeff looked up at the tori.

The smaller torus had extended the larger one by several meters since he regained consciousness after the blast. At that rate, it wouldn't take more than a few hours to finish construction.

The site around them had come alive. Every floating structure moved on its own, some of them bobbing up and down in place, others tumbling in an arc from one point on the ground to another, and then back again. A faint vibration coursed through the ice under their boots.

They had only seen several of the human drones since arriving on Titan, but now more gathered under and above the larger torus. The suited figures hovered over the ice and above the top of the alien artifact, facing inward. Jeff tried to count them, but lost track after fifty.

"How many of them do you think are me?" Riley asked.

"None of them," said Jeff. "There's only one you. Fortunately."

"Har har."

Commander Brighton took a step closer and shielded her eyes as she peered at the suited figures. She moved to take another step, but Jeff put a warning hand on her arm.

"I don't know about the larger one," he said, "but there's some kind of gravity well that surrounds the little tori. It could pull you in."

Brighton took a step back, still squinting up at the nearest drones. Then she looked at her wristpad and pressed her comm button.

"Dex, how's it coming along?"

"Ship's computer is in a slow reboot," he said. "Even if I can get it back online, we're still gonna black out again when we hit that barrier. We'd fall right back down to the surface."

"Do you think we can disable the barrier?" asked Ward.

"Not unless you guys see a big neon sign that says 'this way to barrier generator'."

"I think the structures in the upper atmosphere are maintaining the barrier," said Piper. "They share the same purple lightning."

"If that's the case," said Brighton, "we can forget that option."

"Then we can forget getting off this rock," said Ward.

"Alright, Dex," Brighton added. "You might as well join us."

"We're just gonna sit here?" asked Will.

"Until we find a better plan," said Brighton, "that's exactly what we're going to do."

"We may as well poke around in the meantime," said Will. He took a step toward her and the ground cracked under his feet. He slid his foot back slowly. "Did you guys feel that?" he asked. "Something moved down there."

"Don't just stand there right on top of it," Ward growled.

He grabbed Chapman's arm and pulled him away. At that moment, the ground cracked open and a stream of water ice exploded upward, taking Ward with it. Chapman fell back and rolled away from the geyser. Ward screamed as he tumbled through the air. He hit the ground face first and his helmet split open with a loud crack.

He flipped onto his back and fumbled at the crack in his face shield, trying to cover it with clumsy, gloved hands.

"Don't move!" yelled Commander Brighton, rushing toward him.

She patted several pockets of her suit, but couldn't find what she was looking for.

"Patch kit!" she shouted at the others. "I need a patch kit!"

Ward writhed on the ground, his boots pounding the ice.

"*Carol! Carol!*" he screamed.

"I'm here!" yelled Brighton.

Piper found a patch kit in one of her pockets and quickly handed it to Brighton.

"But it's only for cloth!" she said as Brighton snatched it away.

"We have to try."

Brighton ripped open the pack and removed the adhesive from one of the square strips. As she bent over Ward's helmet and prepared to seal the crack, he reached up and grabbed her wrists. She tried to break his grip, assuming he was panicking so close to death, but he held firm.

Then he chuckled.

Brighton slowly lowered her arms to look into his helmet. Ward sat up, grinning through the crack in his face shield.

"The air is breathable," he said. Despite the damage to his helmet, his comm system still worked. "Doesn't get much closer than that."

Commander Brighton collapsed to the ground next to him, breathing hard. Ward patted her knee and nodded his thanks.

Jeff looked up at the sky, then down at the large torus. "They lowered the atmospheric pressure," he said. "They raised the surface temperature. They changed the composition of the air. It's no wonder the cryovolcano erupted so close to their site."

"Are they terraforming?" asked Riley. "Making this place more like their home?"

"I think they're just passing through," said Jeff.

"How could you possibly know that?" Chapman asked.

Jeff shrugged. "Just a feeling. Titan seems more like a layover than a final destination."

"Then why go through all the trouble to change so much?" Piper asked.

Jeff studied the ring of human drones encircling the large torus. The way they faced the interior of the torus was unusual by itself, as if they were waiting for something to emerge.

"I think that whatever is coming through the big torus when it's complete needs this specific kind of atmosphere," said Jeff. "The same kind we have on Earth."

"Uh, guys?" Dex said over comms. "I have company."

He sounded as if he'd been running. Jeff turned to face the direction of the lander and saw Dex approaching. He jogged on the ice, looking back over his shoulder at the half-dozen human drones following him. They hovered over the ground, keeping pace.

"What did you do to make them angry?" Ward asked.

"Nothing! They were waiting outside the lander when I left."

"Have they made any threatening movements?"

"Well, no…other than chasing me."

"Then don't sweat it." Ward turned away as if the conversation was over.

"Don't sweat it?!" Dex repeated.

Commander Brighton took a step in his direction. "Just bring 'em here, Hollander. Hit the deck when you get close."

"Okay," he huffed.

When he was near the group, he did as she instructed and dove to the ground. The six floating human drones went right past him, heading for the large torus.

Commander Brighton studied their suits as they went past, as if she were looking for something specific. She seemed to have found it, because just as they began to rise farther off the ground to join the ring of human drones surrounding the torus, she ran toward the nearest one and jumped on its back.

They both came down fast and hit the ground hard. The drone made no attempt to throw her off. It simply lay there while she straddled it. Then she grabbed its shoulders and turned it onto its back. Its black face shield stared up at the sky impassively.

She was panting like she had just run a marathon. She pushed her palms down on the drone's chest, flattening out the section of spacesuit displaying its name badge.

"No," she whispered.

Carol slid off the drone like one defeated. She sat on the ice, staring off into the distance with a blank look on her face.

The drone remained on the ground, unmoving. Jeff knelt next to it and looked at its name badge.

The letters were faded and scratched, but he could still read them clearly.

"Dolan, who is it?" Riley asked as he helped Dex to his feet. "What does it say?"

Jeff looked at Carol, who was shaking like she'd just seen a ghost.

"It says Brighton."

48

Kate dried her hair with a towel as she entered the control room. She almost felt like a new person after her hot shower. Almost.

Tom waved at her from his chair. He leaned back precariously, legs propped up on the desk in front of him, staring at Kate over the top of his magazine.

"Close call there, missy," he said gravely. "Glad you're okay."

Dominic walked right up to her and gave her a big bear hug, his wet eyes sparkling above his rosy cheeks.

"I owe you my life," he said.

"I'll settle for a beer."

"Anytime, anywhere."

The colonel nodded at her from the middle of the room. He stood rigidly, his hands clasped behind his back. Several of his staff scurried about, setting up additional workstations.

The viewscreens displayed a collection of camera feeds from around the facility along with a static feed of the two tori in the water. A black funnel extended from the smaller torus, narrowing down to connect with the open end of the larger one.

"Huh," said Kate. "That's new. Is Noah still not back yet?"

"Haven't seen him since you returned with the sub," said Colonel Brighton. He cleared his throat. "Ms. Bishop, I wanted to ask you something."

She finished drying her hair and laid the towel across the back of a nearby chair.

"Sure."

"Do you remember the specific communication frequencies your team used during the first mission?"

"What?" she asked, confused. "Yeah. I mean, yes. I remember. Why?"

The colonel's jaw tightened, as if he didn't want to say anything more. He glanced surreptitiously at his staff, who pretended to be ignoring him.

"Because I want to talk to my daughter," he said.

Kate stepped closer to him. "I'd really like to make that happen," she said. "On the first mission, we had no control over the instantaneous communication. One moment we were on a standard delay, the next moment we could speak to them as if they were right next to us."

The colonel nodded. "And it was only after they were closer to a torus that the instant communication became possible?"

"That's correct."

"I have a theory," he said. "Would you like to hear it?"

She gestured for him to proceed. "By all means."

"Based on your earlier conversation with Jeff Dolan from this very facility, I theorize it is the *ball of light*, and not the torus around it, that allows instant communication between great distances. Yet I don't think you'd be able to talk to anyone, anywhere, without sharing a previous link…perhaps a link over an identical comm channel frequency."

"But I wasn't talking to Jeff over the intercom," said Kate. "We were video chatting directly through the ball of light."

"Which means Dolan himself had to be standing near another ball of light," said Brighton. "I'm working off the hypothesis that if someone on Titan can get on the same frequency on which we're broadcasting, we'll be able to communicate on our own, without talking directly into one of the spheres."

"That's a long shot," said Kate. Then she hesitated and looked closely at Colonel Brighton. "Unless someone on Titan knows to scan those specific frequencies."

The ghost of a smile touched the colonel's lips. "I suppose that would be very clever indeed."

"In that case," said Kate, "we'll start broadcasting as soon as your people are set up."

"What are we going to do about the Nautilus?" Tom asked. "Can't just leave him to get banged up on the surface."

"I think we'll have to," said Kate. "I don't know about anyone else, but I certainly don't have any plans to get back into that thing."

"Someone does," said Dominic. He nodded toward one of the viewscreens.

Kate scanned the mosaic of camera feeds from around the facility. In the lower left corner of one screen, Noah walked across the helicopter platform, wearing a full dive suit, heading for the *Nautilus*.

He had a helmet under one arm and he seemed to be smiling.

Kate tried to raise him on comms, but without his helmet on, he couldn't hear anything.

"Where does he think he's going?" asked Colonel Brighton.

Noah stopped at the edge of the helicopter platform and pulled his helmet down over his head. While he fumbled with the slide lock, Kate tried him again on comms.

"Hi, Kate," he said easily. "Guess I changed my mind about securing the sub."

"I think you had it in your head all along."

"Guilty as charged. I'm just taking it out for a little spin."

"If you're thinking about going near the torus, don't do it, Noah. It's active now. One of them killed Riley and the entire crew of the North Star."

"I haven't forgotten," he said.

He climbed onto the side of the sub and opened the top hatch. "I know you'll take good care of things while I'm gone," he said. "Give my best to Jeffrey when you see him."

Noah dropped down into the sub and shut the hatch behind him. His comm signal went silent.

Everyone in the control room sat in stunned silence as Noah piloted the sub into deeper waters, heading straight for the large torus.

"What happens now?" Tom asked.

No one had an answer.

The back of the *Nautilus* flared brightly as Noah passed the truss of floating halogen lamps and approached the larger of the two tori.

Noah suddenly pulled up, moving above the large torus, heading toward the smaller one. He guided the sub in a wide arc, coming at his target from the side.

"Do you see that?" asked Dominic.

The water in the immediate vicinity of the smaller torus appeared to be vibrating. Horizontal bars of static shot through the grainy video feed.

Just before the *Nautilus* slammed into the side of the torus, a shadow bloomed on the surface of the artifact, and the sub disappeared.

The video feed cleared, and the water was still once again.

"And there he goes," said Tom, spreading his arms out in a grand gesture. "Into the great beyond."

Kate sat down, staring blankly at her desk, her mouth open in disbelief.

"Why would he do that?" she whispered.

Colonel Brighton walked over. He cleared his throat politely. When she didn't acknowledge him, he pulled up a chair and sat beside her.

"Ms. Bishop," said the colonel, "Noah asked me to pass on a message in the event of his abrupt departure. A message just for you." He leaned closer and lowered his voice. "He wanted me to tell you that he's better off out there than he is stuck in some hospital bed."

She looked at Brighton, feeling completely lost.

"Hospital bed?"

"Noah is dying," said the colonel. "He has an inoperable brain tumor, and he doesn't want to spend the rest of his life lying down."

"But why wouldn't he just tell me?"

"He didn't want you to worry," Brighton replied. "And he didn't want you to stop him. He says you could have, if you wanted to."

"I...I wouldn't have tried to stop him," she said, realizing it was true. "Was he in pain?"

Brighton hesitated. "Not when we spoke, no. He was...hopeful."

Kate took a deep breath and let it out slowly. "Thank you, Colonel."

Brighton stood to leave but Kate rested her hand on his arm.

"What did Noah mean when he said I should take care of things until he got back?" she asked.

"Apparently, you signed a truckload of paperwork when you first took this job," the colonel replied.

"That's right."

"And did you ever read it?"

Kate shook her head. "Not line by line."

"Well, Ms. Bishop," said Brighton. "You might want to. Noah left you in control of this team, and he gave you Diamond Aerospace."

49

"That's gotta be a mistake," said Ward.

"It's no mistake," Jeff said. "It says Brighton on the name badge, clear as day."

He knelt next to the human drone Commander Carol Brighton tackled to the ground. The drone hadn't moved an inch.

Jeff unsnapped the catch at the bottom of the drone's black sun visor and slid it up.

The drone was a young man, perhaps in his early twenties, with a buzz cut and void-black eyes that filled his sockets.

Brighton took a shuddering breath and looked away.

"It's my brother," she said softly.

"Was he on the North Star?" Jeff asked.

She nodded.

"North Star?" Piper asked. "What's that?"

"One of the two ships in orbit around Titan during the first mission," said Jeff. "It was owned by a company called MarsCorp. I was on Explorer One with Riley."

"The crew of the North Star had already met a torus by the time we got there," Riley added. "They didn't survive."

"One of them made it back," said Brighton. "Carlo Moretti. But none of the others." She tried to look at the drone lying on the ground, but her face twisted with sadness and she turned away. "And not my brother." She stood up suddenly, fists clenched, and screamed at the smaller torus, "*Why didn't you send him back?! Why not him?!*"

The torus remained silent before her.

She fell on her knees, staring at the alien object. Tears streamed down her cheeks, but her jaw was set in defiance and her eyes brimmed with rage. Ward walked over to stand beside her and put his hand on her shoulder. To his credit, he said nothing.

Jeff and the other astronauts stepped back as five drones broke from the ring of suited figures above the large torus and drifted in their direction.

The drones descended upon their fallen comrade. They picked him up and positioned him vertically in the air, as if reattaching him to some invisible support apparatus. Then the six of them floated back to the torus.

"He was out of place," said Dex. "He was out of place and they fixed him!"

He looked around quickly, then set off in the opposite direction.

"We need to stick together!" Ward shouted.

"Be right back, Commander!" Dex replied excitedly.

He jogged to one of the nearby free-floating structures: a car-sized pyramid of matte-black cubes. The pyramid tumbled slowly in midair a meter off the frozen ground. Dex reached up and tapped it experimentally, and the direction of spin changed slightly. Growing bolder, Dex grabbed one corner of the pyramid and shoved. It floated away from him, slowly losing altitude until it bounced off the ice and began to drift up toward the sky.

No less than twenty of the drones hovering above and below the large torus broke away from their group to pursue the errant structure. Within a minute they had retrieved the pyramid of cubes and placed it back where Dex found it, spinning the same speed and in the same direction.

"Sticklers for detail," Riley observed.

"Perhaps that is their function," said Piper. "Like an automated program that finds and eliminates bugs in a computer system."

Ward frowned up at the large torus. "That thing's going to be finished in a couple of hours, and we still have no idea how we're getting off this moon."

"I've been thinking about that," said Piper. She turned to Dex. "You said even if we take off, we will fall right back down after we hit the barrier."

"That's right."

"What if we flew to the edge of the barrier, close to the ground? We could land and turn off the systems, then reactivate them on the other side."

"How do we get the ship through the barrier?" asked Will.

"We push it," said Piper. "It has sleds, after all."

"I like this plan," said Riley, looking at the others for confirmation. "The barrier is a dome, right? It's gotta end somewhere."

"We have no idea *where* it ends," said Ward.

Commander Brighton got to her feet and finally broke the murderous stare with which she had fixed the smaller torus.

"Ward is right," she said.

Riley threw up his hands hopelessly. "Doing *any*thing beats sitting around here."

"And you're right, too, Riley," she added. "What do you think, Hollander?"

"Well," Dex said, "there's still the problem of making the lander actually, you know, *fly*. I was getting close, but I can't know for sure unless I spend more time with the system."

"We all won't fit in the lander," said Jeff, finally voicing his earlier concern.

"It's officially rated for five, but unofficially, it will take all of us," said Dex.

"Not if you hope to see orbit, Junior," said Riley with grim acceptance. "You might skim the moon's surface for a while, but you won't get higher than that." His eyes met Jeff's, and Jeff nodded. "Dolan and I will find another way home."

"And how *exactly* do you plan on doing that?" Ward asked.

Jeff shrugged, trying to appear nonchalant.

"We've done it before."

"The five of you get to the lander," Riley said. "We can handle ourselves."

Dex stepped forward. "There's no need for this! The lander will take all of us."

"I don't like it either," said Jeff. "Believe me, I wish there was another way. I really do. But either Riley and I stay behind, or none of us get back home."

"Then leave Chapman," said Piper.

"Hey!" Will shouted.

"I won't allow *anyone* to remain behind," said Commander Brighton. She jabbed a finger in Jeff's direction. "Not anyone. Ward and I will carry you to the lander if we have to."

"I say let them stay," said Ward. "If they're so stuck on the idea, then yeah, let 'em stay."

Brighton glared at him. "That is not an option, Commander."

Ward shrugged. "Solves two problems."

Jeff turned to Riley. "Now you know what it's like having a jerk for a commander."

Riley grinned but Ward raised a warning finger. "Now listen here, you smug little—"

"Carol," said a disembodied male voice over the

comm system.

"Who said that?!" asked Riley, looking around for the source.

"This is Colonel Brighton."

"Dad?" said Carol in disbelief. "Where...where are you?"

"Still on Earth. Still sorry I couldn't be with you."

"How is this possible?"

"That would be my doing," another voice chimed in. Jeff smiled when he realized it was Elizabeth. "Got a ping from your dad on an old comm frequency. Took me a hot minute to realize there was no delay. I'm actually talking to you through a relay on Earth, and I'm right over your heads. Blows the mind, doesn't it?"

"But if you're talking to Earth instantaneously," said Jeff, "that would mean—"

"That's right," said Elizabeth. "There's a torus up here with me. Showed up right after I lost contact with the lander. Hasn't done anything other than stare at me. There's one over by the Catalyst as well."

"Commander Ward, what's your status?" asked the colonel.

"Seven survivors on the surface, sir," said Ward.

"Two casualties from the Catalyst."

"I'm sorry to hear that."

"Actually, sir, it's a miracle we're not all dead."

"Colonel Brighton," said Jeff. "Any change in the Earth torus?"

"It's active," the colonel replied.

"I believe you have your man Will to thank for that. He turned our radio into a bomb and almost blew up the torus here to free it from a block of ice."

"Did he hurt anyone?" the colonel asked.

"Only himself."

"Then he did what he was supposed to. I'm sorry I couldn't have been more transparent about his orders, but that was out of necessity."

Will stood cradling his right arm. He still wore the spare oxygen pack Jeff gave him after the blast. Jeff had expected to see a look of victory on the pencil-pusher's face, but instead, Will looked at him with uncertainty.

"How long until the Earth torus is complete?" Jeff asked.

"Our best guess has the smaller one finishing the larger one in just under two hours."

"Any theories on what happens after that?"

"I was hoping you could tell me."

"Either something big or nothing at all," said Riley impatiently.

Jeff smiled. "What he means, Colonel, is that our guess is as good as yours."

"Surely you can do better than that, Jeffrey," said Kate.

He took an involuntary step back, as if someone had just punched him in the chest.

His mouth hung open for a long moment, his words stuck in his throat, until he finally managed to say, "I never expected to hear your voice again."

"I'm sorry I couldn't call sooner."

"I hate to interrupt," said the colonel, "but I really need to talk to my daughter before we lose the signal."

"I'm here," said Carol.

The colonel hesitated, then asked, "Did you find your brother?"

Carol turned around to look at the human drones surrounding the large torus.

"Yes, I found him."

"And?"

"And he's gone, Dad. He's gone."

50

Colonel Brighton plopped down into a chair like he'd been shot. He slowly lifted a shaking hand and covered his mouth.

The few members of his staff that he brought with him from his ship silently left the room. Tom and Dominic remained with Kate, watching the colonel.

"Thank you, Carol," he said quietly. "Be safe down there. We'll talk again soon."

He leaned forward and cut the comm signal as Carol was saying, "But Dad—"

"I'm sorry," said Kate. It was the only thing she could think to say.

The colonel was silent for a long time. Kate and the others looked at each other uncomfortably, not sure if it would be inappropriate to continue their work.

Finally, Brighton spoke.

"For a parent to not know what happened to their child...for a child to simply vanish...it's worse than knowing they were dead." He closed his eyes. "I was angry at first," he said. "So, so angry. And why wouldn't I be? The tori sent back Dolan and Riley from Explorer One. They sent back Carlo Moretti, who was on my son's own crew. So why not my son? Was my boy not special?" The colonel bit his lower lip and shook his head to fight off tears. After a moment, he took a deep breath and continued. "Were the others chosen for a purpose? Or was it random? Oh yes, I was angry. If I had found out about the torus on Earth six months earlier, I would not have hesitated to destroy it. But then I learned they were sending people *back*...people who were lost on the first mission."

Kate shivered and folded her arms over her chest. She vividly remembered finding Jeff washed up on the beach in Florida, rocking unconscious in the surf.

"As I searched for my son on Earth," said the colonel, "and as I learned more about the first mission and what Jeff Dolan saw on Titan, I began to realize it was bigger than my grief. Whatever is happening out there, my son is part of it now. He *must* be. Otherwise he will have died for nothing." He opened his eyes and looked at Kate. "I'm not going to stop it unless I have no other choice. That's a promise." He stood up straight and smoothed down the front of his uniform jacket. "If you'll excuse me, I need to rest. Please wake me if anything changes."

"We will," said Kate.

After he left the room, Tom said, "Man, that was heavy."

"A lot of that going around," Kate muttered. She looked up at the viewscreens. "Any sign of Noah?"

"Nada," Tom said. "No video or audio."

Kate sighed and rubbed the heels of her hands into her eyes.

"You should get some rest, too," said Dominic.

Kate smiled tiredly. "I wouldn't be able to sleep."

"In that case," he said, picking up a stack of printed photographs, "take a look at these."

She walked over to his desk while he laid the pictures on top of his clutter. They were images of different animals: elephant, goat, field mouse, and on and on.

"This is what the ball of light showed us?" she asked.

"Just before it turned into a meteor and ripped a hole in our wall. Notice anything?"

She picked up the goat picture and studied it. The animal looked like it had just eaten a big meal, but beyond that she couldn't draw a connection to the other images. Then Dominic set the last picture on top of the others. It was a blurry photo of a woman walking in the park on a sunny day.

"She's pregnant," said Kate.

"So are all the animals," Dominic told her. "Every single one."

She set down the picture of the goat. "Is that all you have?"

Dominic looked hurt. "For now."

She rested her hand on his shoulder.

"I'm really sorry, Dom. I didn't mean it that way. I'm getting upset at every little detail I don't catch."

He patted her hand. "It's okay, I get it."

Kate went back to her workstation and sat down heavily. Half-buried under stacks of facility printouts was the thick binder of documents she signed when she agreed to work with Noah Bell for the second time. She rescued it from the bottom of the pile and flipped it open.

The first few pages were boilerplate non-disclosure agreements to which she had hastily added her signature. On the back of the last one was a sticky note that she hadn't noticed before. In tight cursive, it read: *Make it last. Noah*.

Kate shut the binder and leaned back in her seat. If what Colonel Brighton had told her was true, she now owned what had once been the world's most famous, or infamous, private space company. She felt as if someone just handed her the keys to an aircraft carrier and said, "Good luck".

Tom had been drumming his fingers on his workstation when he abruptly stopped. He pointed at the image of the large torus on the wall screen.

"So what happens when that thing's completed?" he asked.

"I imagine we'll find out," said Kate.

"Yeah, that's what got me thinking. Given the inherent unpredictability of our current situation, I was wondering if maybe we shouldn't hightail it to one of the colonel's fortified military vessels."

"You think we could be in danger?"

"I just think the ships have *engines*, you know, in case we needed to skedaddle in a hurry. The most we could do *here* is run to the other side of the room."

"Or swim," said Dominic.

"That, too."

"There wouldn't be any hard feelings if you wanted to leave the facility," said Kate. "You don't have to stay if you feel unsafe."

Tom looked between Kate and Dominic hesitantly. "Y'all wouldn't miss me?"

Kate smiled. "That goes without saying."

"I'm not going anywhere," said Dominic.

Tom sighed in defeat and crossed his arms. "Well now I can't have guilt on top of everything else. They were *right*, man. Peer pressure is the real deal. Looks like I'm sticking around, too."

"In that case," said Kate, "I'm going to leave things in your capable hands and take Dominic's advice to rest. But if I'm not back here before the big torus is complete, I want somebody to come get me. Or if anything else happens, for that matter."

The viewscreens flashed red and an alarm blared from the ceiling speakers.

"Does this count?" Tom shouted over the noise.

"What's happening?!" yelled Kate.

Dominic swiped papers off his workstation keyboard and started typing.

"It's the smaller torus," he said.

The grainy video feed of the alien artifact filled the center viewscreen. The water around it churned as if it were being heated to the point of boiling.

The floor shifted under Kate's feet, and she stumbled sideways, grabbing her bolted-down workstation for support.

A second alarm sounded, higher-pitched than the first.

"The facility is moving!" Dominic shouted.

"What do you *mean* it's moving?!"

The walls rattled and the floor shook. Monitors slid off workstations and crashed to the floor.

"The little one's sucking in water!" said Tom.

Kate stared at the viewscreen in horror, realizing what that meant.

"It's pulling us in," she whispered.

Metal groaned from somewhere outside the control room.

"It's twisting us like a corkscrew!" said Dominic. "We can't stop it!"

"Everybody topside!" yelled Kate.

Colonel Brighton stumbled into the room, pulling on his jacket. "What in God's name is going on?!" he barked.

Just then the vibration stopped and the room fell silent. On the viewscreen, the water around the smaller torus calmed. The only evidence that it had just been a roiling mass was a single stream of bubbles rising quickly to the surface.

"The big torus isn't complete yet," said Kate, "so what was that about?"

"I don't know," Dominic replied, "but if the smaller one did that, imagine what the bigger one can do."

51

"But Dad, wait!" said Commander Brighton.

The line went dead.

Ward tapped on his wristpad. "He terminated the signal."

"That's kinda rude, isn't it?" Riley offered.

"We go back to the lander," said Brighton. "All of us. We try Piper's plan: land right next to the barrier, shut down our systems, and push the ship through."

"What if the barrier kills us?" Dex asked. "We were shielded inside the lander last time."

"Once we get it moving, it should only take one or two people to push it across the ice. If I'm not mistaken," she said, turning toward Jeff and Riley, "we already have a couple of volunteers."

Riley shrugged. "Worth a shot."

Commander Brighton walked away, heading back in the direction of the lander. The rest of them formed a single-file line behind her.

The ground rumbled and a square meter of ice to their left exploded upward, tumbling through the air at the head of a geyser. Chapman yelped in surprise as two more geysers erupted to their right.

"We need to hurry," said Ward. "This place is changing fast."

Brighton picked up her pace, moving at a light jog.

There was a deafening boom from behind. They turned back to look and the icy ground suddenly dropped away beneath their feet. With a crack, it snapped back into place, slamming against them as they fell.

The blastwave hit them, pushing them across the ice. The force of the blast spun Jeff around as he slid.

In the distance, beyond the construction site, a wide column of blue-white ejecta shot up from the cryovolcano, almost as wide as the base of the volcano itself. Half the mountain had been completely torn away, leaving behind a jagged husk that spewed water ice into the atmosphere.

The ground vibrated under Jeff's gloves as he pushed himself to his feet. There was another loud crack from somewhere nearby as a geyser erupted from the ice.

"Run!" Brighton screamed.

Gray water poured out of the center of the smaller torus like a dam had burst. It splashed down onto the icy surface and froze on contact.

The large torus began to spin.

The smaller torus had completed its job. It spun in tandem with the larger one, giving the impression of two gears powering a large machine.

"We had two hours!" Riley shouted, standing next to Jeff.

"We don't anymore."

Jeff noticed Riley was carrying six spare oxygen packs slung over his shoulder. Jeff took three of them to Riley's relief, then they set off after the others.

They caught up with them shortly after, standing at the base of a crooked hill of ice directly blocking their path. A deep chasm surrounded the hill like a wide moat.

"The entire landscape is changing," said Piper loudly. "This wasn't here earlier."

"Let's go around," said Chapman.

"No time!" Ward shouted. "Up and over. Let's go!"

He jumped the chasm at its narrowest point and started up the ice hill, searching for a safe path. The others climbed up behind him, using the same jagged handholds. They made it up to a narrow ledge which extended to the far side of the hill and back down to solid ground.

Ward pressed his stomach against the wall of ice and scooted carefully along the ledge. His boots sent small shards of ice tumbling down the vertical cliff behind him, into the deep chasm.

Brighton climbed out onto the ledge, hugging the wall. After she had taken only a few steps, there was a loud crack from above.

A large chunk of ice fell toward the ledge.

Ward looked up just as the ice hit his broken face shield. He fell off the ledge with the chunk of ice embedded in his helmet, disappearing into the chasm below.

"No!" Brighton screamed. She looked down after him, breathing hard, then stood up straight and pounded the wall of ice with a closed fist. Turning back to the others, she shouted, "Keep moving!"

Piper went first, stepping hesitantly onto the ledge. She scooted along quickly, without looking up. Dex followed after her, then Chapman.

Riley gestured for Jeff to go first.

Jeff hugged the wall as he walked the ledge, keeping his eyes focused on the backs of the others and trying to forget that Ward had just fallen into the deep chasm below.

The six of them made it to the far side of the ice hill. Commander Brighton referenced her wristpad and adjusted their heading.

They trudged across the frozen tundra in silence. Flurries of snow pushed across the white surface.

"Can you hear me?" Kate said. Over the static-laced comm system, her voice sounded far away.

"We hear you," said Jeff.

"Things are happening quickly here. The big torus is complete, and the smaller one broke apart. The big one is spinning."

"Same here," Jeff said.

"There's something else," Kate added. "Another big torus came down from the sky."

Jeff turned around.

Sure enough, a second large torus had emerged from Titan's atmosphere, passing the dome-shaped barrier and steadily descending toward the first.

A third one emerged from the orange, hazy sky.

Then another.

They descended in a vertical line, like ring supports for an invisible tunnel.

Tunnel, thought Jeff. *A tunnel to Earth.*

"Are you there?" Kate asked.

"We're heading for the lander," said Jeff, turning back around to jog after the others. "Have to make it into orbit before this whole place is destroyed. How many big ones are there?"

"Just two, so far, including the one in the water."

The ground shook violently and Jeff stumbled to the side. Farther ahead, past the others, he could see the dim outline of the lander on the ice. He could also see that it was surrounded by humanoid figures hovering just above the ground.

Jeff ran past several floating structures. The edges of the structures seemed to pulse with a dark energy as they tumbled in place.

"We have company," said Riley. "Ten of them."

"More than that," Piper said. "Look up."

High above the lander, floating in the air, were dozens of the human drones.

"They don't want us to leave," said Chapman.

"No," said Piper. "They don't want us to interfere."

"Either way," said Riley, "they're blocking the hatch."

Jeff caught up with the group, breathing hard.

The human drones closest to the lander had formed a barricade, hovering in a ring around the vessel. They faced inward, as they had when they stood vigil over the large torus.

Jeff looked back at the floating structures he had just run past.

"I have an idea," he said. "Dex, can you get the engines going?"

"If the system has rebooted, then yes. But that's a big 'if'."

Jeff turned to Brighton. "Commander, as soon as the drones leave the lander, fire it up."

He started walking toward the nearest floating structure, but someone grabbed his arm and turned him back around. Riley held him there with an iron grip.

"This one's on me," he said.

Jeff tried to pull free from his grasp, but Riley wouldn't let go.

"I'll do it," said Jeff. "You get on the lander with the others."

"What are you two talking about?" Dex asked.

"No, Dolan," Riley said. "You have a good reason to get back to Earth. The best of reasons. All I have is an ex-wife who was happy I never came home." He squeezed Jeff's arm even harder. His eyes were fiercely adamant. "Let me do this."

"What if you don't make it back?" Jeff asked.

Riley grinned. "Haven't you heard? I'm already dead."

He let go of Jeff's arm and jogged away.

"Where is he going?" Piper asked.

"To give us a chance."

Riley ran up to the nearest floating structure and threw his body against it, smacking against the black surface with his shoulder and sending it tumbling away.

Several of the human drones surrounding the lander broke from their formation and floated in that direction.

Riley wasn't waiting around for them to arrive.

He ran across the ice to another structure and kicked it out of place.

"You don't like that, do you?!" he yelled, taunting the drones. "You want me to stop? Come and stop me!"

The snow flurries had intensified over the past few minutes. As Riley ran farther away from the lander, he soon became lost in the mist. His comm signal crackled and went off-line.

More of the human drones near the lander floated after him, two at a time here, ten at a time there, until only one remained, hovering directly in front of the hatch.

Jeff walked over to it and spun it around to face him.

Its name badge read DOLAN.

Jeff took a step back, too shocked to think straight. The drone floated away from him until it bumped against the hatch, where it remained.

"Oh, man," said Dex when he read the name. "I wonder what Freud would think of this."

Jeff stared at the drone. "Freud wouldn't think anything. He's dead."

He stepped forward and grabbed the drone by its shoulders, then yanked it away from the hatch and gave it a hard shove.

"Everybody inside!" he said.

The drone coasted several meters away, then stopped in midair and drifted back toward the lander. Jeff intercepted it and shoved it away again.

Behind him, Commander Brighton got the hatch open and the others went into the lander. Dex whooped with joy from the cockpit.

"Back online!" he shouted. "We're in business."

As Jeff struggled to push the drone away from the lander yet again, something in his periphery caught his attention.

The other drones were coming back, floating quickly toward the lander.

Will bolted out of the hatch and ran toward the approaching swarm.

"Chapman, get back in there!" Jeff yelled.

Will ignored him and ran at the drones.

"We are *leaving!*" Brighton roared from inside.

Jeff gave the drone he was struggling with one last, hard shove, then sealed the hatch from the outside. He slapped the lock control on the hull and jogged away from the lander.

"Dolan, you open that hatch," growled Commander Brighton.

"They'd bring you down if I don't distract them," he said. "You get through that barrier."

Brighton cursed him passionately.

"I'm sorry," he said. "I don't see any other way."

He ran after Will, in the direction of the large torus, searching for more structures to displace. If he could keep the drones occupied long enough, the lander might have a chance of making it to the barrier, and then back to *Explorer II*.

"Will!" he shouted.

Chapman looked back. Ahead of him, the drones were rapidly approaching.

"We have to distract them."

Jeff pointed at one of the nearby floating objects. Will looked in that direction, then gave Jeff a thumbs-up and started running.

Jeff shifted course and headed toward a black, refrigerator-sized ovoid floating inches off the ground.

A plan formulated in his mind as he ran. He knew it was a long shot, but, given his current situation, a long shot was better than nothing at all.

52

"Elizabeth, did you catch all that?" Kate asked.

"I got it," she said over the research facility's comm system. "I'll be ready for them, as long as my visitor doesn't have other plans."

Kate knew she was referring to the torus that had kept her company since her team went down to the surface of Titan.

The facility groaned around her. Kate looked up at the viewscreens. Most of the feeds showed only static. Only a few cameras on the truss encircling the larger torus were still operational. The artifact spun in place like a giant wheel.

Tom hurried into the room. "Colonel says wheels-up in five. Last ride to safety."

Kate nodded. She picked up the binder of paperwork Noah had given her and held it to her chest, feeling like a lost child in a crowded marketplace.

"I'll be right there," she said.

Tom ran out, leaving the door open behind him.

Kate sat in her chair, still clutching the binder. Then she picked up a microphone and hooked it over her ear.

"Jeff, can you hear me?" she asked.

All she heard was static. She was reaching up to remove the microphone when his voice came through, loud and clear.

"I hear you even when you're not talking," he said, out of breath.

"We're evacuating to one of the colonel's ships," she told him. "I don't know if we'll be able to communicate."

There was a pause, then he said, "I understand."

She clutched the binder tightly. "Why didn't you get on that lander?"

"I wanted to. More than anything. Hey, you know what? I realized something right when I got here."

"What's that?"

"All of my answers are back there, with you."

The line hummed with static, and she thought she lost him.

"Jeff?"

"I'm sorry I drifted away," he said. "Give me another chance?"

She smiled and wiped away a tear that spilled onto her cheek. "You come on back, and we'll see."

"Careful, though. If I get back in one piece, I'm never leaving."

"Promise?"

"There might be—way to—nly I—"

"Jeff?" Kate said loudly, leaning forward to adjust the signal.

The line went dead.

Dominic hurried past the open door to the control room, struggling with a pile of his notes. A second later he ran back into the room.

"What are you still doing here?!" he asked, exasperated. "The last helicopter is leaving right now. We gotta go!"

Kate stood up slowly, taking one last look around the control room. Then she followed after Dominic, heading topside to the helicopter platform.

The colonel stood on the deck, staring out at the giant, bowl-shaped indent on the surface of the ocean. Floating nearly a thousand feet above it was another large torus, identical to the one beneath the water. In the distance beyond it, the colonel's ships waited.

Kate ducked and followed Dominic beneath the helicopter's spinning rotor blades. She squinted against the blasting wind as she climbed up into the cabin and sat next to Tom. He was already buckled in. He smiled at her, but looked terrified.

The colonel hoisted himself into the cabin and sat across from Kate, next to Dominic. His jaw was set, determined, and Kate thought he didn't look afraid at all. He looked ready.

Tom pointed out at the water and said something, but Kate couldn't hear him over the noise of the rotor.

She bent forward to look out the window.

The torus above the water projected a force of air downward, blasting the surface of the ocean. The edges of the wide concave bowl on the surface were being pushed outward, creating large waves, but the bowl itself remained glassy and calm.

The air above the bowl distorted. Kate had the distinct impression a massive pressure bubble was about to pop.

She leaned toward the colonel to voice her concerns when it did just that.

Wind blasted in all directions from beneath the large torus, smacking into the research facility like a blastwave. The landing platform cracked in half and the helicopter listed violently. Its spinning rotor blades sliced into the surface of the platform and snapped off. Kate grabbed for a handhold as the craft slid down and crashed nose-first into another chunk of broken platform.

Metal squealed as the helicopter came to a rest.

Kate and the others hesitantly climbed out of the wrecked craft, scrambling up the broken platform. Several of the floating decks atop the research facility had been ripped off. They drifted away, into the churning sea.

Kate and the others gathered on the widest of the remaining platforms to look at the ocean.

The concave bowl on the surface had dropped deeper into the water until it nearly touched the torus beneath it. The large torus was barely visible under the surface, turning in place. The torus in the air far above spun in the opposite direction, shedding water from its hull.

"Where's that water coming from?" Tom asked.

"From wherever the upper torus is linked to," said Dominic. "Presumably, from the one in the water right below it."

Behind Kate, one of the colonel's staff spoke loudly into his radio as he called for another helicopter.

"There's nowhere to land, man!" Tom shouted.

"We'll have to use the gurney," said Colonel Brighton.

"What do we do until then?" Dominic asked.

The colonel looked out to sea. "Try to enjoy the show."

PART III

53

Before Jeff's eyes, the landscape of Titan changed.

Clouds appeared in the lower atmosphere, glowing orange as they burned with inner fire.

The once-smooth expanse of ground that had stretched in all directions was cracked into a chaotic network of razor-sharp spears, thrusting up as if hammered through the ice from below.

Jeff and Will ran as fast as their bulky suits would allow, heading for the larger torus. They jumped over deep cracks and dodged geysers erupting in their path. Chunks of ice the size of basketballs fell from the sky, exploding on the surface and pelting their suits with frozen shards.

Jeff risked a quick glance behind him and saw a squadron of human drones still in pursuit. His boot hit a protruding slab of ice and he fell forward, barely getting his hands in front of him as he smacked against the uneven ground.

Will helped him to his feet and they kept running.

So far, the drones had shown no aggression, but that didn't mean Jeff wanted to hang around and wait for them to catch up. He and Will had pushed more than a few floating structures out of place, and he figured it would only take so long before the drones stopped treating the symptoms of the disturbance and went straight for the cause.

In the sky above, fiery clouds swirled around the highest torus. It hovered just below the artificial barrier. Purple lightning crackled between the outer edge of the torus and the surrounding clouds. As Jeff watched, a black film spread across the opening of the torus, like ink spilled on a glass table, covering it completely.

A thick haze crept in and settled over the surface of Titan. It glowed a dull orange like the atmosphere above the barrier.

A geyser erupted to Jeff's left. He glanced at it with wide eyes as he ran past. The plume of water ice shot high into the air, sparkling in the hazy light.

Four large tori loomed in the sky, aligned on top of each other a mile apart to create a passage from the barrier down to the surface.

The black film that spread across the opening of the highest torus bulged in the middle, distending downward as if something were trying to break through from above.

"Do you see that?" Will asked, looking up.

"I see it."

Lightning crackled across the sky, bathing the landscape a brilliant purple. As Jeff's vision adjusted after the flash, he saw something emerging from the highest torus.

The pointed end of what looked like a gigantic meteor slowly broke through the bulging, black film. Purple lightning arced inward from the edges of the torus to probe the exterior of the meteor like searching fingers.

As more of it descended from the void, Jeff could just barely make out large pits in the surface, almost as if a web of rock-like material were wrapped around a glowing red core.

At last it completely emerged, floating slowly down from the highest torus. To Jeff it looked like an asymmetrical wedge of rock, one side mostly flat, one side curving outward in an arc that met two pointed ends at the top and bottom.

Jeff had to look down as he scrambled over a narrow crevice in the surface. The depths of the crevice glowed red far below.

His suit beeped a low oxygen warning at him. He ignored it as he ran, patting his shoulder to make sure the three oxygen packs he had taken from Riley were still there.

"How's your air?" he asked.

Will consulted his wristpad. "Fifty percent."

The lowest torus loomed above, blurry in the fresh haze that had settled over the landscape.

One of the nearby half-buried black structures broke free of the ice and drifted upward. As Jeff watched, more of them floated into the haze, rising toward the alien object.

With a quick glance behind him, he realized the drones were no longer in pursuit. They rose into the sky, heading for the highest torus.

Black film stretched across the opening of the second torus in line as it prepared for the arrival of the meteor-like object.

As it descended, Jeff began to grasp its size. The larger tori were more than ninety meters in diameter, and the emerging object barely fit through the center hole. The human drones and the smaller floating structures were tiny specks in its shadow.

The drones and structures swarmed around the object as it descended, forming a dense, swirling cloud. Purple lightning erupted from the shell of the alien object and hit the swarm. A moment later, the lightning shot back and crawled over the pitted surface like snakes.

The drones and the smaller structures fell from the sky and disappeared into the black maw of the torus below.

Jeff and Chapman were now almost directly beneath the torus closest to the surface. Jeff looked around frantically while the ground shook beneath them, threatening to crack open and swallow them at any moment.

Then he saw it.

A shelf of ice had thrust upward from the ground, creating a steep ramp that almost connected with the exterior of the nearest large torus.

"That's your plan?!" Will shouted, noticing the ramp of ice.

The ground rose beneath them, throwing Jeff forward to crash against a wall of ice. He rolled quickly to the side as the ground he was just standing on cracked against the wall he had just hit.

Will stood with his back to the ice, his eyes wide with terror. Jeff grabbed his shoulder and they ran for the ramp. Above them, the torus spun faster, emitting a high-pitched whine and producing a steady downward current of air.

They leaned into the wind and crawled up the ramp on all fours. The edge of the torus was a blur in front of them. Jeff braced his boots against the ice and motioned for Will to do the same.

"Ready?" he asked.

Will shook his head, no.

Jeff shot forward with a burst of speed and leapt over the edge of the ramp. He wasn't able to look back to see if Will had followed him.

A fragmented shadow appeared on the blurry surface of the torus. For a moment, Jeff thought he was going to fall back down to the ground and impale himself on one of the jagged spears of ice.

Then the shadow violently pulled him closer to the torus and swallowed him into darkness.

54

Crushing pressure ripped Jeff's breath away as he fell through a universe without stars.

There was a flash of light and he slammed to the floor. His forehead cracked against the inside of his face shield.

Wincing in pain, he slowly got to his feet, fighting against an exponential increase in gravity.

Chapman screamed from above and crashed into Jeff, sending him back down to the floor.

Jeff stood once again, struggling to catch his breath.

"You're...a real...pain...Mr. Chapman."

Will groaned and rolled over onto his stomach. He pushed himself to his hands and knees and remained there, panting.

"Hard to breathe," he said in a rush.

Jeff grabbed him under the armpits and hoisted him up.

They were in a long, curved hallway that stretched away in both directions. Soft blooms of blue-green light danced languidly beneath the hard, semi-translucent green floor. Jeff took a step and the floor glowed brightly under his boot where it made contact.

Jeff frowned, trying to connect two distant dots in his mind. This arched hallway was roughly four meters wide and three tall, just like the hallway in the torus he had entered in orbit around Titan during the first mission. Yet *that* torus was a third the size of the one he had just been pulled into.

A hollow track, like a small tunnel, ran along the peak of the hallway, curving away into the distance parallel to the floor. On the first mission, a sphere of light traversed that tunnel, stopping to parrot snippets of the crew's recorded conversations. Jeff waited, but no sphere of light arrived this time.

He and Chapman trudged down the hallway like a couple of zombies, feeling as if they were walking through waist-high mud.

Jeff's suit beeped another warning at him. Though he wanted to keep moving, he forced himself to stop. He shrugged off the spent oxygen pack and detached its tube. Alarms blared inside his helmet as he attached the tube to a fresh pack and slung it over his shoulders. There was a hiss of air from somewhere inside his suit and the alarms flicked off. He checked his wristpad: two hours of oxygen remaining.

If anyone were to ask him what he planned to do next, Jeff doubted he could've given a straight answer. His initial plan hadn't extended beyond getting off the surface of Titan before it melted away beneath his feet.

"You've been here before," said Will.

"Or somewhere like it," Jeff replied. "Will, why'd you leave the lander?"

Chapman shrugged helplessly. "I really can't say. It's all a blur when I think back on it. All I remember is thinking that the lander would crash if I didn't help you and Riley with the drones."

Jeff grunted. "Be sure to mention that in your report."

After several minutes of walking, a room opened up on the interior of the hallway. They stood at its entrance, looking within.

The room was a large cube, its walls pitted by shallow bowls. A dim network of lights, like optical cables, threaded the walls, connecting the bowls. Within each bowl was a different material. One contained a puddle of swirling blue jelly. In another, a pile of yellow spheres stacked themselves into a pyramid, flattened out, then melted together and formed a larger sphere.

Jeff's crewmate on *Explorer I*, Gabriel, had described this room as a specimen lab.

He motioned for Chapman to wait, then he walked inside, waited a moment, and stepped back out again. As soon as he left the space, the walls changed. The bowl cutouts were in the same place, as were the snaking lights that connected them to each other...but the materials were different. The bowl that had contained the viscous jelly now held a fibrous orange vine. The bowl with the little yellow spheres was now filled with a purple cloud of dust which swirled gently at the base of the bowl.

Jeff repeated the process of stepping into the room and back out. The materials changed again.

"Fold space," he said out loud, recalling Gabriel's term for it.

"What's that?" asked Will.

"We encountered it during the first mission. I didn't know anything about it then, but my crewmate did."

"What is it?"

Jeff sighed as he tried to think of a way to explain it.

"There's an empty room," he said. "You put an apple on the floor. You leave and come back, the apple is gone. Leave and return, it's back. You're switching between two rooms that share the same fold space. They exist on top of each other."

"Like an alternate dimension?" asked Will. "How do you switch between them?"

"Beats me. Seems random, but that wouldn't make sense if you stacked a thousand rooms and needed something specific from one of them."

He looked down the hallway as a dim light glowed from around the corner. It brightened and shot past overhead in a streak. They instinctively ducked from it, but it was gone faster than they could react.

The light dulled around the curve of the hallway, then reappeared at the other end behind them. It stopped directly overhead and resolved itself into a glowing sphere of light, spinning quickly within the narrow track at the peak of the hallway.

Multicolored light rippled over their spacesuits like moonlight reflections on water.

"Is this normal?" Will asked.

A sharp pain stabbed Jeff in the back of the skull and he collapsed to his knees, screaming. The high-pitched noise threatened to burst his eardrums. Will ran to his side and was yelling something at him, but Jeff couldn't hear.

Then there was silence, and the pain was gone.

Will had vanished.

"Chapman?" Jeff called as he stood slowly.

The hallway looked the same, but there was an opening in the outer wall that hadn't been there before. It led to a new specimen room, much like the one they had just investigated.

"Will?"

No response on comms.

The rippling light flashed across Jeff's spacesuit in a different pattern. The pain stabbed at the back of his skull, but this time he managed to stay on his feet, wincing and putting his hands on the sides of his helmet until it passed.

When it did, Chapman was standing next to him, looking around like he was lost.

"What's going on?!" he said loudly. "You just disappeared!"

"You can see me now?"

"Yes!"

"Good. I don't know—"

The knife jabbed into his skull. He reached out and grabbed Will's arm for support.

When the pain subsided, Jeff let go and stood up straight. His head throbbed and he heard a constant whooshing noise in his ears, as if his suit were submerged in rushing water.

"Are you okay?" Will asked. "That looked like it hurt. You want to tell me what—"

He broke off suddenly and looked around.

"Wait a second. The hallway's different."

The specimen room that had just been there was gone, its opening replaced by an unbroken wall.

Yet farther ahead, there was another room, and this opening was twice as wide.

The ball of light shot down the tunnel and stopped on a dime in front of the room, shimmering and twirling in the ceiling.

"Do you know what's happening?" Chapman asked.

Jeff shook his head. An echo of pain lingered in his skull.

"I really have no clue."

They walked toward the room hesitantly, breathing hard against the heightened pressure inside the torus.

The room itself was unremarkable. The walls, floor, and ceiling were all a matte black edged by thin white lines.

Something floated in the center of the room, a kind of transparent matrix, almost like an enlarged three-dimensional image of a DNA strand. Jeff took a step sideways, keeping an eye on the projection. It shifted as he moved, some parts of it extending and some parts disappearing.

He stepped into the room and waved his hand through the floating projection, to no effect. Then he knelt down next to it. Parts of it extended up toward the ceiling, spreading out into a wide network of fibrous strands. He leaned sideways and those strands disappeared, but more became visible at the bottom of the projection, growing down like roots to connect with the floor.

Chapman whistled. "That's...I don't know *what* that is, but it's impressive." He looked up at the ceiling. "I can't see any kind of projector."

Jeff stood up and faced the ball of light in the hallway.

"What do you want from me?" he asked in frustration.

He felt a tingle at the back of his skull, like a low-grade electric current.

Jeff suddenly realized it was emanating from the small sphere that had been implanted into his brain sometime before he returned from the first mission.

He swallowed thickly and looked up at the impassive sphere of light.

"So that's what it's for," he whispered.

Chapman waved his gloved hand through the shimmering strands of the three-dimensional projection as they reached toward the ceiling.

"I figured it out," said Jeff.

Chapman walked over to him.

"Figured what out?"

"I think I know how they move between different fold space rooms."

"We did it earlier, remember?"

"We moved *randomly*. I know how they pick and choose."

"How?"

"They use something like the sphere they put inside my head. This hallway is stacked, like the specimen room. When you saw me disappear, I switched to another hallway that shares the same space. I snapped back, and you saw me appear exactly where I'd been standing."

"Okay..." Will said uncertainly.

"Then I grabbed your arm and you came with me to another hallway. I want to try it again, but I think we need to make physical contact for you to come with me."

Will put his hand on Jeff's shoulder.

"Then let's do it."

Jeff tried to remember exactly how the pain had felt, how it sliced through his mind like a sharp knife.

The high-pitched whine in his ears returned, the invisible knife stabbed through the back of his skull, and he screamed.

When he opened his eyes, the hallway had shifted again. Will stood next to him, and the wide room behind him was still there. Several other entrances had opened along the inner wall, revealing more specimen rooms.

"It worked!" said Chapman in disbelief.

Jeff went back into the wide room. The floating projection had also changed. Parts of it were moving before his eyes, flowing like tiny rivers. Other pieces snapped off and drifted away, only to reconnect with another section.

"What are you trying to show me?" Jeff whispered.

He turned around to face the hallway. The ball of shifting light in the ceiling spun so quickly it glowed solid, like a small star.

"I don't understand!" Jeff shouted.

The room around him exploded in a white flash and something shoved his chest. He fell backward into the three-dimensional projection and became trapped in it, like a fly in a spider's web. Gnarled branches of it protruded from his arms and his legs. There was no pain, just a deep and endless terror that he would be stuck there forever.

Impossibly, the light grew even brighter until it made no difference whether or not he closed his eyes.

Memories played in his mind like movies on a screen, but they were not his own.

He saw a world that was not Earth: a red, volcanic world with a thick, gauzy atmosphere. Shapeless behemoths floated in the mist, rolling lazily above the free-flowing lava that covered the surface. One of the creatures floated past something familiar to Jeff. It had the basic shape of a large circle, but it was obviously unfinished. It hovered in the sky in a nascent, skeletal form as tiny multi-armed figures moved around it—building it, making it whole.

In the distance behind it, more unfinished circles floated in the mist.

Jeff realized he was looking at a shipyard, except the workers weren't building ships.

They were building the tori.

55

Jeff dropped from the three-dimensional projection as if the floor had just fallen out from under him.

He landed on his shoulder with a yelp of pain. Will quickly knelt next to him.

"What happened?!" he asked excitedly. "There was a light and I couldn't see anything. I thought you went somewhere else again, and I…hey, the projection's gone."

Jeff glanced up. The center of the room was dark and empty.

He wanted to stretch out on his stomach, just lie there and revel in the blissful feeling of doing absolutely nothing, but then Riley's voice interrupted his reverie.

"I can hear you breathing, Dolan."

Jeff didn't have enough energy to be surprised.

"How do you know it's me?"

"Because you're the only person who can make breathing sound like a complaint."

"Are you okay?" Jeff asked out of the corner of his mouth. It felt like an elephant was standing on his chest. "What happened?"

"Yes, yes. I'm fine. I did the same thing as you, I'm guessing. Jumped out of the frying pan and into the fire."

"Where are you?"

"In the big torus."

"*Where* in the big torus?"

There was a pause. "A long hallway."

Jeff shook his head as Will helped him off the ground. "We'll find you."

"We?"

"Hi, Riley," said Will.

Riley grunted. "With all possible offense, you couldn't have brought Piper instead?"

"She didn't bolt from the lander at the last minute, like Chapman did," said Jeff.

“That’s because she’s smart. By the way, you might want to brace yourself for a bit of a shock when you get here.”

“I’m already used to your ugly mug. You don’t have to warn me.”

“It’s not that.”

“Then what is it?”

He hesitated again, then said, “Noah Bell is with me. And he has a submarine, if you can believe it.”

Jeff and Will found them after ten minutes of walking along the curved hallway.

Riley and Noah sat with their backs against the inner wall. Soft lights pulsed from within the translucent material. A submersible the size of a large SUV rested in the middle of the hallway atop a puddle of water.

Noah wore some kind of heavy dive suit. While not as bulky as the Constellation-class spacesuits, it looked like it had been designed to withstand very deep water.

“Quite a reunion, huh?” said Riley as Jeff walked over and rested his hand on the sub’s bulbous front window.

He had felt tired for quite some time, but now he was truly exhausted. His experience inside the projection room seemed to have sapped his energy almost to the point of collapse.

"Hello, Jeffrey," said Noah. "It's nice to see you again."

Jeff sat next to him with a sigh, leaning back against the wall.

"Hello, Noah. I take it the torus pulled the sub in."

"Just like it did to you and Gabriel near Titan."

"Guess you should have kept your distance."

"I did it on purpose."

Jeff studied his pale face, and said, "Couldn't just take my word for it?"

Noah smiled. "There's nothing quite like experiencing it in person."

"How are you feeling?"

Noah looked into his eyes and realized he knew his secret.

"Like I'm ready, I suppose," he replied. He looked up at Will. "You must be Mr. Chapman. I've been working with your boss."

"How is he?" asked Will.

"Better than some."

Will nodded. "That's actually a pretty good description."

"How did you get away from the drones?" Jeff asked Riley.

"I jumped in here. It's all I could think to do. After a while they stopped breaking off to fix the structures and started going straight for me. What's happening outside?"

"Something is...*emerging*...from a torus."

Noah's eyes sparkled with interest. "You mean, something from..."

Jeff nodded. "Elsewhere."

Noah leaned back until his helmet rested against the wall. He looked up at the ceiling. "Is this truly what you and Gabriel saw when you went into the first torus?"

"Yes," Jeff said. "It's *exactly* the same, as a matter of fact."

"But the torus we jumped into is bigger," said Riley.

"You haven't puzzled that one out yet?" Noah asked with a mischievous grin. "They all share the same interior. The simple fact that we're all sitting here together is proof of it. You two entered a torus on Titan. I entered one on Earth. And now we're all in the same hallway."

"We didn't start out in this hallway, though," said Jeff. "Not this exact instance of it, anyway." He looked at Riley. "Did you feel anything after you got here? A sharp pain in your skull?"

Riley frowned. "How did you know that?"

"It happened to me, too, when I switched hallways. They're stacked on top of each other using fold space. We could all be standing in the same spot in different hallways and never see each other."

"And yet, somehow," said Noah, "we all ended up here."

"I think we were helped," Jeff said. "Who knows how many hallways there are? Perhaps millions. You're right that the tori share the same interior space, but the space...this hallway...is actually *many* hallways. Each one has its own door that leads to a different torus, and they're all stacked in the same physical location using fold space. So that means," he continued, "if you came here from Earth, we can use the same door to go back."

"*If* you can find it," said Noah. "I made a few laps around the place when I arrived. There is nothing resembling an exit anywhere. It *should* be in the ceiling right above us, because I fell straight down to the floor."

"I might know a way to find it," said Jeff. "I figured out what they put inside my head." He nodded at Riley. "And yours."

"Is it a bomb?" Riley asked.

"It's a fold space manipulator. It allows us to move between the stacked rooms."

"But you said there could be millions of hallways!"

"There must be a way to choose a specific instance."

"How do you know all of this?" asked Noah.

"Well, that part I figured out on my own," Jeff admitted. "But I was shown other things while I was suspended in some kind of information matrix."

"Like what?"

"They are not on Earth to steal our water or to enslave us."

"Do you think that's why they told you?" Noah asked.

"What do you mean?" said Jeff.

"So far, they've done a really poor job communicating their intentions. Maybe they haven't known how to talk to us until recently, or maybe they expected us to be smart enough to figure it out. But if they finally got a message across to someone," said Noah, gesturing at Jeff, "then that someone might be able to prevent a certain first contact situation on Earth from going sideways."

"You think they want me to carry a message back to Earth?" Jeff asked.

"I think there was no point in telling you they meant no harm unless they wanted you to do something with the information."

Reluctantly, Jeff stood up. He grabbed Noah's outstretched arm and helped him to his feet.

"How many people does your sub hold?" Jeff asked.

"Three," Noah replied. "But I'm not going back."

Jeff looked around. "There's nowhere else to go."

"Sure there is," said Noah, smiling. "Elsewhere."

Jeff shook his head, confused. "But you don't know what's out there."

"Exactly."

"Does Kate know about this?"

"I'm sure she's figured it out by now."

Jeff turned to Riley and Will. "Guess it's just us, then."

Riley sighed. "Actually, Dolan, I'm going with him."

"You're *kidding* me."

"What am I gonna do back on Earth, watch television? After everything that's happened? No way. I got the bug now. I'm peeking behind the curtain."

Jeff stood there for a long time, stuck halfway between anger and compassion. Finally, he sighed and unstrapped his spare oxygen packs.

"These will get you a few extra hours."

Riley accepted the packs with a grateful nod. "I just want to go have a quick look around," he said. "See how far the rabbit hole goes."

"That's exactly what I was thinking, Commander," said Noah.

"And who knows?" said Riley. "We might be back before you know it."

"You're being serious?" asked Will, gaping at them in shock.

Riley slapped his shoulder. "Don't try so hard, Chapman."

Jeff climbed up on the side of the sub, then stopped. He told Riley everything he knew about his interaction with the ball of light, and how he learned to use the fold space technology.

He finished by saying, "Hold on to Noah when you try it. Otherwise you'll leave him behind."

"Even a lunk like me should be able to figure it out," said Riley. "Eventually. You take care of yourself, Dolan."

"You as well."

Jeff climbed up on top of the sub and opened the hatch. He lowered himself into the narrow airlock without looking back at the other two. By the time he sat in one of the two seats behind the sub's bulbous front window, Noah and Riley had disappeared down the curving hallway.

Will dropped into the sub behind him, muttered a curse as he fell sideways, then pulled himself into the seat next to Jeff.

"You know this is crazy, right?" he asked.

They strapped in, and Jeff wondered if the safety belts would make any difference. He studied the controls before him. A warning light flashed, alerting him that he needed to connect his suit to the sub's air system before launch. He dismissed it with a swipe. Then he gripped the control stick and settled deeper into his seat.

"Okay," he said. "Here we go. Grab my shoulder."

Will did, and Jeff wasn't surprised to feel his hand shaking, even through all of the suit fabric.

He closed his eyes and focused on the small area inside the back of his skull, bringing up the memory of stabbing pain. He concentrated on Earth, imagining blue skies, green forests, sandy beaches...

The pain was less intense than the last time, and he thought it didn't work. Yet when he opened his eyes, there was a shadow in the ceiling farther down the hallway.

An exit.

Jeff tried it again. The shadow vanished. He craned his neck and saw a dark patch behind the sub now, half on the floor and half on the wall.

He closed his eyes and thought about Kate.

He held her face in his mind's eye, filling his thoughts with the singular desire to see her again.

When he opened his eyes after the third attempt, there was a shadow directly above the sub. Seawater dripped from its blurry borders.

Jeff sat there, waiting.

"Now what do we do?" asked Will.

Just then, a streak of light shot past on the ceiling. The sub lurched upward as the shadow lunged down for it, swallowing it in darkness.

56

The sub tumbled wildly in a void, and the only things Jeff could see were the flashing lights of the instrument panel.

Something hit the sub and he was thrown forward against his harness. He heard a rush of water around him, and silvery bubbles flowed over the front window.

The sub was in the ocean.

As the bubbles cleared, he saw the large torus below, its ring disappearing to either side as it extended into dark water. It turned rapidly, churning the ocean around it. The sub rode backward in the current, revealing the smaller torus from which they had emerged.

"Did it work?" Chapman asked excitedly, leaning forward to look out the window. "Are we back?"

"We're back."

Above them, the surface of the ocean was pushed down like a bowl toward the center of the torus. Sunlight hit the bowl, turning it into a sheet of beaten silver.

Jeff let the current carry the sub farther away from the large torus. He pushed a small button that said IGNITION, and a mechanical *whirrrrr* filled the cabin as the motor kicked on. Grabbing the control stick, he gently turned the sub around.

Ahead of him in the murk, the outline of a floating structure extended below the surface, tapering down to a point. He accelerated toward it, then checked his wristpad to make sure his comm channel was open.

"Elizabeth, are you there?"

He was playing a hunch that he could still talk to the ships in orbit around Titan based on his proximity to the large torus.

"I never left," said Elizabeth. "Kinda boring all by myself up here, though."

Jeff's smile hurt his cheeks as relief washed over him. "Any chance you'll get some company?"

"I imagine so," she said. "The lander popped out a little too far ahead for a quick pick-up. I'll catch 'em when they swing back around."

"But they're okay?"

"Near as I can tell. What about you?"

"I'm in a submarine, with Chapman."

"On Earth?"

"That's right."

"You took a shortcut home and the rest of us have to sleep for five months?"

"I didn't know it would work at the time."

"Is Riley with you?"

"No," said Jeff. "He stayed."

She was silent for a moment, then said, "I see."

"Elizabeth, thank you."

"You can thank me if the torus hanging right outside my window doesn't gobble all of us up before we get back."

"Fair enough. I'll talk to you again soon."

He was close enough to the facility to make out some of the details. It had been recently damaged. The hull was torn open in several places, and he could see debris floating within the compromised rooms. He guided the sub toward the top of the facility, rising slowly and steadily.

When he finally broke surface, he piloted the sub to the edge of a floating platform. After a quick trip through the sub's airlock, he opened the hatch and took off his helmet.

Kate's head appeared in the opening above him, rimmed by golden light.

"Ah, look," he said, "an angel."

She grinned at him and shook her head, then disappeared from the opening. Colonel Brighton's stern face replaced hers.

"Where's my daughter?"

Jeff climbed out of the airlock, taking a deep breath of salty air. The colonel helped him step from the sub to the platform.

"According to Elizabeth McCall," Jeff said, "she and the rest of the crew are on their way back to Explorer Two."

Brighton sighed with no small amount of relief. Then a thought occurred to him and he looked at Jeff sharply. "You couldn't bring them back with you?"

"Colonel, I didn't know I was going to make it back at all. But I *did* find a stowaway."

He turned back to the sub as Will Chapman emerged clumsily.

"Well, I'll be," said the colonel.

Will took off his helmet and saluted Brighton. "Back in one piece, sir." He grinned broadly. His short auburn hair was plastered to his forehead.

The colonel pulled him close for a gruff hug, then pushed him away just as harshly and smoothed down the front of his own uniform.

"Welcome back, Mr. Chapman. What did you bring me?"

Jeff's gut clenched as Will glanced in his direction, remembering he knew the purpose for the sphere in Jeff's head.

"Sir," said Chapman, facing the colonel, "there was no way to take samples on Titan. We were lucky to make it back at all."

Brighton turned that over in his mind for a minute, then nodded reluctantly.

"How about you, Dolan?" he asked. "Figure out what's in your head?"

Jeff was about to attempt a very shaky lie when Chapman said, "It's a dud, sir. The tori put one of those spheres inside everyone they bring back. It's some kind of identifier. Purely vestigial."

"Vestigial," said the colonel, chewing on the word.

Jeff looked past him, out over the water. A large torus hovered in the air above the bowl in the surface, turning in the opposite direction as the one under the water.

A steady breeze was being generated by the spinning torus. It pushed Kate's hair to the side as she walked up to Jeff and stood in front of him.

"This is the second time you've come back from Titan," she said.

"And both times I've ended up in your arms," he added. He looked down in mock surprise at his empty hands, and said, "Oh, wait."

Kate slipped her arms under his and pressed her cheek hard against his spacesuit. He returned the hug as best he could while wearing the bulky suit.

She finally released him and took a step back.

"This is my team," she said. She gestured to a hippie and a jovial man with a bushy black beard. "Tom Willis and Dominic Wright."

He shook each of their hands in turn, and nodded greetings.

"Now that's out of the way," said Brighton, "you want to get us up to speed? What are we dealing with here?"

"We're dealing with a species far older than we could possibly imagine," said Jeff. "Their homeworld suffered a great cataclysm several millennia ago. They knew they would all perish, so they built the tori to search the cosmos for a way to bring them back someday. The machines have been traversing the universe ever since, gathering materials and building outposts like the one on Titan to recreate the exact circumstances that existed on their homeworld. Each new outpost extends the tunnel they're building. Earth is at the end of the tunnel."

Purple lightning crackled from the large torus hovering above the water. A black film spread from one interior edge to the other, and the ring spun faster. Low-hanging clouds swirled around it.

"You said they were recreating exact circumstances," said Dominic. "Circumstances for what?"

Jeff looked down into the bowl on the ocean's surface as something began to emerge from below.

"Birth."

57

Kate hugged herself tightly as she watched the alien object slowly rise from the ocean. She hadn't grabbed her jacket from below deck, and the stinging rain kicked up by the spinning torus made her shiver.

Jeff put his arm around her shoulder and she leaned into him.

The alien object was easily the size of the research facility, if not larger. It emerged slowly, as if it were being lifted by an elevator from below. Gray seawater sluiced out of deep pits in its rock-like surface. The pits glowed bright red, contrasting the dull brown of its exterior.

More of its bulk rose from the deep.

"My God," said Colonel Brighton. "It must be six-hundred feet tall."

The bottom of the object cleared the water's surface.

One of the colonel's aides stepped forward and spoke at his shoulder.

"Do we tell the ships to fire, sir?"

Jeff scanned the horizon, seeing the cluster of military warships for the first time in the distance.

The object rose higher, on a direct course to plunge into the center of the torus above it.

"Wait," said the colonel.

His aide appeared blatantly perturbed by the colonel's hesitation, but he stepped back.

"Why would they tell you all of this?" the colonel asked abruptly, looking at Jeff.

Jeff chose his next words very carefully.

"You have all of your weapons trained on the object, right?"

"That's right."

"I think they knew that would happen," said Jeff. "Or they were at least prepared for it. I think they wanted me to give you a message."

"Which is?"

"Don't use the weapons."

The colonel turned away to stare at the object. He seemed completely in control of the situation, the very picture of stoicism. Yet Jeff noticed that the colonel was holding a pair of dog tags in one hand, and he rubbed his thumb over their surface with a furious intensity, pressing so hard his knuckles turned white.

A crack like the calving of a massive glacier rent the air, and everyone ducked instinctively.

The top of the object split open, emitting a pulsing red light that bathed the bottom of the torus above it.

"So the tori are recreating the exact circumstances required for the birth of one of these creatures," said Dominic.

"That's what I took away from my little history lesson," said Jeff.

"But you also mentioned their homeworld was stricken by a great cataclysm millennia ago. In that case, the species would be long-dead."

"What's your point?" asked Brighton.

"They're immortal!" Dominic said excitedly. "They found a way to conquer death, which is something we've been trying to do for decades. And they did it from beyond the grave!"

"They had a pretty good head start," said Kate.

She held Jeff tighter as the top of the object vanished into the black hole of the large torus. After several more minutes, its entire bulk had risen into the circular black void and disappeared.

Water rushed back into the bowl on the surface of the ocean, violently crashing in from all sides until no evidence of its existence remained.

"Tom, are any of the underwater video feeds still working?" Kate asked.

"Yes, ma'am."

He dug into his backpack and handed her a tablet. She turned on the screen and cycled through all of the video feeds, most of which showed only static, until she found one that was active.

In the dark water, the smaller torus was nowhere to be seen. The larger one slowly broke apart, releasing chunks of itself to the deep. They tumbled slowly down to the ocean floor a mile below.

Kate looked up at Jeff. "Can you still talk to the Explorer?" she asked.

He checked his wristpad, then picked up his helmet and spoke into it.

"Explorer, do you copy?" he asked. "Are you still there, Elizabeth?"

"Still here," she replied. "And you wouldn't believe what I'm looking at."

Kate leaned closer to speak into the helmet. "Is the torus breaking apart?"

"Piece by piece," said Elizabeth. "About half of it ha—bro——way—ar—"

Her signal cut off.

Jeff lowered his helmet. "No nearby torus," he said, "no instant communication."

"So, it's over?" Tom asked.

"That one is still intact," said Colonel Brighton, nodding toward the large torus hovering well above the water.

Something about the destruction of the underwater torus had triggered a cascade of jumbled thoughts in Kate's mind. The pieces floated around each other like a maddening puzzle, refusing to fit together.

She looked up at Jeff again.

Something about *him*. Something about Jeff and Riley and their return to Earth after the first mission. Kate looked at the torus, thinking hard. The ball of light had shown them pictures of pregnant animals.

Okay, she thought. *The tori are giving birth to one of the beings that created them, and then the tori are dying.*

Their main purpose had been fulfilled, and that purpose was to give birth to their creators.

"Colonel," she said slowly, "how many astronauts on the first mission to Titan had children?"

He frowned as he considered the question. Realization dawned on his face as he looked at her.

"All but three of them. Jeffrey Dolan, Tag Riley, and Carlo Moretti."

"And from a strictly biological perspective," she said, "if you strip away society and culture, what is an organism's number one directive. Its *top* priority?"

"Procreation," Dominic said. "The continuation of its species."

"That's right," said Kate. "The tori only sent people back that hadn't yet fulfilled their biological imperative."

The colonel looked down at the dog tags clenched in his hand.

"My son had a baby girl."

"Except we weren't simply sent back," said Jeff quietly. "We had to die before they knew whether or not we had children."

Kate put her hand on his chest.

"You mean it just killed whoever already had kids and sent the rest back to Earth?" Tom asked in disbelief.

"Not maliciously," said Dominic. "At least, there's no evidence of that. It would be more like a series of program checks once they encountered another organism. Has organism procreated? If no, return to point of origin. If yes, disregard. I would imagine it's more of an extension of their original programming, like a side effect, as opposed to a primary directive."

"In their culture," said Kate, "the parents might die after giving birth. The destruction of the tori supports that theory. They might consider any organism that survives childbirth to have outlived its usefulness."

"But we don't suddenly up and die after we have kids!" said Tom. "People can still be useful for decades afterward."

"It's not just a different species were looking at," said Dominic. "It's a different culture with different perceptions, different traditions."

"It happens on Earth, too," Kate said. "The female octopus dies shortly after giving birth. Salmon die after spawning."

"It's coming back," said Jeff.

They all turned to look at the last torus as the top of the rising object peeked out of the black void, ascending toward the sky.

This time it was different.

Gone was the pitted, rock-like exterior. What remained was decidedly more organic. Red light moved in undulating patterns beneath the surface of its slick, textured skin. Chunks of the shell it had been contained within floated around it in a shimmering cloud.

"That was an egg," said Dominic in surprise. "Or a cocoon."

More of its bulk rose from the black hole, but that didn't help Kate to identify any recognizable shape.

In one moment, it pulsed and contracted like a giant muscle. In another, its mottled brown body elongated, becoming sinewy and graceful, as if it were swimming through the air.

There was no obvious eyes or mouth, no clear top or bottom. Yet Kate noticed it preferred to maintain a slightly elongated shape. She wondered if that was the result of Earth's specific atmosphere or gravity, or if that was the creature's natural form.

The lowest portion of its body emerged from the black hole, and the film covering the opening immediately vanished. The torus broke apart, heavy chunks falling down to splash into the ocean and sink below the surface.

The creature rose higher into the sky, leaving behind the sparkling cloud comprised of its shell fragments.

As Kate watched, its skin changed texture as easily as that of a cuttlefish, assuming a hard, jagged appearance. Its color transitioned from lightish-brown to almost black, and thin streams of glowing red, like lava, shot through its crevasse-ridden surface.

Colonel Brighton's aide stepped forward once again.

"Do we open fire, *sir?*" he asked pointedly, putting too much emphasis on the sir.

The colonel watched the creature ascend, a sense of pure wonder on his face. Kate thought she had never seen anyone look more at peace.

"No," Brighton said quietly. "No, we let it go."

Jeff squeezed Kate's shoulder. He looked up at the creature as it rose into the distant sky. She wondered what he was thinking, if he had found any of the answers he went looking for on Titan. Would he be happy here, back on Earth? Would he ever be able to accept all that had happened to him, and move on?

She wanted to ask him all of those questions and more, but felt it wasn't the right time. Perhaps later, back on the mainland.

Kate hugged him tightly.

As if he could read her mind, he said, "I'll be okay."

Then he looked at her and smiled, and she knew he was telling the truth.

EPILOGUE

Jeff lifted his feet off the coffee table as Kate hurried into the room, pulling her hair back in a ponytail. She picked up a magazine with a picture of herself on the cover from the table where his feet had just been and stuffed it into her shoulder bag.

"Keys!" she said excitedly. "Keys, keys, keys!"

"On the dining room table," Jeff said, watching her with amusement.

It wasn't often that Kate Bishop ran late, and it always made for quite the spectacle.

"I already checked there."

Jeff put down the book he was reading and stood up.

"Even behind the flowerpot?" he asked.

She stopped long enough to give him her patented *yes-even-behind-the-flowerpot* look.

"It's *your* press conference," he said. "They'll wait for you."

"Is that what you're wearing?" she asked as she rushed out of the room.

Jeff looked down at his classic T-shirt and sweatpants combo.

"I'm going?"

"Jeffrey! You're the company's lead engineer. Of course you're going."

"You mean *your* company," he said, smiling.

She poked her head around a corner to look at him as she put on her earrings. A proud smile tugged at the corners of her lips.

"That's right. *My* company."

Jeff gave the dining room table a passing glance as he walked into the bedroom to find his nicer sweatpants.

"Slacks and a blazer!" Kate called from the living room.

Jeff dropped his other pair of sweats on the bed and went hunting for whatever people who attended press conferences should wear.

The truth was he had been looking forward to seeing his old crew. Jeff's debriefing had taken place completely separate from theirs since they returned to Earth five months after he did. He had barely spoken to any of them in the meantime, other than a few tentative emails regarding possible job offers from the quickly-expanding offices of Diamond Aerospace.

Jeff tucked his white collared shirt into his black slacks and pulled on his blazer, thinking about the crew members who didn't come back from Titan.

There had been no word from Riley, or from Noah Bell. He wondered if there ever would be.

He thought about them often. What did they find out there? Were they still searching?

If Colonel Brighton knew anything, he wasn't telling. Jeff had asked him several times during his debriefing, and as often as he got the chance afterward. The colonel turned mute at the slightest mention of Riley, Noah, or the creature that had risen from Earth's ocean. After a sharp warning in the form of a visit from two armed security officers reminding him he signed a dictionary-length non-disclosure agreement, Jeff quickly learned not to broadcast his knowledge of that particular encounter. Most of the time, he and Kate simply pretended it never happened.

Yet sometimes, in the quiet hours of the night, they would speculate.

Jeff frowned at the dining room table, certain that was where he dropped the keys when he returned from the grocery store earlier. He snapped his fingers when he realized what must have happened. He jogged to the front door and left the house. Then he went immediately back inside and looked at the dining room table.

No keys.

He went out and came back in again, and there they were, right where he left them.

Jeff scooped them off the table and whistled a tune as he walked toward the front door, tossing the keys into the air and catching them again with a flourish.

He hesitated for just a moment as he opened the door. He looked around the living room with the faintest hint of a knowing smile on his lips, then closed the door behind him, whistling as he walked down the driveway to join Kate.

A warm salty breeze ruffled his hair. Jeff looked up at the clear blue sky.

It was going to be a beautiful day.

Printed in Great Britain
by Amazon

71480652R00284